VELVET CRUELTY

EVE DANGERFIELD

Eve Dangerfield

For my Zias.
Blood is blood.

PROLOGUE

Adriano Rossi

A GIRL BARELY old enough to be called a woman is sitting on a bench two hundred feet below me. She's laughing, a cutesy box of cupcakes on her knees. I adjust my lens scope and her face comes into focus. Green eyes, pale skin, and a wide, soft mouth with lips as red as blood—a color I've seen more of than most. She picks up a cupcake and holds it away from herself, as though afraid to taste it. Knowing her stepmother, she probably is.

Parker says something and she laughs, her long ebony black hair catching the light. People stare as they walk past, their mouths falling open. The girl's always been pretty but since she turned eighteen, no one can take their eyes off her. I move my scope half an inch to the left and find Parker. Clean-shaven with a hint of baby fat around the cheeks and chin. He looks younger than thirty-eight. And soft. The kind of guy you'd size up if you were looking to jump someone at a train station.

My finger brushes the rifle trigger. One squeeze, the whisper-jerk of a bullet, and he'd be gone. But a quick death is better than Zachery Parker deserves.

He can't take his eyes off the girl either. From forty stories away I can tell he wants to grab her hair and pull her mouth onto his cock. He won't, though. Two benches away, not bothering to look like anything but muscle, are her bodyguards. Kurt Cooper and Theodore Murphy. Their Rugers are in full view at their sides as they chat and eye up female joggers. I could be killing John F Kennedy behind them, and they wouldn't notice. They're there to stop Parker from grabbing teenage tits and that's all.

I'll see Cooper and Murphy soon. Show them exactly how bad they are at their jobs.

The girl stops laughing and brings the pink cupcake to her lips. Her small tongue flicks at the frosting and Parker almost nuts in his jeans.

She's not teasing him. She's just fucking clueless. A doe-eyed little girl. Never been on a date. Never had a friend sleep over. Her mom dresses her in shirts that puritanical grandmas wouldn't be caught dead in. Whenever anyone talks to her, those big green eyes glaze over. Bobby says she's pretending to be clueless, Doc and I think she's the real deal. If she had a different last name, she'd have flunked out of high school. But when you know you'll be married before you can buy beer, why bother learning?

Parker moves to wipe the pink frosting from her nose and the girl glances at her bodyguards. They snap to attention and Parker's hands fall to his sides. He's smiling, but it's fixed. Irritable. He doesn't like being told what to do, but rules are rules, and no one touches January Whitehall. He's lucky to sit next to her. When the girl graduated from Trinity Grammar, she received her diploma offstage. She's danced at the New York Ballet Academy since she was nine, but no one's ever seen her perform. A kid once tried to film her riding a horse at Kensington Stables and Murphy hit him so hard, he got a concussion.

Parker's spent millions gaining the stepmother's loyalty and that bitch has made sure no one's so much as brushed up against the girl's side. She's as pure as snow and in four weeks she'll say 'I do' and belong to Parker forever.

Or so he thinks.

Parker's security team is almost invisible. Two guys in the skyscraper across the road. Two more in a Buick idling by the curb. A sniper on top of St. George's Episcopal Church. If I shot Parker this morning, I'd have to execute five men in under a minute to get away. Not impossible, but messy. I shift my position, easing the ache in my spine as the girl finishes her cupcake. She sucks leftover frosting from her fingertips and a throb runs down my cock. There's a body begging for corruption under those ugly clothes. It'd be fun to tear her out of them. She'd cover herself with her hands, but that'd only make it hotter, her tits jiggling as tears ran down her face. I'd feed her Orchard, so she'd be wet and writhing, whatever her prissy little mind told her. I'd pin her to the floor, shove her thighs wide with my knees, and press into her pussy. I'd watch her virgin blood smear up and down my shaft as I fucked her. She'd fight me the whole way, her little fists pounding against my back as I broke her open.

The perfect Whitehall princess, ruined by a dirty lowlife like me.

But that's not the plan. Whatever Morelli decides to do with the girl, she doesn't really matter. Parker matters. Making him regret the day his father slimed into his whore of a mother matters.

There's a chance I'll fuck January Whitehall, but it's more likely I'll kill her. Kill her, cut out her heart, and feed it to Parker. And it won't be personal. As Parker taught us a long time ago, sometimes you're in the wrong place at the wrong time.

4

CHAPTER ONE

January Whitehall

*I*T'S MY WEDDING *day.*

I've thought it a hundred times since I woke up, but it still doesn't feel real. Maybe it never will. Maybe I'll float from the cathedral to the reception to my new married life without having to do anything at all.

Anita's brush sweeps lightly across my closed eyes. "Okay, January. Open."

I look at myself in the special dressing room mirror and see my eyelids are now peachy pink. "What a beautiful color!"

"Well, you're a beautiful bride."

Anita's trying to sound happy but the skin between her eyebrows is pinched. She's done my stepmom's makeup for years. I'm sure it's strange that the first time she's doing mine, it's for my wedding. I wish I could talk openly. If I could, I'd tell Anita that what's happening isn't so strange, that arranged marriages are still common in other places. But I'm not allowed to talk openly. My marriage is family business and Anita isn't family.

I watch as she puts away the eye brush and selects a pot of shimmering powder from the dozens lining her flat leather satchel. "Highlighter," she explains. "Let's make those cheekbones pop."

My sister, Margot, shakes her empty glass at me. "JJ, have some champagne…"

She's been drinking since we arrived in the suite to get our hair done. That was five hours ago. I take her glass and put it on my side table. "Maybe you should have a Coke?"

"Maybe you should have a drink?"

"I'm only eighteen."

"Yeah, and you're getting *married*. You can have one glass of fucking champagne."

I look around, praying no one heard her curse. "Margot, please chill?"

She sticks her tongue out at me but doesn't say anything else. Margot is braver than I am—and tipsy—but she knows about family business too.

She yawns, stretching her arms over her head, and her platinum bangle tumbles down her wrist. She catches me looking. "As soon as the wedding's over, I'm selling it."

Anita moves in front of me, blocking Margot from

view, and I'm glad I don't have to answer. The bracelets are Mr. Parker's gift to my bridesmaids. Around the hotel suite, identical bangles are sparkling on the wrists of my cousins Sadie and Penelope and my school friends Giuseppina, Darcy, and Quinn. All of them are getting their makeup done, sipping champagne, and having a far better time than Margot.

When Anita is done highlighting my cheeks, she moves back to my eyelids and applies black winged liner and false lashes. "You sit like a statue, January."

I look at my hands. "Thanks. It's probably because of ballet."

"Well, half the girls I work with wriggle more than you. You should be a model."

I smile. I'm sure Anita is just being nice but the idea of me being a model is crazier than me going to the moon. I get overwhelmed when two people speak to me at once. I can't imagine going down a runway with hundreds of cameras flashing in my face.

Kurt, my bodyguard, barks out a laugh that makes everyone in the room jump. "… I said, *'Go fuck yourself, Hardaker!'*"

Theodore, my other bodyguard, slaps his thigh. "Fucking asshole. You should have done it again."

The two of them are tucked away in the corner of the suite, a bottle of Glenfiddich on the clear coffee table in front of them. I'm sure mom wouldn't like them drinking on the job, but in a few hours, they won't be my bodyguards anymore.

Margot bends her head toward me. "At least after today, you won't have to deal with those chucklefucks."

"Shhh!" I say, suppressing a smile. Kurt and Theodore are nice, but they're also loud and kind of rude. It'll be good not to worry about what they're saying to the girls at ballet anymore. A clock on the wall chimes, announcing midday. There's less than an hour until the ceremony. My nerves sizzle like strip steak.

"Nervous?" Margot asks.

"A little. But I bet Mr... I mean Zachery, is nervous too."

Margot scowls. "First of all, who cares? Second of all, you still call him 'Mr. Parker?'"

"Sometimes! He's intimidating, I guess."

"Bullshit. It's because your nanny calls him 'Mr. Parker.'"

My body temperature ticks up a notch. "Margot, for the millionth time, Zia Teresa isn't my nanny."

"No, she's *mom's* housekeeper."

I look over my shoulder. Mentioning mom always makes me feel like she's going to show up and scream at someone. Probably me. But the room is as friendly and mom-free as ever. "Zia Teresa is my friend," I tell Margot. "And she's yours too. Do you remember how she helped out when you threw up on mom's chintz lounge?"

Margot clicks her fingers at her makeup artist, Helen. "Hi? Yeah, can you bring me more champagne?"

Helen purses her lips, but she puts down her eyelash curler and leaves. I wince. It isn't like Margot to be rude, but she's scared, and I have no idea how to help her. If Zia was here, she'd know how to calm Margot down. She knows how to do *everything*. I wanted her to come to the wedding, but mom refused. "What would people think, having a servant at a formal celebration?"

But Zia—Auntie—Teresa isn't just a servant. She was my father's housekeeper when he was young and when my real mom died giving birth to me, Zia Teresa bottle-fed me and read me stories, and sang to me in Italian. She's tiny, less than five feet tall with a beautiful, wrinkled apple face and the sharpest, funniest tongue in the world. She smells like DNKY's Be Delicious and Pond cream and Newport menthols, even though I always ask her to stop smoking. For her not to be here today... It's just wrong.

Anita pats my shoulder. "Okay, baby girl, almost done. We just need setting spray."

I close my eyes and Anita blasts me with so much wet mist, I'm surprised I'm not dripping. I imagine being sealed in a cocoon, a clear plastic barrier so that when Mr. Parker kisses me at the altar, he won't really be kissing *me*. But when I open my eyes, I'm not in a cocoon. I'm just me, but shiny.

Beside me, Margot sips her fresh glass of champagne, her face gleaming with the same setting spray. She looks fierce and gorgeous. I reach out and touch her arm. "You look beautiful, M. I'm so glad you're here."

Margot sighs. "I wish daddy were here. If he were, this wouldn't be happening."

I fight to keep the smile on my face. "I wish daddy were here too, but I'm happy to be marrying Mr. Parker."

"You have no fucking clue. This isn't *fair*."

I return my gaze to my mirror. "Margot, when Zia Teresa was fourteen, her dad pulled her out of school and sent her to work for our grandma. He took three-quarters of her paycheck until she got married and then her husband took her whole paycheck."

"So?"

I straighten in my makeup chair. "So, I'm sorry today is hard for you but I have to get married."

"God, January… *whatever*." Margot fumbles with her purse and pulls out her neon green vape. Mom would go crazy if she knew Margot vaped but if there's something risky that she hasn't specifically banned, Margot wants to do it. As she blows out a dragon-like puff of smoke, Fabrizia from Abbagliante Bridal glides through the door in a silver power suit. "Good afternoon, ladies! Prepare to be amazed!"

A team of assistants carries in dresses, each carefully sealed in opaque protectors.

Giuseppina squeals. "Oh my God, it's time! January's getting married!"

It takes five assistants to bring in my wedding gown. One on each corner and an extra at the end. I have no idea how much the dress costs, but from the assistants' terrified expressions, a lot.

"Up, January," Fabrizia calls. "To the dressing area."

She ushers me behind a small curtain where I take off my satin robe. Mr. Parker chose my wedding lingerie and two days ago, I was taken to a salon where every hair below my neck was waxed away. I'm still getting used to the bareness, but it does make the underwear, a short white corset and skimpy panties, look nicer. I try to imagine Mr. Parker seeing me half naked like this and my stomach turns over.

One of Fabrizia's assistants lifts a pair of kitten heels from a shoe box and hands them to me. I slide the patent leather onto my feet and grow an inch taller. Originally, Fabrizia wanted me in high heels, but mom freaked. "Do you want my daughter to tower over her fiancé?"

My dress is hung on a wooden frame beside me, and the assistants stand around it whispering nervously like it might come to life and run away. Fabrizia unzips the opaque sleeve and I see a stretch of white lace and pearls. My stomach contracts. "It's gorgeous."

"Hmm." Fabrizia stares at me in the mirror. "So, the princess is still marrying the goblin?"

Unlike everyone else, Fabrizia doesn't hide her disapproval of Mr. Parker. Probably because she's even scarier than my mom.

"I'm very excited to get married."

Fabrizia makes a 'pffeew' noise. "Dutiful, *bella*, but you'll need to give a better performance in bed tonight."

My cheeks burn under all Anita's makeup. I know there's a chance I might not be a virgin tomorrow, but I've never even been kissed before. Surely Mr. Parker won't take things that far. Maybe we'll get to the bridal suite at the Ritz Carlton and just talk and hold hands?

My wedding dress is cool against my skin. I've had lots of fittings, but it's different today. Heavier. Fabrizia slides up the zipper, but her progress halts halfway along my back.

"Oh my gosh, what's wrong?"

"Nothing." Fabrizia calls an assistant over and the two of them delicately but firmly urge the zip toward the hook and eye.

"I'm so sorry. Mom made sure... I mean, I haven't eaten in two days."

Fabrizia tuts. "It isn't your weight, silly girl. You've grown since the last fitting."

"Grown?"

"Your *il petto*." *Bosom.*

I look in the gilt-framed mirror and see Fabrizia is right. Cleavage swells over the sheer lace cups of my dress. "Do we have time for an alteration?"

With a tiny grunt, Fabrizia manages to close the zip. She snaps the hook and eye with her efficient fingers and steps back, wiping her hands on her suit. "Your fiancé will not have complaints. What do you think?"

I bite my bottom lip. I've never shown off my collar-bones, let alone my breasts, and the ivory lace make me look even paler than usual. I normally wear my hair up for special events, but Mr. Parker wanted it down in loose curls. I don't look *bad*, but I don't think I look very bridal. At least not the way I imagined I would for my wedding.

"It's a beautiful dress," I tell Fabrizia. "I hope I can make it look good."

She makes the 'pffeew' sound again. "I shouldn't be asking you your opinion, should I? Nothing about this wedding is for you."

Before I can reply, Fabrizia strides away, barking at her assistants in Italian. One of them brings forward the veil Mr. Parker chose. My hair stylist Monika fixes the diamond circle around my head and the Venetian lace falls almost to my feet.

I study myself in the mirror, rearranging my face into a shy smile. This is how I'll look as I walk down the aisle. I transition into a toothy beam. This is how I'll look as the Archbishop announces us Mr. and Mrs. Parker. I touch a hand to my cheek. This is the blissful astonishment I'll hold through our first dance, giddy at what a fairy tale this has turned out to be.

"January," Sadie calls. "Can we come see the dress?"

"Of course," I say, letting my face relax.

By the time everyone has admired the dress, there's only twenty minutes until the wedding cars arrive. Staff bring out flutes of champagne and orange juice and Kurt and Theodore pour themselves one last whiskey.

"Cheers," Penelope says, and we clink glasses. I take a small sip of my cocktail and put it aside. Margot downs hers and reaches clumsily for mine. As Margot chugs it back, there's a sharp tap on my shoulder. It's Fabrizia. "Come with me," she says.

I follow her to a corner of the suite hoping mom hasn't called with some insane last-minute request. But Fabrizia points to a small person slipping through the door. My mouth falls open. "Zia!"

I run toward her, but Fabrizia clutches my wrist. "Don't ruin your dress."

I pull up short and stand there waving at Zia Teresa like a moron. She seems smaller than usual and kind of withdrawn. Only her brown eyes are the same, bright as a sparrow's. She looks me up and down with the same assessing look she used to give me before school. "You're magnifica, *bella,* but what is…?"

She gestures at my breasts.

I raise a hand to my barely covered chest. "It wasn't my idea, Zia! Mr. Parker chose the dress."

"He could have chosen a little more of it."

I grin even though my heart is tearing open. I want to hug her so badly, it hurts. By the time I was nine, I was already taller than Zia and I started picking her up and crushing her to my chest. She pretends to find it annoying, but I know she loves it. If it wasn't for this stupid wedding dress, I could do it again.

"I can't believe you came to see me!" I say.

"Of course, I came. Nothing could keep me away." Zia looks at Fabrizia and I wonder if she's about to criticize her for showing off my cleavage, but their eyes meet in some mutual understanding.

"I'll give you a moment," Fabrizia says and walks back to everyone else.

Zia takes my hand. "I can't stay long. If your step-mother knew I was here…"

"I know."

She turns her head and coughs. A long, wet cough I could recognize in my sleep. "Zia, please quit smoking."

"Bah, what's the point?" She looks around then stands on tiptoe and kisses my cheek. "You look beautiful."

I try to smile but my face won't move. "I wish you could come to the wedding."

"What do we say about wishes?"

"They're for fools."

"That's right." Zia pushes her tiny shoulders back. "Stand tall."

I lift my spine, imitating her.

"Better. Now smile."

I try again but it makes the corners of my eyes sting. Zia Teresa has the heart of a soldier and today, of all days, I don't want to disappoint her, but the thought of what will happen once I'm Mr. Parker's wife is terrifying. "Zia—"

Her hand tightens on mine. "This is not the place."

"I know, I just wish I could make brodo with you."

Zia stares at me and to my horror, her brown eyes gloss over.

Zia Teresa hates weakness. She finds art pretentious, music sentimental and she scoffs at romantic comedies. We've spent thousands of hours together and I've never seen her cry. "Zia…"

She raises her fingertips, squashing the tears away. "Tell me the recipe for brodo."

"But—"

"The recipe, *bella*. Now."

I swallow. "Boil three osso bucco and two chicken breasts in salt water. Skim the fat and add garlic, onion, celery, carrot, potatoes and Roma tomatoes. Simmer for an hour then strain the broth and serve it with pastina.

When everyone is done with pasta, you serve the meat."

She gives me a curt nod. "You can use gravy beef if you can't find osso bucco, but the marrow is better for colds."

"Yes, Zia."

"And buy fresh parmigiano. None of that disgusting supermercato cheese."

"Of course, Zia."

"You should make brodo in your new home, just like I showed you."

"I will."

We look at one other and I want to say that I love her, that she is my mother and that she taught me everything I know. But we both already know it and a better gift to Zia would be to stay strong. I lift my chin. "I'll see you soon."

"Of course." Zia digs into the pocket of her heavy brown coat and pulls out a gold coin. "This is for you."

I take the coin and see a little man engraved into the side. There's a bubble on top, a place for a necklace to thread through. "Is it a medallion?"

"Si. A St. Christopher. Protection for whenever you journey from home. I gave one to all my girls when they went to Foggia for the first time. It should be on a chain, but…" Zia shrugs.

But then my mom would see it.

I tuck the medallion into my bodice. I'll have to find

somewhere safe to hide it later but for now I need it with me. I take Zia's hand again. "I'm so sorry you can't come today."

Zia shakes her head. "Do not blame yourself for what other people do. Just focus on your own survival."

My own survival? That seems a little melodramatic, even for Zia Teresa. "What do you—"

Another tap on the shoulder. Fabrizia's mouth is a thin line. "Miss Whitehall, we need to leave."

"Okay."

I turn to hug Zia Teresa but she's already slipping out the door, her hand fumbling in her purse for her menthols. I watch her leave, heaviness washing over me.

"You ready?" Fabrizia asks.

"Of course." I throw my shoulders back. I will be a flawless bride. I will make Mr. Parker happy, and he'll give me permission to bring Zia Teresa from my stepmother's household into my own. Then I'll pay Zia to drink espresso and watch E! entertainment news and tell me my hair is getting too long. I touch the medallion resting against my right breast. I don't know what I'm scared of, but I hope Zia is right and the St. Christopher will protect me anyway.

CHAPTER TWO

January Whitehall

S T. MICHAEL'S CATHEDRAL towers above me, rising into the light blue sky. I feel like an ant quivering before God. The air is icy and the maple trees lining the street are bare. Margot and my other bridesmaids stumble out of Cadillacs behind me, shivering and huddling close to each other.

Penelope moans. "Who gets married in winter?"

Someone who turns eighteen in late autumn, I think and chew my lower lip. I'm about to marry Mr. Parker. Mr. Parker with his silk shirts and crow's feet. Inside the cathedral, four hundred guests are waiting for me to say, 'I do.' Margot moves toward me, turning her bouquet so white petals sprinkle her feet. "Still time to run, JJ."

I imagine sprinting down the street, my priceless train swirling into filthy gutters, the leather on the bottom of my shoes rubbing away on the pavement.

The back of my neck prickles and I turn.

"What?" Margot asks.

I want to say 'I feel like someone's watching me' but that's stupid. People *are* watching me. All around us New Yorkers are pointing at me, the bride on her wedding day as though I belong to all of them.

"Did you hear what I said?" Margot mutters. "You can still get out of here."

"Where would I go? The train station? Starbucks?"

"Anywhere. Just run."

I know Margot means it, that she would even try to help me, but it doesn't matter. It would take Kurt and Theodore five minutes to find me, and then what? I touch my bodice, feeling for the St. Christopher. "Margot, I can't wait to be married."

She rolls her eyes and I poke her cheek the way Zia Teresa did whenever I questioned her. Margot swats me but she's smiling. "Your nipples are coming right through your dress."

"It's the lace! It's chafing me!"

"You better hope Billionaire Boy has no complaints or mom's gonna kill you."

Carolyn, the wedding planner, rushes down the cathedral stairs to meet us. "Hello, girls! Get in the order we rehearsed, please!"

I know the signs of someone being bullied by my stepmom and Carolyn has all of them. Her voice is high, her perfect eye-makeup is smudged at the corners, and she's sweating buckets. My bridesmaids and I arrange ourselves in a line and climb the steps to the cathedral. I can already hear the respectful murmur of the guests inside, politicians, Mr. Parker's business associates, and the entire Whitehall family.

A string quartet begins to play a light, hopeful song.

"Okay, girls," Carolyn says. "Time to go. Giuseppina, you're first."

There are 'ohhs' and 'ahhs' from the crowd as Pina disappears into the cathedral. Queasiness builds inside me as Darcy and Quinn go next. The aisle at St. Michael's is very long. It's a full five minutes and a new song before Sadie and Penelope air-kiss my cheeks and depart. They're Whitehalls and the sight of them makes the crowd murmur even louder. They know the main event is getting close. Me.

Goosebumps rise on my arms. I've never been the main event. I'm the youngest of my family, the least important, and the worst at school. The freak with bodyguards who until last year didn't know what a passport was.

Margot kisses my cheek properly, lips to skin. "I'll see you soon."

It feels like a lie. I squeeze her hand as she slips away into the church.

"Oh my fucking Christ, she's moving too fast for the

music," Carolyn moans. "Oh *God,* your sister's moving too fast!"

Yup, mom definitely told Carolyn she'd be planning debutante balls in Idaho if she screwed this up. I smile reassuringly at her. "Everything's going to be okay."

"Shh!"

Behind us, Kurt and Theodore are leaning up against a bridal Cadillac and drinking out of a flask. When I walk into the cathedral, it will be the furthest I've moved in public without them in almost ten years. My stomach twists. I wish I wasn't alone. My brother Harris wanted to walk me down the aisle, but mom said no. I'm not sure why. Maybe it was my daddy or no one for Mr. Parker.

"January?" Carolyn tugs my arm. "You're shaking. Are you okay?"

I think of Zia Teresa, of the St. Christopher medallion against my chest. *Protection for whenever you journey from home.* "I'm fine. I'm wonderful."

The music changes to a slow, melodious song. I haven't heard it before, but it feels familiar. Inevitable. As though in the back of my mind, it's always been playing. The song I'll walk down the aisle toward Mr. Parker to.

Carolyn looks like she's about to pass out. "Okay, January. Now!"

I move automatically, slowly in time with the music. I'm aware of my whole body. My feet in my kitten heels, the lace shifting across my thighs, the air brushing my bare shoulders, the circle of warm metal at my breast.

The crowd turns to face me, a thousand-headed monster. I keep my gaze unfocused and walk forward, one step at a time. The aisle is so long, Mr. Parker and his groomsmen are just tuxedoed blurs. I haven't met any of his friends before. Maybe we'll become friends too and I'll entertain them and their wives at dinner parties. I could make arancini and stuffed artichokes.

I pass Senator Billingham, Princess Clara of Sweden, my father's old friend Joshua Price the third, and Uncle Benedict, the patriarch of the Whitehall family. He gives me a small smile and relief floods through me. Whatever else happens, I'm making my family proud.

My stepmom stands in the front pew, flawless in her lavender Chanel suit. Her eyes sweep me for imperfections, narrowing when they fall on my cleavage.

Sorry, mom. Not my choice.

Her gaze flicks from my chest to Mr. Parker and I know what she's trying to say. *Look at your husband. Do your duty.*

I obey and meet Mr. Parker's eyes. His round face shines with sweat and he's smiling so hard his cheeks are apples. The song swells around me and I smile like I practiced in the mirror, but inside my stomach turns over.

Mr. Parker's tongue flashes out, licking his lips, and

my left heel turns underneath me. I stumble sideways and gasps echo around the cathedral.

"January!" Mr. Parker makes a nervous motion forward, but my gaze is caught by a flash of gold. Behind the alter, a blond priest grins at me. I know that man. I met him once during pre-wedding counseling. Archbishop Bancroft said he was Father Monastero and said he was there to take notes. But why is he here now? And where is Archbishop Bancroft?

Cursing myself, I straighten and continue my way down the aisle. A murmur of relief rings around the church and Mr. Parker steps back into place.

I glance at the priest, hoping I imagined him out of wedding nerves. But there he is. He doesn't look like a priest; he looks like Zia Teresa's forever crush, Elvis. He has the same razor cheekbones, sneering mouth, and bright blue eyes. If his golden hair was black, he'd be a dead ringer. I sneak a peek at my bridesmaids. They're staring at the priest too, but none of them look worried. Margot's cheeks are pink, and Penelope is running a finger over her lips.

I reach the base of the marble altar, my bridal smile glued to my face. Someone—Sadie?—takes my bouquet and Mr. Parker steps toward me, his pale eyes scrunched in skin. "January. Finally."

He holds out a hand and I wish I'd run. To the train station. To Starbucks. To anywhere. I think of the St.

Christopher medal and pray that someone will help me.

A crashing roar tears through the air, and I stagger backward, my ears ringing. The walls are shaking and the carpet moves beneath my feet. I've done this. I wished on St. Christopher and now he's bringing down the cathedral.

All around me people are screaming, pushing, running, knocking over pews, and crashing into each other. Mom. Giuseppina. Strangers. Hats fall, mouths freeze into wide O's. Mr. Parker is balled up in front of the altar, his tuxedo's arms over his face. I whirl around looking for his security team. For Theodore and Kurt. For anyone. A rough palm closes over my mouth, another around my waist. "You're coming with me."

A man is touching me. A man is touching *my mouth*. I try to scream but the sound is swallowed by his palm.

"Shut the fuck up," he hisses in my ear.

The arm gripping me has white and gold sleeves. It's Father Monastero. My stomach knots. Are priests allowed to curse? He drags me backward past the altar and toward the tabernacle. His arms are hard with muscle, and his cologne is heady, almost boozy. My blood turns to ice. A priest might swear in an emergency, but he'd never, ever, smell like that.

I pull at the gold-lined sleeve. Wrapped around his wrist is a snake tattoo, its fangs dripping black blood. "You're not a priest."

He laughs in my ear. "Nice work, idiot."

I struggle as I'm dragged through a small door at the back of the cathedral, kicking his shins and tossing my head, trying to bash his nose.

"Bitch!" He lifts me off my feet as easily as if I'm a doll and carries me into the room. The door slams shut, and he drops me like I used to drop my schoolbag. I hit the carpet gasping for breath. The room is small, the walls covered in bookshelves and priest robes. Father Monastero's blue eyes glitter down at me. "Don't move."

A second explosion rumbles the cathedral. The floor shakes and heavy books fall from the walls. It must be terrorists. Men who want to kill the senator or the princess or uncle Benedict. How many bombs do they have? Are we all going to die? I think of Zia Teresa and her small, beautiful face. Thank God she's not here, thank—

Pain explodes in my head as I'm yanked upward. Father Monastero grins at me, his hand tight in my hair. "Hi."

"H-Hi," I say automatically.

He jerks his head at the back of the room. "Two minutes and we're going through there."

"The... wall?"

"Fuck you're even sillier than you look. The door."

I blink and see the outline of a second door embedded in the stone. A secret passageway. My mouth goes slick with fear. The priest shakes me by my hair. "Hey. Focus. If you pass out, I'm gonna have to slap you."

I let out a dry sob. "Who are you?"

"Just some guy."

"Well, what do you want?"

"Don't worry about it. I'm not worried about it." His gaze travels down my body, a shark's smile curving his mouth. "Nice dress."

"I… I didn't pick it."

"I know you didn't, moron. It's what *he* wanted. A pristine little virgin gliding toward him with her tits out."

My scalp is on fire. I try to pry his fingers out of my hair but they're like iron bands. "Excuse me?"

The not-priest throws his head back, cackling at the ceiling. "Let me guess, how dare I speak to precious little January Whitehall that way?"

I don't say anything, but he must read the answer in my eyes because his fist tightens in my hair. "Welcome to the real world."

He traces a fingertip along my collarbone, and my skin feels like it's melting. Since I became engaged to Mr. Parker, no man has touched me. Even my brothers stopped kissing my cheeks. It was like I had a barrier around me. Like men couldn't touch me even if they wanted to. But this false priest's finger is trailing down into my cleavage.

"Does that feel nice?"

"N-No."

He grins, and his handsomeness flashes out at me like a knife. "You think I'm sexy, huh?"

Shame heats my insides. I look away, trying to find sense in this whirling nightmare.

"Hey." He taps my cheek hard. "Don't be embarrassed. It'll be more fun if you like it."

The door leading back to the cathedral bursts open. It's Mr. Parker. His hair is on end, his face bright pink.

"Oh my God, help me!" I scream.

Mr. Parker isn't listening. He's staring at the priest. "*Stop touching her!*"

The priest's free hand slides down my back to my bottom. "Sorry, Zach. No can do."

Mr. Parker's face goes white. "Who...?"

"Don't recognize me, do you? I don't blame you, it's been a long fucking time. Here's a little reminder. *Alessia Valente.*"

Mr. Parker withers like sped-up footage of a plant dying. "You."

"Not me," the priest says. "*Us.*"

A window opens in my head. This isn't an accident. The fake priest didn't drag me in here to help me, or even hurt me. The explosions, whatever's happening in the cathedral... it's because of Mr. Parker. I'm not the main event, not even on my wedding day.

"Just let her go," Mr. Parker shrieks. "Give me January and I'll—"

The door opens again and a giant man ducks under the frame. His face is hidden under a black balaclava and before I can shout a warning, he wraps an arm around Mr. Parker's neck and forces him to his knees.

"Let go of me," Mr. Parker gurgles, his hands slapping frantically at the giant's.

The priest laughs. "Hey, Zach. Watch this."

He turns me to face him and his mouth crashes onto mine. He kisses me deeply, the sharp scent of him wrapping around me like a thorny rose. His lips take on a soft, coaxing quality and my own part in shock. The second they do, his tongue is in my mouth. I try to pull away, but his hand is still clenched in my hair, trapping me. Heat surges through my body and all I can think is that *this* is my first kiss. Not Mr. Parker in front of the altar. A crazy not-priest in the back room of a cathedral.

I don't want to kiss him back but I'm already doing it, pressing my lips to his, touching his tongue with mine. Something in me knows what to do. More than knows. *Wants.*

A high, awful scream rips through the air and the priest laughs into my mouth. He pulls away and the desire I feel to keep kissing him is a hundred times worse than his hands on me. He leers like he knows exactly what I'm thinking. "You kept this pussy on ice too long,

Zach. One little kiss and she's butter."

The huge man still has Mr. Parker in a chokehold. My fiancé writhes and jerks, tears streaming down his dark red cheeks. "*January! January!*"

My heart slams against my ribs. "Please let him go?"

The priest ignores me, spinning me around so his hips press into my backside.

There's another explosion. A thick book bounces onto my foot, but I barely feel it. The priest's hand is sliding along my stomach, rising to cup my left breast.

"Let's see what we have here," he mutters.

"Nnnggijos," Mr. Parker moans.

"Yes," the priest says, caressing my breast. My legs go weak. I want it to feel bad, but it just feels wrong. Like saying the alphabet backward. Everything inside me is hot and ringing with fear, but I know it's not my fault. I don't want to do this. He's making me.

The priest nuzzles his face into my neck. "Me and the boys are gonna have fun with her, Parker. But don't be jealous, you'll get to watch."

Mr. Parker makes a high, whining noise like a dying insect.

The priest's fingers toy with my nipple through my dress. "We'll break her in, Parker. Fuck her every way a girl can be fucked."

The man in the balaclava gives a rumbling laugh and I stop breathing. Thinking. I try to disappear inside myself.

"You think you know what's gonna happen, Zach," the fake priest says in my ear. "You're wrong. You've got no imagination. The things the four of us have dreamed up to do to your little virgin... you're gonna blow your brains out just to end it."

Two loud bangs from behind us. Someone knocking on the hidden door. The fake priest lets go of my breast. "Time to leave."

Balaclava man raises a fist and brings it down on the back of Mr. Parker's head like a hammer. He slumps to the floor.

I scream but my throat is too dry for noise. Mr. Parker's eyes are still open, but he isn't looking at anything. He's like a fish at a market.

"The fuck are you doing?" Father Monastero snaps.

I jump but he's not talking to me. Balaclava man is unzipping his fly.

I cry out and manage a second of sound before the priest grips my jaw and forces it shut. "Hurry the fuck up."

I watch as the balaclava man pees all over Mr. Parker, the stream running over his face and soaking his wedding tuxedo. I want to scream again but my body is floating apart like dandelion seeds. The urine stream ends, and I'm left staring at a stranger's penis.

I've only ever seen one penis. Paul DeLuca took his

out during science class as a joke. But this penis is nothing like that short pink thing. It's long and fleshy and covered in tattoos. Balaclava man has tattoos on his penis. He shakes his penis, releasing droplets onto Mr. Parker's unconscious face. The scream that wouldn't come before makes another attempt against the priest's hand.

"Shut up," he hisses, pressing harder against my mouth.

I want Zia Teresa to snap a tea towel at these disgusting men. I want Margot to swear at them. I would even take my stepmom, her face tight, screaming at me as much as anyone else. I want Theodore and Kurt. The police and the army and the FBI. I want this to *stop*.

The balaclava man looks from Mr. Parker to me. His eyes are electric green, so bright they look fake. And the *way* he looks at me. He hates me. No... that's too personal. He *nothings* me. He could kill me, crush my throat underneath his foot and it would be like swatting a bug. My knees buckle.

"Shit," the priest snarls, hauling me up. "She's gonna faint. Are you done?"

"Yeah," balaclava man mutters.

The fake priest carries me through the secret door and into the cathedral courtyard. It's empty though the air is full of sirens and screams.

"Margot," I mumble. "My brothers. My cousins. Is

everyone okay?"

The priest ignores me. "Where's the van?"

"It'll be here." It's a third man, shorter than the others, but with muscles that are almost bursting through his tight black turtleneck. There is a gap between it and his balaclava, and I can see a tuft of dark brown hair. I wish I couldn't. I don't want to be able to identify any of these men.

A white van whips around the corner, driving across the smooth concrete of the churchyard. I want to struggle but my legs are noodles. I try to toss my head against Father Monastero, but he just laughs. "Careful with the veil. I want you wearing it when we get home."

Home. The word sends a jagged bolt of fear through me. Where do men like this even live?

The van screeches to a halt and I'm tipped onto my feet. "Time to get in, Tesorina."

Tesorina. That's an Italian word.

"What?" The priest raises a blond brow. "You want another kiss?"

"We don't have time," balaclava man grunts.

He picks me up as the back of the van slides open and tosses me inside. I fall onto a pile of what feels like towels. "Help," I whisper to no one.

The van sinks as the balaclava man climbs in, settling into a seat built into the wall. He glares down at me. "*Stronza piagniucolosa.*" *Whining little bitch.*

Fear shimmers through me like fog and I ball my knees into my chest trying to fold myself into nothing. The van sags lower as the priest and the third man climb in.

"Who we waiting on?" the priest asks. "Morelli?"

"Yeah." The third man bangs the panel behind my head. "Get ready to drive."

He glances at me and quickly looks away, but not before I see his eyes are dark brown. A jolt goes through me. Do I know him?

Father Monastero slaps the third man's arm. "What's wrong, Basher? You don't want to look at the sweet little virgin?"

"Don't use my name."

"Ah but you're not really Basher, are you? Besides..." Father Monastero's gaze finds mine. "... January Whitehall's gonna know all our names soon. And a whole lot of other things."

Terror wraps its icy fingers around my throat. I'm going to die today. On the day I was supposed to get married. There's a loud rap at the back of the van and the door slides open again. A fourth man stands backlit by the afternoon sun. His balaclava is pulled on top of his head and even my panic-fried brain recognizes he's gorgeous. Tanned with thick brown hair and a perfect angular face. The kind of handsome that makes your tongue go numb.

"Fucking shit-show," he says in an accented voice. "Give me a hand with him."

The van sinks another inch as a body is hauled in beside mine.

"Who's that?" Father Monastero asks, but I already know. Kurt's face is turned toward me, dark blood running from his forehead to his ear. I clap my hands to my mouth.

"Go," the handsome man says, climbing in and shutting the door.

Basher pounds the back of the van three times. We jerk forward and I grip the floor, trying not to slide into Kurt. I can't tell if he's alive.

The handsome man makes a talking gesture with his thumb and two fingers. "Doc? The girl."

"Right." Father Monastero pulls a white bag from the wall.

"Doc?" I say. "Like 'doctor?'"

The handsome man smiles at me. "You didn't think he was a real priest, did you?"

Even in all the chaos, my stomach surges with excitement. I don't think I've ever seen anyone so beautiful before. "I... Who are you?"

The handsome man laughs. "A question for another time, *bella*."

He's Italian too. He sounds exactly like Zia.

Father Monastero grabs my chin, turning it to expose

the side of my neck. There's a huge needle in his hand. "Don't worry," he says. "This'll only hurt a little."

I scream and hands come down from everywhere, pinning my arms, my legs, my stomach. Father Monastero hovers above me, smiling his sneering Elvis smile. "Sweet dreams, Tesorina."

CHAPTER THREE

Doc Valente

J ANUARY IS BALLED up on Morelli's dark red carpet, still unconscious from her sleeper injection. I lean against the banister of the main staircase, waiting for her to wake up. I've heard all brides are beautiful on their wedding day, but she's a pretty little thing. She reminds me of a colt, all legs and lashes and long, dark mane. And those tits... Mama Whitehall did a good job hiding them away. My eyes almost fell out of my head when the brat walked down the aisle toward me.

A moan falls from her red lips. Even twitching on the carpet, she looks too pure to exist. Like she's been kissed by angels. It makes a man want to violate her. Or at least it makes me want that.

On the other side of the room, her useless bodyguard is still out cold. He didn't get a sleeper injection; Adriano just kicked him in the head. I would have slit his throat and pushed him out of the van, but Morelli wants him alive for now.

"Mmmmff." The brat turns over, her fingers contracting like kitten claws. Her eyes flick open. They're green. Not psycho green like Adriano. Pale green with a dark ring. The kind that make you think of hills and secret gardens. I push myself off the banister. "Evening, Tits."

January squints at me. "Father Monastero?"

I grin. When we got home, I changed into black jeans and a T-shirt. I'd have kept the priest robes on but Morelli told me to quit showing off. "Not a real priest, dipshit."

Her lower lip trembles and I watch as today's events replay in her brain. She touches the side of her neck. "You drugged me."

"I did." The needle pierced her so easily. I'll never get over how simple humans are to penetrate. How quickly you can turn the living into the dead.

January sits up, her wedding dress spread around her like a white puddle. Her eyes scan the entrance hall, lingering on the oil paintings and the fire roaring away in the corner. "Where am I?"

I yawn pointedly. The kidnapped are so fucking boring. 'Why am I here?' 'Please let me go?' 'I have a family…' Things won't get fun again until the others are back downstairs.

"Mr..." She blinks at me. "I don't know your name?"

"You can call me Doc."

"Doc, can you please let me go?"

With a sigh, I pull my butterfly knife from my pocket and flick out the blade. "What was that?"

She shuts up.

I pick my thumbnail with the point. There's a little blood under the nail. Not from today. Probably from when Adriano and I worked over Nicci Fattore. I wish I'd cut Parker, sliced his eyelid, or taken a finger. But I did tongue his virgin bride and Adri pissed in his face. We have plenty of time to make the ugly fuck pay.

I can feel the brat watching me. I count the seconds until she asks another stupid question. *One, two, three—*

"What are you going to do to me?" Her voice is clear but there's a little wobble at the edges. She's a minute from tears, max. "Can you please tell me where I am?"

"Stop talking."

"Please just... Why is this happening?"

"Tesorina, I don't know why you think I carry a knife, but keep talking and I'll bleed you all over the carpet."

Her mouth snaps closed, and she starts whimpering into her hands like a bunny. I like when girls cry, but she's not doing it properly. She's sniffling like a five-year-old who lost her teddy bear.

I groan at the molded ceiling. "Fucking hell, can you quit your whining?"

She looks up at me. She's even paler now—and she didn't have a lot of color to lose. She looks half-dead. But then maybe she'll be entirely dead by the end of the night. That's Morelli's call.

"How many people died?"

I frown. "The fuck do you mean?"

"The explosions. How many people died? Do you know?"

I lower my knife. I could tell her that her whole family's dead, but looking at her grey complexion, the news might kill her, and then I'd be in the shit. "No one died, Tits."

"But… the explosions?"

"C4 down in the sewers. So, I guess some NYC plumbing died. You gonna cry about it?"

January stares into the middle distance. "Everyone's safe?"

"Yup. You're the only person who got fucked over in this arrangement."

"Oh."

I expect her to start bawling, but she just blinks rapidly. "So, are you really a doctor?"

I stare at her. For a girl with unicorn stickers on the back of her phone, I wasn't expecting this much backchat. "Does it matter if I'm really a doctor?"

"I... No. I just don't know what to call you."

I grab the front of my jeans. "You can use Father Monastero, if you want. That got me hard."

She flinches. "I don't..."

I laugh. "Or you can keep playing innocent, *lurida sgualdrina*. That gets me hard too."

"I'm not a whore." Her eyes widen and she claps a hand to her mouth.

For a second, I don't understand, then it clicks. "You speak Italian?"

She shakes her head.

"You speak Italian," I repeat more to myself. "*Capisci cosa ti sto dicendo, vero?*"

She keeps shaking her head, but I can see the comprehension in her eyes. I swear under my breath. How could we have missed this? She's Anglo. Her whole family is Anglo. Mentally scanning our plans, her speaking Italian doesn't change anything, but how did we miss it? "Who taught you Italian?"

She shoves herself backward on the carpet. "No one."

I point the blade at her. "Who. Taught you. How to speak. Italian?"

"My Zia."

"Your *Zia*?"

"Well, I mean she's not really my auntie. She's my housekeeper. My nanny. She's lived with me my whole life. I call her Zia Teresa."

There was an old woman around the house, but neither of us gave her a second thought. "Dyed hair? Smokes cigs?"

January blinks rapidly. "Yes. How—"

"This old girl taught you how to say, 'filthy whore?'"

"No. Our gardeners… they were Sicilian. I used to overhear them sometimes."

"Yeah, that makes sense. Sicilians are swine."

A small smile creases her mouth.

"What?" I ask.

"Why do all other Italians hate Sicilians?"

She's trying to be funny. Sweet. I drop to my heels beside her and flip the knife over my knuckles. Her eyes go glassy. *Better.* I jerk my head at the blackened windows. "It's dark now, Tits. If you'd stayed at your wedding, you'd be married. Eating crab while Zachery Parker gropes your thighs under the table."

She swallows, her eyes fixed on the blade. "I… I guess."

"I know. And in a few more hours, you'd be on your way to the Ritz-Carlton to suck your ugly husband's cock. Do think Parker'd fuck you like a dog the first time? Bend you over and nail you from behind?"

Her gaze skids away, coming to rest on the wall behind me.

"No, he'd want to see that perfect rack. But then he'd only last thirty seconds."

I can almost see her thinking *'don't let him upset you.'* I laugh. I could tear her apart and watch her piece herself together again all night long. "You're in luck, Tits. All four of us are better-looking than Parker and we all know how to make it last hours."

Her ruby red lips tremble. I remember pressing my mouth to them at the cathedral. I was mostly focused on Parker, but it was a sweet kiss. Sugary. She didn't want to like it, but she couldn't help herself. I bet she's the kind of girl who soaks her underwear while you're making out. "When I stuck my tongue down your throat at the cathedral, was that your first kiss?"

She blinks her doe eyes at me. "I… What?"

"Was it your first kiss? Or did you practice with the girls at school?"

Her mouth twitches and I know she wants to tell me I'm disgusting. My cock thickens in my jeans. I lift the knife, examining the point again. "Tesorina, if you don't tell me about your first kiss, I'll give you another one. And this time I'll bite."

She shudders. "It was my first kiss."

"Glad to hear it. I know Tweedledee and Tweedledum didn't let anything with a cock within ten feet of you, but there's always a chance someone slipped under the ropes."

Redness rushes into her pale cheeks. I want to make her cry and then eat her pussy. Listen to her sob while she comes all over my face…

"Mr. Parker never kissed me," she whispers. "He was a gentleman."

"He was a weirdo playing fucked up games with his cock."

Her face registers only confusion. Fucking virgins. "He was edging himself. Waiting for you to grow up. Fantasizing over your jailbait pussy like it's an apple getting ripe enough to eat. He's a freak."

She shakes her head, dark curls whipping around her shoulders. "You're a psycho."

I roll my tongue across the inside of my cheek and grin. "Yeah, but I'd never piss ten years away waiting for a girl to get legal. Now you're eighteen, I don't plan on waiting 'till the end of tonight."

"Please leave me alone," she whispers, beautiful tears collecting in her eyes.

I look up the stairs. Where the fuck are the others? I was planning on saving this bombshell until my brothers were around but they're taking too fucking long. For years I've watched this brat float around with her head in the clouds. Pearl earrings; summers in Paris; parties with nine different fucking birthday cakes. She's a spoiled bitch. Already crying when nothing's happened yet. She's not cut or shot or getting it in all three holes.

I get to my feet. "Quick question. Do you think the first time I saw you was when you met with the Archbishop for marriage counseling?"

Her hand jumps to her throat. "What do you…?"

"If I could extort my way into being the priest at your fucking wedding, who do you think you've been confessing your boring, petty sins to?"

Horror stretches across her face. "No, you can't…"

"I can't?" I tap my chest. "I dunno. Do you have a weird thing about secretly eating Tiramisu that you feel the need to tell priests about?"

She throws herself on the carpet and resumes her silent snuffling. My enjoyment is slightly deprived by realizing I should have put two and two together about the Italian housekeeper. This bitch had way too much access to tiramisu.

"Doc?"

Basher bounces downstairs, buttoning the sleeve of his navy shirt. He reeks of Tom Ford and his dark hair is ruffled with wax. I know exactly what he's doing. "Dressing up for the little brat?"

Basher looks pointedly at my bare feet. "You know you're not seventeen, right?"

"You know you're not the bass player in a Midwestern wedding band, right?"

Basher rolls his eyes. "At least you're not in the priest outfit."

He doesn't know January's awake, otherwise he'd be making soppy eyes at her like always. I smile at him.

"Whaddya think of the girl up close? Pretty scrawny, huh?"

"Have you gone blind? She's stunning."

I want to turn and see January's reaction so bad, but I keep my eyes on Basher. "You get the tarp?"

He takes the wad of clear plastic from under his arm. "Where does Adriano want it this time? Because last time—"

"Bobby?"

The tarp falls to the ground. Turning on my heel, it's hard to see who looks more horrified, him or her.

"You're… awake," Basher says in a strangled voice.

"Yes. What are you doing here?"

Basher doesn't answer, just stares at her like her pussy invented cold fusion.

I clap my hands. "We're losing traction here. Tits, your precious algebra tutor shouldn't have been teaching you math any more than I should have been taking your confession. Basher, she's been awake the whole time, sucks to be you."

January looks like she's going to pass out. Surely, she can't be far from it. How many rugs can someone get pulled out from under them in one day?

"Bobby…" she whispers.

"It was his idea to tutor you," I say, because I'm a prick.

Basher shoves me, but he can't deny it. It *was* his

idea. We needed someone in her school, and he had the master's in computer science, so he bought some slacks and registered with the New York Board of Education. We laughed about it at the time. Then he actually started teaching Miss Priss quadratic equations and everything got a lot less funny.

Bobby presses a hand to his heart like he's Romeo or something. "January, I mean it. I'm so sorry."

I elbow his side. "Hey Basher, remember what she said about you in the confession box?"

January claps her hands to her mouth. She's already learned it's pointless to try and stop me. She braces herself for impact instead. Maybe she's not so stupid after all. "You should have heard her go on about you, Bash. 'He's so nice, I hang around the library asking him about axels and shit just to see if he'll talk to me.'"

Basher's face is scarlet and he's looking anywhere but at January.

"I wanted to know if she was rubbing her virgin kitty thinking about you. But they don't let you ask questions when you're the priest."

Tears splash down January's cheeks and into her tits. I could rub my dick through those tears. Make her taste them.

"How long have you been watching me?" she whispers.

"Years," I say. "How do you think I know what your

Zia Teresa looks like?"

Heavy footsteps pound down the stairs behind me. Adriano in a green Henley, heavy canvas pants, and boots. Looking, as always, like he shops exclusively at the military surplus store. I raise a hand. "Evening, brother."

He ignores me, looking at Basher. "Tarp?"

"Here." Basher bends and collects the plastic sheet.

There's a strangled sound from January but Adriano doesn't seem to notice. "Where's Eli?"

"Still on his way," I say. "You ready?"

He doesn't reply. Adriano's never been one for talking. At school, he was everyone's pick for 'most likely to shave his head, climb a cell tower and start gunning down strangers.'

January is looking at him like he's Frankenstein come back to life. Which isn't far from the truth. Adri's not bad-looking, but he got cut in Bolivia. Now there's a silvery scar from his right eye down his cheek. It doesn't do his 'serial killer' vibe any favors. But even before the scar, he scared the shit out of girls. I used to have to give them an ounce of weed before they'd agree to fuck us both.

Adriano points to the bodyguard piled in the corner like firewood. "Awake?"

"Nope," I say. "The girl is, though."

Only then does Adri turn to take in the slumped figure of January Whitehall.

She stares back at him as though she's going to puke. "You're the janitor from my dance studio."

Adriano's lip curls, revealing his gold incisor. "Is that right?"

I laugh. "January confessed about you too, Adri. She felt bad about your fucked up face. She was too scared to say hello. It's probably the tatts."

Adriano looks down at his hands, covered in mementos to hate and revenge. "You feel sorry for me, girl?"

"No!" she squeaks, but there's an unmistakable softness in her voice. Pity is something we can sense like blood. We exploit it in others; we conceal it in ourselves.

Adriano takes a step toward her. "You talked about my scars?"

"N-No."

I laugh. That's the thing about Adriano. No matter who you are, he's fucking terrifying, which means you can always count on him to liven things up. It would be something to watch him fuck her. That does it for me sometimes, watching ugly and pretty get crushed together. And God how precious January would cry getting fucked by Adriano Rossi.

"Adriano," Basher warns. "We're waiting for Eli, remember?"

"Eli's taken long enough."

"Have I?"

I sigh. Say what you will about Morelli, the prick

knows how to make an entrance. He glares down at us from the top of the stairs in his tight white shirt and charcoal three-piece suit. His gaze finds January. "Miss Whitehall, you're awake."

January still looks terrified, but her eyes are feverishly bright as she takes in Morelli's stupid mug. He smiles at her, and she looks like she's going to swoon. I roll my eyes. Morelli has this effect on women. He's pretty as a picture and the extra years in Naples gave him an accent that makes American pussy cream itself. I have to keep him away from the clubs on busy nights or the girls get distracted, and the bottom line goes way down.

Morelli comes down the stairs just slow enough to piss me off, adjusting his sleeves so his platinum cuff links glint like morse code in the fire light. January can't tear her eyes off him, which is exactly what Eli wants. He reaches the landing and gives her one of his 'come suck my cock' smiles. "Miss Whitehall, my name is Elliot Velluto Morelli. It's a pleasure to have you in my house."

Her lip twitches. I bet some inborn politeness is trying to make her say *'thank you for kidnapping me at my wedding.'*

Morelli stares coldly at her. "I'm speaking to you."

"H-Hello, Mr. Morelli."

"Better. You've obviously already met my associates." He waves a hand toward Adri. "This is Adriano Rossi."

Again, silence, but now the girl is visibly shaking.

Morelli snaps his fingers. "Greet Adriano, Miss White-hall."

"Hello, Adriano."

"Good girl." Morelli turns to me. "This is Domenico Valente—"

"Doc," I snarl. "You're not my fucking mother."

"Domenico Valente who we call Doc," Morelli finishes irritably. "He played the part of your priest today."

January's green eyes fill with tears, probably remembering her pathetic confessions—staying up too late on school nights, being jealous of her friends for going to the movies. I wave at her. She says nothing.

Morelli sighs. "Miss Whitehall, I was told you were polite. Do I need to teach you manners?"

She looks at Basher in a wordless plea for help.

"Do not look at him," Morelli says in a silky voice. "Look at Domenico and greet him."

January addresses my chin. "Hello, Domenico."

I grin. "I've changed my mind. She can call me that all day."

Morelli puts a hand on Basher's shoulder. "And this is—"

"Bobby," Basher interjects. "Just Bobby."

Morelli pauses. Usually when people interrupt him, he has Adri break their fingers, but he loves Basher, treats him like a baby brother. He gives him a small nod. "Fine. Miss Whitehall, this is Bobby. Sometimes we call him Basher."

January tucks a strand of hair behind her ear. "Good evening, Bobby."

Basher goes bright red. He thinks an anglicized name makes him her type. He's deluded. She doesn't have a type. She's a pretty little girl who doesn't know her asshole from her elbow. The irony is, the only one with an Anglo name is Morelli. His dad called him 'Elliot' after a business partner. Word is, when the epidural wore off and Morelli's mom saw the birth certificate, she went for his eyes.

A current is passing between January and Basher. She's still screaming at him to rescue her. Makes sense. She's spent the most time with him and now that we're all together, she trusts him the most. It's high time someone took a shit on that.

I whistle. "Hey, Whitehall. Did you know we call Bobby 'Basher' because his real name's Roberto Bassilotta?"

January's eyebrows pull together.

"Also, his parents farmed pigs in Ohio and his nonno fought for Mussolini."

Adriano lets out a snort of laughter. Basher looks like I stomped on his puppy. I shoot him a wink. "Sorry, Bash, but you need to have more pride in your heritage."

"*Puttaniere psicotico*," Morelli mutters. *Psychotic who-remonger.* He flicks a finger at January, who's risen to her knees. "You. Get back on the floor."

She obeys, lowering herself down onto her ass. "Mr. Morelli, can I ask why I'm here?"

"You're questioning me?"

He says it as though it's a throwaway line, but the undercurrent zaps her. "No. Not at all, I just…"

He walks toward her, studying her face, her body. He's fussy, Morelli. His taste in pussy is more expensive than his taste in clothes. And unlike the three of us, this is the first time he's seen January up close. Unless you count her sliding around the van unconscious.

He takes her chin and turns her face this way and that. "Why did you have security guards, *bella*?"

January seems dazed by his attention and his touch. "To… keep me safe?"

"No. Lie back on my carpet."

January's eyes scan the room for an escape that isn't going to come. Finally they land on Bobby. He jolts like an electric shock's gone through him, but he doesn't move. He's not stupid. Even in his crushed out little heart, he knows January might come out of this evening a corpse. It would be revenge for him as much as any of us, but he looks fucking miserable all the same.

January's gaze drifts back to Eli. "Mr. Morelli—"

"Is there a reason why you're not doing what you're told?"

She recoils and I'm sure she's going to break—

scream or jump to her feet and try to run. But then she lies back like a snow angel on the carpet. I head to the side table and pull out a chair, ready for the show. Adriano posts himself by the fire and Basher stays near Morelli, as though he still might be able to stop what's about to happen.

Morelli studies the girl before him. "Since you're determined to be helpful, Bobby, pull Miss Whitehall's hem to her thighs."

Basher's mouth twists. I can practically taste his dilemma. He wants to protect January. He wants to obey his boss. He wants to see January's body. He hesitates, before kneeling at her side, turning his face away as he tugs up the lace of her gown. I lean forward as January's long legs are exposed.

She lets out a soft whine. The sound heats me through like whiskey. For years I've run strip clubs and pussy palaces, handled thousands of gorgeous women, but none have had this one's palpable innocence.

I want to ruin her.

"Move away," Morelli says.

Basher retreats, his face shadowed. He's angry, but I'm pretty sure he's hard behind his chinos too. How could he not be after finally laying hands on the girl he's panted after for years?

Morelli steps between January's legs. "Are you going to misbehave?"

She shakes her head, making her long hair rush against the carpet.

"Good." He nudges her legs wider with the tip of his shoe. "Open."

January squeezes her eyes shut, but she obeys, spreading her thighs.

"Good girl." He presses his wingtip to her pussy and she lets out an involuntary moan.

I grin, shifting in my chair as I adjust my swollen cock. I wish I hadn't worn jeans.

"This..." Morelli says, stroking his shoe against her. "*This* is why you had bodyguards."

She screws her eyes up tighter, her cheeks flushing crimson. Across the room, Adriano growls. I know exactly how he feels. It would be one thing if she was scared, but she's scared *and* turned on. We can all see it.

Morelli slowly rubs his shoe against her cunt. "I'll tell you why you've come to us, *bella*. You were promised to a man my brothers and I have an unresolved conflict with."

January's eyes snap open and I can see her straining to concentrate on something that isn't her virgin pussy being rubbed. I laugh. "Does that feel nice, Tesorina? Are you getting wet?"

Her head rolls across the carpet. "Leave me alone!"

Basher lets out a shocked laugh and Morelli smiles. "Doesn't like you, does she, Doc?"

I scowl. "She liked me fine when I was her priest."

January wriggles back from Morelli. "Mr. Parker *isn't* a bad man."

Morelli's smile fades. He presses his shoe a little harder against her. "What are you basing that on?"

Her lip quivers. "He knew my father."

"Ah, your beloved daddy. Not to be insensitive, but your father died when you were eight. Your stepmother engineered your engagement to Zachery Parker against his wishes."

Adriano spits into the fire.

"My mom wouldn't do that."

I snort. Her stepmother is a stone-cold bitch. If she wanted a smoke, she'd have sold January's pussy for half a pack of cigarettes. Girls like January can never see that, though. They believe in happy families and forever love no matter how much evidence there is to the contrary.

"Mr. Parker and mom arranged a marriage for the benefit of both our families, but that doesn't make him a bad person."

Morelli smirks, working his wingtip a little faster between her legs. "I appreciate your loyalty, Miss Whitehall, but do not speak to me about Zachery Parker. The four of us have known him much longer than you have."

January's eyes are glazed. She looks like she's about to come right on his shoe.

"Doesn't that feel good, *bella*?"

She shakes her head as though she can wish this all away. I picture her little cunt swollen, tingling. Excitement mixing with panic and fear. Across the room, I hear Bobby swallow.

"I asked you a question, Miss Whitehall. Doesn't that feel good?"

Her gaze moves from Morelli, to Basher, to Adri, to me. I'd give a lot of money to know what she's thinking and exactly how tingly those thoughts are making her.

"You little liar." Morelli removes his shoe from between her legs. "Here are the facts. You've been taken as an act of war. You are now the property of Velvet House. Mine and my business partners."

January stares unseeingly at Morelli. "Are... Are you going to kill me?"

Adri gives a low chuckle. Morelli smiles. "You have no rights here. You are not a guest, you are our prisoner. If you do what you're told and act as a woman should, then no harm will come to you. If you don't behave, Miss Whitehall, then yes, we will kill you."

Tears burst from her eyes like a broken dam. We watch her cry. Basher looks like he wants to hug her. Adri is disgusted—he can't stand women's tears—but Morelli just seems bored. "Stop crying."

January sobs harder, her little shoulders shaking.

Morelli kneels beside her, cupping her cheek with a

gentle hand. She looks up and hope flares in her eyes. The handsome man is being nice to her. Morelli traces a thumb over her upper lip. "My scared little girl…"

January's mouth quivers so sweetly, I wish I had a cigarette.

Morelli stares into her hypnotized face, and then he slaps her. The sound snaps around the room like a firework.

"You will not manipulate us," he says quietly. "You will not control us with tears. You'll do what you're told, or you'll suffer. Understood?"

January raises a trembling hand to her face. "Yes, Mr. Morelli."

"Good girl," he says, and a smile curls the corner of his mouth.

He likes her. Fucking hell. I want Weepy Big Tits to myself. I've already got Basher sniffing around, I don't need Morelli throwing his hat in the ring too.

"People will be looking for me," January whispers. "The police. Mr. Parker…"

Morelli turns his back on her and points to Adriano. "Wake up the bodyguard."

Adri yanks him up by his shirt collar and smacks him in the face. Cooper yelps, his eyelids flicking open. A scream slices through the room as January struggles to her feet. "Let go of him, please?"

"Doc, take care of her," Morelli says, walking away.

I stride forward, pulling her back against my body.

"Don't kill Kurt," she gasps. "Please."

I clap a hand over her mouth and the feel of her lips against my palm sends another hum through me.

Adriano drops Cooper onto all fours. He kneels, sputtering like a busted engine.

"Good evening, Kurt," Morelli says as though the two of them are old friends.

Cooper's face contracts. "You…?"

"Me. Welcome to Velvet House. You won't be staying long."

Cooper tries to scramble to his feet, but Adri puts a boot in his back.

January screams again into my hand. The sound is muffled but Cooper still hears her. His bloody face goes rigid. "January?" He looks at Morelli. "You took her."

"We did."

"Look, you can have her. You can do whatever you like, just let me go."

January sags in my arms. Poor little Tesorina. Betrayed by the man who's protected her half her life. Even I didn't see that coming. I haul her upright. "It's okay, baby. He'll pay for saying that."

But the little brat shakes her head. "Nuuuh. Pleaghs?"

I press my hand harder to her lips.

Morelli smiles at Cooper. "We expected security to

be weakened by the handover, but you and your partner were an embarrassment. Drunk in broad daylight. And why were you hanging around the back of the cathedral? I assume you were calling your dealer?"

Cooper's expression is pleading. "Mr. Morelli, you can have her. You can—"

Adri kicks him in the side. He collapses onto the carpet, spitting blood.

Morelli raises a furious hand. "Christ, Adriano! Where's the tarp?"

"Shit. Here." Basher rushes forward with the plastic wrap.

"*Jesu Cristo.* What's the point now?" Morelli says, pinching the bridge of his nose. "You're supposed to lay it out beforehand."

I can't help but laugh.

"You think this is funny, Valente?"

"Obviously." I take my hand off January's mouth. "What about you, Tits? Do you think this is funny?"

"Please! *Please* don't kill Kurt."

"Thank you, Janie," Cooper slurs, dripping blood. "Thank you!"

Adriano kicks him again, and there's an audible crack of ribs.

"Nice one," I say.

January gives a yipping little scream. "Mr. Morelli, please let Kurt go!"

Ell frowns. "*Bella*, this man was assigned to protect you and not only did he fail miserably, he just betrayed you. He doesn't deserve to live."

"But you can't kill him!"

I lower my mouth to January's ear. "What do I get if I help you? Will you blow me in front of your bodyguard while everyone else watches?"

She squirms and I tighten my grip around her.

Morelli clucks his tongue. "Doc, stop teasing her. Basher, get the plastic under Cooper before the carpet becomes even more fucked. Adriano, kill this idiot."

"What about me?" I ask Morelli. "Why can't I kill Cooper?"

"Because I'm not staying up all night, watching you flay this moron. I need some fucking sleep."

"Killjoy."

January lets out an ear-splitting scream. Adri looks murderous. If there's one thing he hates more than women crying, it's women shrieking. I clap a hand over her mouth. "Sorry about that."

Adriano shakes his head and turns to Morelli. "Make Basher do it."

"Fuck off," Basher says at once. "You fucking do it."

Morelli holds up a hand. "Why Bobby?"

Adriano jerks his head at January. Morelli looks from her to Basher, who's too slow to get the look of righteous horror off his face.

Morelli inclines his head. "Bobby, kill the body-guard."

All the color rushes from Basher's face. He glances at January. "Can she go in the other room?"

"No." Morelli reaches into his waistband and hands him his Walther PPS. "Now."

"But—"

His nostrils flare. "Think of your mother. Your sisters. This is everything. Ten years of planning. *Don't* fail us."

Basher's face hardens. He's a cute kid. A nice guy. But that's not all he is and no one struggles with that more than him. He gives January one last look and then his shoulders slump. "Fine."

She struggles against me as Bobby approaches Cooper, her ass rubbing against my jeans. I press into her, and she bites me. Hard.

"Ow," I say, shaking my palm. "Little bitch!"

"You're evil," January spits. "Evil, horrible men!"

I press my hand back over her mouth. "You think we mind being evil, Tesorina? You think we care?"

Morelli pulls a handkerchief from his jacket. "You don't know what you're talking about, Miss Whitehall. You've been sheltered your whole life. Told what's right and wrong. Your morals are like your pussy. Completely untested. You've never had to make a choice. Doc, take your hand away."

The moment I do, January screams and Morelli shoves the cloth between her lips. She gives a noise of muffled outrage, and he slaps her again.

"Remember what I said, Miss Whitehall. Behave yourself and live or disobey and die." He turns to Basher. "Kill him."

Basher presses the gun to Cooper's head. The plastic contains the spray and the body jerks twice before going still.

January slumps in my arms. I'm pretty sure she's passed out.

"So that's done," I say. "Can we eat? I'm fucking starving."

Morelli sweeps a hand through his model-perfect hair. "Not yet. Set up a camera and put a chair into the middle of the room. Time to show Parker what we've done."

CHAPTER FOUR

Adriano Rossi

CALM FOLLOWS THE death of the bodyguard. The girl lies passed out on the floor, while Doc and I set up the room and Basher methodically mops up brain splatter. He won't look at me. I don't care. It was the right decision. Whatever Basher thought was happening, it isn't. The girl doesn't belong to him, and she never will. I've done him a favor.

"Where the fuck did we get this ring light?" Doc asks, adjusting the tripod.

Ell looks up from his seat by the fire. "Why?"

"Because it's for teen girls who do makeup videos."

"That doesn't mean it won't work."

Doc glares at him. "Would it kill you to help us?"

"You've got everything under control."

"You're a lazy fuck, Morelli."

Ell sits in a chair by the fire doing clean-up of his

own: contacting our NYPD rats, confirming no one tied us to what happened at the cathedral. But Doc knows that. He just likes to take swipes.

The pearls on the girl's wedding dress and the diamonds in her hair keep catching the light. Fucking ridiculous, her getting married. She couldn't get through a sleepover without calling her whore of a stepmother to take her home. I don't want to look at her, but she keeps catching the light too—milk-pale skin and long lashes. She sets my blood boiling when usually it moves like mud. I want her gone. Wrapped in the same plastic sheet as Cooper and thrown into the freezing Atlantic.

"Zia?" She shifts on the floor, swaying herself up onto her palms. "Zia?"

Her voice is so soft. Fluttery. I turn away from her. "Girl's awake."

Ell stands. "Good. Miss Whitehall, how are you feeling?"

She doesn't answer. Her gaze falls on Cooper's body and the color drains from her face. Doc abandons the tripod and bounces over to her. "Are you gonna puke? Because your only options are down your dress or on your former bodyguard."

Her delicate throat contracts. "Could I please have some water?"

"Of course." Eli gestures to Basher. "Bobby, get Miss Whitehall some water."

Basher heads to the wooden bar and returns with a crystal tumbler full of water. She could smash it and try to cut us, or slash her wrists, but all the little girl does is sip her drink. She's only half-finished before Morelli takes the tumbler from her. She left a red lipstick mark on the rim. The sight of it makes my cock ache.

"Now, Miss Whitehall, we must discuss business."

"W-What kind of business?"

Ell raises her glass, drinking from the place her lips stained. The girl's face goes as red as her lipstick. Typical. Eli Morelli's need to know he can seduce any woman in his path is pathologic. But it doesn't matter. She doesn't belong to him, either. I clear my throat.

Ell glances at me, amused. "Forgive me. We have business with Zachery Parker. Business you will help us with."

Her eyes are so clear you can read them like a book—all fear and guilt and hope. It was like that when she danced too, you could feel her feelings. Her joy, her sorrow.

"What do you want me to do?"

"Take off your dress."

The room fills with a silence cold enough to cut skin.

"Please," she whispers. "Please, Mr. Morelli?"

Ell holds out the tumbler. "Bobby?"

Basher steps forward to take the glass. His face is blank and I'm glad. If he looked the way he did before,

I'd force him to do the honors again. But maybe he'd like that. He usually does, even if he won't admit it.

Ell smiles down at the girl. "You remember what I told you before your bodyguard was killed?"

She bows her head.

"Then you know better than to refuse me. Take off your dress."

She looks up, all trembling lips and watering eyes. "Mr. Morelli... I *can't*."

"Have it your way. Doc?"

Grinning, Doc pulls his revolver from the back of his jeans. "Get in front of the camera, and strip."

Her pleading eyes dart around the entrance hall.

"January Joy Whitehall, I will blow your brains out and Bobby will be the only one to mourn you."

She looks to Basher, his face skull-like in the flickering firelight. Her gaze falls on me. Those eyes like big green worlds asking if it's true if she could die tonight. At least she's asking the right person.

Doc presses the barrel to her head and I feel the sensation against my own skull, a cold ring of steel. "Last warning, Tesorina. I'll waste you, then fuck your corpse. Stand up."

She blanches but doesn't get to her feet. There's a backbone in this girl. We didn't see that coming. Maybe I should have. I watched her dance a thousand times, repetition and strength and control.

Ell walks back to his chair by the fire. "Hit her."

Doc lowers the gun and backhands her. The girl's head snaps sideways.

She touches her cheek. "You're a beast."

Doc laughs. "Take off your dress and I'll show you how much."

"Never."

He slaps her again but this time and this time, she glares at him. "You're *insane*."

Doc shakes out his hand. "Get your tits out and stop wasting my time."

"No!"

I cross the room to Eli. "We should kill her."

"We brought her here for a reason."

Doc drags the girl toward the chair in front of the camera. Her hands slapping at his arms. "Let me go!"

Give her a little longer and she'll be spitting and scratching. I grit my teeth. "If you're determined to do this, I can control her."

"How?"

I pull the platinum bracelet from my pocket. "Read the name."

Ell squints at the little heart charm. "Where did you get this?"

"Stopped her while she was running out of the church."

Ell smiles. "Beautiful work. Go take over."

The girl is slumped on the chair. Doc scowls when he sees me coming. "Give me five more minutes."

"No. Move."

I drop the bracelet in the girl's lap. She picks it up with her long, elegant fingers and the fire in her eyes vanishes. "Margot? You've got her too?"

I shake my head. "Just the bracelet. Your sister's alive, but she doesn't have to be. Your choice."

The girl's face shifts. It's an expression I've seen a million times. Revulsion. But my blood is thick and steady. Let her hate me. It doesn't matter. I return the bracelet to my pocket. "What'll it be?"

Her hand lifts to her left breast, cupping it lightly.

Doc sniggers. "Gonna give us a show, Tesorina?"

Color flares in her cheeks but she ignores him, letting go and lifting her hands to her veil. Eli clicks his tongue. "Leave that, Miss Whitehall. The dress."

She reaches behind herself for her zipper. The sound of it coming down is like a tongue along my cock. Her fingers fumble and she looks up at the ceiling. "It's stuck."

"Would you like some assistance?" Eli asks. He sounds gentle. Deferential. That's how he is with women. Letting them think everything will be easy.

She hesitates. "Yes, please?"

Ell smiles. "Ah, *bella,* it's charming when you're polite. Turn around."

She trembles as his fingers brush her porcelain skin.

Doc's teeth are bared as his gaze flicks from her face to her chest and back again. He wants her tied to his bedhead so he can cut her, fuck her, starve her into savageness.

The wonder that vanished from Basher's puppy dog eyes when he killed Cooper is back. He'd carry the girl to bed and fuck her gently, make her believe she'd found a man who'd treat her that way for the rest of her life—believe it himself for a while.

Eli caresses the girl's waist. He's measuring her. For all his soft words, his goal is always possession. To reduce a girl to an equivalent weight in gold. When he does, he puts a collar on her neck and parades her around until he gets bored. Then she either accepts a few tokens and leaves or exits his company via a more permeant route. These men, my brothers, are idiots, all of them, but it's not their fault. To them, the possibilities of this girl are endless. To me, they point to the same forked road—kill her or suffer. And I won't let that happen. I'll end this before things get more fucked up.

Ell's hands rise to the stuck zipper. A short tug and the fastening slithers down, exposing her back. It's pale and delicate and utterly unblemished. My fingers twitch as I imagine my tattoo gun kissing that flawless canvas.

Doc lets out a low whistle and the girl clutches the loose folds of the dress to her body. Four hundred thousand dollars of Venetian lace and pearls. We won't destroy it. When she's dead, we can fence it to some gangster's girlfriend who thinks she's royalty.

"Miss Whitehall. Let go," Eli whispers.

The dress falls in slow motion like an avalanche and then January Whitehall is standing in her wedding lingerie and heels, her long veil still fixed to her hair. Her body is sleek and well-muscled. Her underwear is sluttier than I expected. Her big tits spill out of a tiny corset and there's barely a scrap of lace between her legs.

Bobby makes a squashed cat sound and coughs into his fist to cover it.

Ell gives her a cold smile. I can practically see the numbers whirring in his head, the girl's value rising higher.

January wraps her arms around herself and tilts her head so the veil falls across her shoulder. It's even more obscene than if she stood there naked. Doc catches my eye and winks. I remember him as a teenager, setting his sights on some Manhattan princess no one thought he could have. Seducing her like someone paid him to do it. The girl needs to die before this gets messy.

Ell gestures to the chair in front of the camera. "Please take a seat."

She obeys—probably welcoming the barest cover it provides from hungry eyes.

"Thank you. Bobby, camera?"

"It's recording."

"Then who should do the honors?" Eli asks.

I frown. "Why not you?"

"I need to talk."

"You can't talk and fuck at the same time?"

The girl lets out a pitiful moan we all ignore.

"It will look better if it's simultaneous," Eli considers Basher. "No, not you."

Doc points to his chest. "Me?"

"You already kissed her you *pezzo di merda.*" *Piece of shit.*

"Fine. Then it should be who Parker wants to see the least. The gargoyle."

Ell turns to me. "Do you want to do it?"

That heat again, boiling through my veins. Setting my muscles twitching. "Whatever works."

"Fine. Use the Walther."

I stride to the table by the fire and pick up the gun. Basher practically lunges for me. "Not that one."

I raise the weapon, ready to crack it over his head but he waves his hands. "I don't wanna stop you. There's blood on it."

I look down. The barrel is flecked with Cooper's gore. "Huh."

I turn to the girl, disgust etched into every line of her pretty, childish face. My chest tightens. For years I've watched her from a distance, but this is hatred at close range. "You still want me to use it?" I ask Eli.

He grins. "You're a sick man. No. Use yours."

I hand Bobby the Walther and unholster my Glock. "You'll do the talking?"

Eli checks his hair in a nearby mirror. "Of course. Let's go."

The girl goes still as I approach. Fixed like a bunny in headlights.

"Open your mouth."

She presses her full lips together. They're so plush it's as if they were designed by a man who spent years perfecting the art. I reach out to pinch her nostrils but before I do, she complies. I stare into the expanse of her mouth and my cock stiffens against my leg. It's not a slow acceleration, I go from detached to hard as if I was sunk into a woman and I imagine fucking the girl's face while the others watch. Coming down her virgin throat.

Instead, I shove the gun in her mouth.

Her arms spring up, pushing against me. I grasp her shoulder and pin her to the chair one-handed. She claws at me, but her slaps and scratches are like kisses on my arms. I shove the barrel deeper. She screams and the revolver catches the sound and gargles it. I pump, but only slightly. The way I would if it was my cock between her teeth.

"Good," Eli says behind me, his voice thick as honey.

"The bitch needs to calm down or she'll choke for

real," Doc says. "Show her, Adri."

I release the girl's shoulder and clasp her neck. It's so slender, it's like gripping a swan. "Stop screaming and suck."

She moans around the barrel. I tighten the fingers at her throat. "You want me to make it my cock?"

"Nnnghh!"

Doc laughs. "Bad luck, big guy."

I ignore him and look right into the girl's eyes. "You wanna lose your virginity to a pistol?"

"Nnnngggghh."

I bend to her ear. "You'll get the barrel first. But if you piss me off enough I'll try for the handle."

A small gasp and the pressure on the gun slackens. Her head bobs back and forth, drawing on the barrel with loud, sloppy pulls. She has no idea what she's doing, but at least she's doing it. I look at Eli. "You ready?"

"I am," he says, amused. "Good work."

"Yeah, not bad," Doc says. "Don't worry, Tesorina. You can't actually suck-start a gun."

The girl makes a garbled sound. I glance at Basher. He looks slightly sick, but he can't take his eyes off her. Whatever he's feeling, he'll be beating off about it later.

I thrust the gun deeper into her throat, and she swallows obediently. Looking across, I see Doc palming his cock through his jeans. He grins. "I'll jack off if you do."

"Wait your turn." Eli steps in front of the camera. "Good evening, Parker."

The amusement goes out of the room like a blown bulb. I twist the gun in the girl's mouth and she slurps like a porn star. I hope Parker sees it. Hope it burns like battery acid.

"As you can see, we have your fiancée." Morelli runs a section of the girl's hair through his fingers. "You've kept January Whitehall to yourself since she was a little girl. But she's ours now."

Doc laughs, the sound more anticipation than genuine amusement.

Ell drops the strands of hair. "We won't fuck her, not at first. But we'll keep you informed of our progress. Little updates, as we help her become a woman."

I push the gun deeper again. She chokes a little, but she keeps going. She is stronger than I thought she was. "Good," I tell her. "Good *Pryntsesa.*"

An icy insect crawls up my neck. I didn't mean to say that but surely no one heard me. Eli is still talking to Parker; the girl is still sucking and gagging.

"… this is only the beginning," Eli says to the camera. "If you're a smart man, you'll eat your gun. But you're not a smart man, Parker. So, enjoy the show."

"That's enough," Eli says. "Bobby, stop recording."

I pull the gun from the girl's mouth and her lips smack together. She looks at me and for a second, it's with something other than terror. My gut drops. *Pryntsesa*. Maybe she did hear me. Then she slides onto the floor, crying in big racking sobs. "I want to go home! I want to go home!"

I wipe the barrel on my T-shirt. "We done?"

"We're done," Eli agrees. "Bobby, take the footage, edit it together and send it. Miss Whitehall, if you can stop crying, you can have a suite upstairs. Clean clothes. A big bed to sleep in."

"I want to go home!"

"She's too far gone," Doc says. "She won't stop whining now."

My Glock is still in my hand. One bullet between the eyes, faster than heaven. The girl never got to dance for an audience. Adulthood is just another stage she'll never perform on.

Ell walks to the wall and presses the intercom. "Gretzky? We're finished. Bring Harvey and Sal and a cleaning kit. I want the girl in the basement and the entrance hall cleared. Now."

The basement. The little cage Morelli built to keep people we're not ready to kill yet.

"I want all of you in the dining room at midnight." Eli heads to the stairs, his mood clearly soured. Bobby follows with the camera.

Doc and I stand in front of the fire and watch Gretzky carry the girl from the room, her limbs swaying like a dead deer. When they're gone, Doc slaps a palm on my shoulder. "Hey, Adri, what's 'Pryntsesa' mean?"

The icy insect picks at the base of my skull.

"Oh, I remember. It's Ukrainian for 'I've fallen for teen pussy. How am I gonna surrender my way out of this one?'"

Rage flares in me like propane. I grab his T-shirt and wind the collar around my fist. "I want her dead."

"Because that would make the feelings go away, wouldn't it?"

I want to kill him, but I force my hand to unclench. There's no point in fighting Doc. He eats anger and drinks frustration. I turn and head for the staircase.

"You owe me a new T-shirt, fuckstain."

I glance back. "I'll pay you in advice. That pussy's more trouble than it's worth."

"Whatever you say, *Pryntsesa*." Doc's laughter follows me out the entrance hall.

CHAPTER FIVE

Elliot Morelli

J ANUARY WHITEHALL. WHEN you first see her, you think 'yes, that's a pretty girl.' But the longer you look, the more the simplicity slides away to reveal a woman shaped by angels. Her skin isn't smooth, it's flawless. Her face isn't lovely, it's that of a goddess stepping off a seashell. Her body isn't decent, it's big-titted, long-legged perfection. The horniest fifteen-year-olds wouldn't have the balls to dream it up. Soon she's so beautiful it almost hurts. Then it *does* hurt. That sparking need to touch her. To make her yours. I have always had control. Always been able to wait for what I need.

Tonight, I offered Miss Whitehall a deal—stand and she could live in my house. Instead, she lay on the floor sobbing for home. I wanted to scoop her up and carry her to the east wing anyway.

"You gonna eat or what?" Doc asks.

I ignore him. He and Adriano are vacuuming up Japanese takeout, but I have no appetite. I can think about January Whitehall. Her round ass, her flat stomach, her gorgeous little face. If only she'd gotten up... but time in the basement will do her good. If she was to be mine, she'll have to learn to behave properly. No tears. No tantrums.

Doc gestures at my Karaage chicken with his chopsticks. "Can I have that?"

I scowl, pulling the plastic container closer to myself. I can't believe he gave the girl her first kiss. He must have forced her into it. Domenico wouldn't know subtlety if he woke up to it sucking his cock. January Whitehall will kiss me of her own accord. I'll coax her into the palm of my hand before I take her innocence.

It was not our original plan to kidnap her. We were going to plant a bullet in her head and try to get as much of her brains on Parker as possible. But after years of surveillance, killing her began to seem wasteful. Like smashing a glass case to seize a five-star dessert. You might prevent the true owner from enjoying it, but you ruin it all the same. We wanted the dessert—if only to taste it before tossing it on the ground.

It was a risk, of course, the Whitehalls are a powerful New York family. But January is a relatively insignificant member. The youngest daughter of a third son. Her unimportance is the only reason Parker was able to buy her hand in the first place. It was worth the risk to abduct her. There would be bad blood, but the Whitehalls wouldn't go to war for one teenage girl. While no single act could ever erase what Parker has done, I thought watching his fiancée get tag-teamed by the men coming to kill him was a promising start.

Tonight I walked into my entrance hall, and I was ready to give her to Doc and Basher to play with, then Adriano to kill. Until I saw her.

For centuries, my mother's family has dealt in precious stones. January Whitehall is *una perla rara*. A once in a lifetime gem. Identifying her potential is the only intelligent thing Parker has ever done.

When I rubbed my wingtip between her legs, I expected to see fear, but when my shoe brushed her panties, Miss Whitehall's eyes went wide and her nipples turned to stone under that ridiculous gown. Her shame was as delicious as her arousal.

I'm going to humiliate her with her own desires. Watch her grind herself on my cock, crying while she comes all over me.

"You sure you're going to eat the chicken?"

I glare at Doc. The table around him is a mess. Loose paper, scraps of wire, tablets, discarded scalpels, and textbooks. The polished oak floorboards are caked with dirt, and the side tables are covered in an inch of dust.

This house is more than two hundred years old and in less than five, my brothers have turned it into a truck stop restroom. My Nonno's houses were always immaculate, not a fingerprint on a mirror or a speck of dust on the mantelpiece. If he saw this place… "This place is a fucking mess."

Doc shoves another dumpling in his mouth. "Why are you bitching at us about it? Hire a cleaner."

"I did. She saw your workroom and ran away."

Doc smirks. "Oh, yeah. Well, hire someone else."

"While we're keeping the daughter of one of New York's most prestigious families in our basement?"

"Well, if you're too paranoid, we can't have a clean house, can we?"

"We have a live-in staff of five. One of them—"

Doc points his chopsticks at me. "You wanna tell the boys to stop making us money and surveilling the people trying to kill us so they can sponge the carpet, be my fuckin' guest. Personally, I'm gonna live with the mess."

I pick up my chopsticks and dig into my karaage chicken. Domenico Valente is as disrespectful now as he was at sixteen. Worse. He used to be at least a *little* afraid of what would happen if he ran his mouth to the wrong person. Bullets would bounce off his arrogance now. Before I can tell him so, Bobby strides into the room. "I've sent the file. Parker's already seen it."

I lower my chopsticks. "He's watched the footage?"

"A couple of times."

I feel a sweet, almost giddy sense of release, and smiles spread across my brother's faces, even Adriano's. I stand and walk to the bar to collect the bottle of grappa I brought from my wing. It was distilled by my bisnonno and I've been saving it since I turned eighteen. It's surreal to crack the seal and smell the sharp-sweet liquor. I pour triple measures and bring the tumblers over.

"Congratulations," I say, raising my glass. "May all our plans succeed, and our lost ones be avenged."

We drink and for a moment no one speaks. We're all lost in our own world. No matter how much time passes, the memories of what led us here never fade. When you're young, things have a freshness you can't reclaim. Your first taste of wine. The first time you know a girl will let you kiss her. The first time a man raises a gun to you and your blood turns to ice.

These days you could strap me to the side of a train, and I wouldn't feel that bright, all-consuming fear. A good thing. But there's something about the old days, the four of us running wild through the boroughs, hatching our first schemes, convinced we were kings. Now my brothers and I *are* kings, but we've fought for every inch of our sovereignty with blood. We're tired, and we don't laugh like we used to.

Bobby comes to my side of the table. "Can I have a word?"

"Of course."

We take our grappa into the hallway. Bobby and I both have dark hair and brown eyes, but no one ever mistakes us for siblings. He is rough-looking with olive skin and thick brows. Common, my nonna would say, but handsome and smarter than anyone I knew until I met Doc.

"Problem with Cooper?" I ask.

"Nope. He's with Harvey and Sal. He'll be in the Atlantic by morning. It's just…" He gazes at a point beyond my shoulder. "Adriano shouldn't have made me kill him in front of her."

My hand tightens around my tumbler. For months Doc warned me Bobby was in love with January, but I took him for a loudmouth asshole. This is a complication I don't need, especially now that *I* want the girl.

"I made you kill Cooper and it was the right decision."

"You could have told Adri—"

"But I didn't." I squeeze Basher's shoulder. "Let's go eat."

He hesitates. "What's going to happen to January?"

Even the way he says her name is a warning. Soft and protective. "We'll discuss it later. Right now, we're celebrating."

Bobby looks like he wants to say something else, but I turn and walk back to the dining room. Doc bangs his empty grappa glass on the table. "Reload."

I pour him more liquor and top up my own glass. Bobby takes his seat to my right, pulling mushroom ramen toward himself. He sneaks his vegetarian meals in the order last, as though we might not notice his diminishing appetite for flesh. We, who know him better than anyone.

Doc's eyes are wild as he raises his glass. "A toast."

Adriano, Basher, and I lift our glasses.

"To pissing in Parker's face and stealing his bride. "Salut."

I grin. "Salut."

Bobby taps a hand on the table. "Gretzky's been listening in at Parker's place. He killed three of his men after he got home from the cathedral."

"He's doing our job for us," Doc says gleefully.

I say nothing. Parker's blind rage will only last a short time. He'll compose himself and come after us.

"Have any of the families called to account for the scene at the cathedral?" I ask.

Bobby shakes his head. "No one's reached out yet."

"They will and when they do, we'll give one answer. We're enacting revenge against Parker. Anyone who stands to lose money from the situation can have a cut of whatever we claim from his estate. The rest can look the other way."

Adriano sucks up ramen noodles. "And if they don't

want a cut? If they want retribution for the inconvenience?"

"We tell them to choose a side. Parker or Velvet House."

Doc smiles dreamily. He'd love a crime family to pick a fight with us. If I gave the word, he'd Jonestown every branch of the New York famiglia. But I'm a businessman. I don't kill for pleasure. I kill when it's necessary and when it benefits me. Parker is the only exception. I built Velvet House with one eye on that animal. To collect enough wealth and power that when the time came to ruin him, we would endure.

I pour us all another round. "Get drunk tonight. Tomorrow, the real work starts."

Doc drains his grappa. "January Whitehall."

Basher's face falls. Even Adriano looks up from his ramen. Trust Doc to mention the elephant in the room in the most disruptive way possible.

"What about her?" I ask.

"I want her. On her back. On her knees. On my face. The fucking works." He looks around the table. "This is me staking a claim and you bastards better respect it."

"Well, that's going to be a problem," I say lightly. "Because I want her."

Doc's eyes narrow. "You said the rest of us could have her."

"True. But now I've seen her, my opinion has

changed."

Adriano returns to eating like nothing has happened, but Bobby looks like he's about to be sick. Velvet House doesn't have a traditional family structure. The rules are the ones we made ourselves. But I am the boss and my brothers know it. Which means if I want Miss Whitehall, she's mine.

Doc lets out a long sigh. "Fine. We can share her."

"You don't share. You can barely let other people choose music in the car—"

"That's not—"

"Besides," I say loudly. "I want Miss Whitehall as my mistress, which means she'll have official standing in my household. She won't be passed around Velvet House like a whore."

"A mistress?" Bobby asks. "But you're not married."

"Not yet, but once this Parker business is done, I'll get engaged."

Doc laughs. "To that watch guy's daughter? You said she smelled like asparagus."

I press my fingertips into my temples. It is a miracle I have not killed this man. Of all the benefits of getting married, not being in daily proximity to Doc is top of the list. Smart as he is, perceptive as he can be, he's an utter lunatic. Without Adriano's protection and my money, he'd have been in Bayview Correctional years ago.

"It doesn't matter who I marry. The point is I'll be married by the summer. Keep your calendars clear."

"So what?" Doc asks. "You get married and kick us all out of the house?"

"What do you think our future holds? My wife and children eating dinner with us every night? The four of us living in a frat house forever?"

"You could not get married."

"I'm almost thirty-four. I need heirs."

Doc rocks back in his chair. "So where will January be while you're out shopping for a wife?"

"My mistress will not be your plaything while I'm away. I'll send her somewhere else."

"Seems like a waste of pussy," Doc mutters. He clears his throat. "I have a better idea. She should come work at Dreams."

Bobby chokes on his noodles. "As a stripper?"

"No, as a fucking bouncer. Of course, as a stripper."

"What's your justification for that?"

Doc shrugs. "She's hot. We can make money off her. And she's had all those dance lessons. Plus, how's Parker gonna feel when we send him vids of her working a pole?"

A valid point. The man spent a fortune in private security keeping boys from touching January's arm in homeroom. He might have an aneurysm watching her give out lap dances, which would be funny.

Doc lowers his chair, his eyes on mine. "I'm thinking long-term. Security at the club's airtight. Parker'd have more luck abducting her out of The Hague. And if anyone threatens her in there, they're asking for trouble with Danil Yamlihanov. Half the pole koalas are sucking off his boys."

I smile. "You're making more sense than usual."

"Just imagine it," Doc says with a grin. "Baby Whitehall, shaking her tits for strangers. She'll be fucking humiliated."

"And you'll have access to her whenever you want. If she's in your clubs, she's as good as yours."

Doc shrugs. "I'm not gonna apologize for wanting to destroy her pussy."

Bobby makes a noise of disgust and Doc winks at him. "Don't be a prude, Basher. You've had plenty of fun at Dreams and you can stop by whenever you want. I'll give you half-off on a dance."

"Fuck you, asshole."

"Bobby, what do you think we should do with her?" I say, cutting off whatever inane retort Doc was about to respond with. "You know the girl. What do you think will work?"

Bobby winds his chopsticks through his noodles. "I…"

"Yes?"

He shakes his head. "I dunno."

"Bobby," I say gently. "You have a right to talk, and I have a responsibility to listen."

He screws up his face like he's trying not to vomit. "I… guess. I guess I wanna marry her."

Doc bursts out laughing. Adriano snorts. I bite the inside of my cheek, so I don't join them. "Bobby…"

He scowls. "Laugh all you want. What's gonna piss Parker off more than knowing his fiancée married someone else?"

"Me fucking her in front of fifty Russians?" Doc suggests.

Bobby's gaze locks on mine. "I care about her. I'll look after her. And we'll start trying for a baby right away."

Doc keeps right on laughing, but I can see where Bobby's coming from. It *would* be humiliating to send Parker pictures of his fiancée heavy with another man's child. If I made January my mistress, I wouldn't get her pregnant. As sweet as it would be to see my child swelling that perfect body, I don't need illegitimate children draining my bank account and compromising my lineage.

Perhaps January *is* better suited to Bobby. And if I gave her to him, maybe he wouldn't be too mad if I had her a few times first.

Doc seems to be thinking along the same lines. "You can marry her, Basher. But the second your back's turned, I'll be coming up the stairs to fuck up the paternity tests."

Bobby snorts. "You think I'll be living here once we're married?"

"What are you gonna do? Drag her back to Ohio? Get her to help you with the pigs?"

"Valente," Bobby says calmly. "You could grease every pole in Dreams with your personality. You're a scumbag, and the day January wants to fuck you is the day I buy a fallout shelter because the fuckin' world's ending."

I look to Adriano. He's working his way down a second bowl of ramen. An outsider would think he was ignoring us. "Adri, you weigh in."

He shakes his head.

"Don't be like that. You helped bring her here. What do you want to do?"

"I think," he says, chewing slowly, "we put her down."

There's a beat.

"The fuck, Rossi?" Doc says. "*Always* with the unfettered fucking murder."

Bobby points a finger at Adriano. "Do not touch her."

I hold up a hand. "I asked his opinion. He gave it. He's as entitled to discuss killing her as either of you are your plans."

"Fuck that," Doc snarls. "The girl's useless as a corpse. Why can't we at least make money off her?"

"Well? Adriano?" I ask.

"Because she's a whining bitch."

Bobby's jaw tightens.

"She *is* fairly whiny," Doc concedes.

Adriano wipes his face with the back of his hand. "She'll make a terrible wife, a useless stripper, and a worse prisoner."

"So we kill her?" I ask. "How is that helpful?"

"It's helpful because it's practical. We only took the girl to break Parker. And all your bullshit ideas—having her strip, keeping her as a whore, getting her pregnant—you think any of that will have the same effect as me cutting out her heart and sending it to him?"

No one answers because no one can. All of us return to our food. When I'm finished, I look around the table. Bobby is moodily spooning up ramen and letting it splash into the container. Doc has his head down, clearly scheming, and there's a hard glint in Adriano's eyes. Tonight was supposed to be a celebration. Instead, we sit here, entirely divided. It's my fault. I didn't intend to take the girl for myself. I'm no stranger to pampered princesses and rarely in the mood to play the dutiful prince. Yet I can't let the others have her. I know from watching fallen bosses that to assume a prize wanted by everyone in your inner circle is to invite distrust. I will make her mine, but it has to look democratic.

The solution comes to me, bright as a bulb. "We should speak to her about this."

Everyone looks up.

"You mean tell January what each of us wants for her?" Bobby asks.

"Yes."

Adriano scowls. "You'll let the girl choose?"

"We're in a gridlock and it would be useful to understand what she wants." And January almost came on my dress shoes. There's no way she won't choose me.

"I like it," Doc says.

I look to Bobby and he nods.

"So, we're in agreement? Tonight, we drink, tomorrow we talk to January."

Doc smirks. "How's Adriano gonna pitch her on getting murdered?"

"He doesn't have to talk to her."

"I want to," Adriano says.

"You will not kill her without my permission."

His green eyes look poisonous and for a second, I think he's going to tell me to go fuck myself, but then he inclines his head. "Fine."

I'm far from reassured but I turn to the others. "I'll talk to her first."

"Why?" Doc demands.

I point to the Velluto crest on the wall.

"Fine. But I'm second."

"Third," Bobby says, a flush working its way down his neck.

"Then we have a consensus." I pour out more grappa. "Cards?"

We call downstairs for cigars and brandy. Doc takes over the sound system playing the kind of jolting acid house that sets your teeth on edge. We talk, tell jokes, go over the interesting parts of the abduction and speculate on whether Parker is slitting his own wrists. Doc robs us blind, as he does whenever we play cards. The tension between us melts away and we laugh together, the way we did when we were boys.

And yet there's another figure hovering by our table, watching silently in her wedding lingerie. I glimpse her in the moments between beats, between hands, between swigs of brandy and puffs of smoke. I feel her there and wonder if she's sleeping or crying in her cage beneath Velvet House.

CHAPTER SIX

January Whitehall

THIS IS WORSE than a nightmare. Nightmares end and this goes on and on and on. What kind of people have a basement cell in their house? Or was it made for me? It's hard to know which idea is scarier.

I lie on the single bed with the limp pillow over my face, waiting for something to happen. My stomach gurgles non-stop. In the corner of the cage is a small, walled-off bathroom with a toilet and sink but no shower. I can drink from the tap, but there's no food. I think it's close to three days since I've eaten. I take out Zia Teresa's St. Christopher and run my fingers around the edges.

When I woke on soft red carpet in a beautiful house, I thought I'd been rescued. Seeing Doc's awful smirk, my hopes died a second time.

Domenico Valente.

A poetic name for a terrifying man. The priest's vestments hid his neck tattoos and his lean, powerful body. In a sleeveless T-shirt and black jeans, he reminded me of an arctic wolf. I remember what 'Tesorina' means now. Treasure. He's mocking me. I don't know much about people, but I know when they hate me for being a Whitehall. *Lurida sgualdrina,* he called me. *Filthy whore.*

But I'm not a whore. I'd never kissed anyone until him. I recall the way he pressed his lips onto mine and heat goes skittering through me like flame across oil.

"I didn't like it," I tell the cell. "He had a knife. He *slapped me.*"

No one answers.

I don't like bad boys. That was Giuseppina. I crossed the street when I heard loud voices or saw tattoos. I like nice boys. Boys like…

Roberto Bassilotta.

In my senior year, I needed help with Algebra. I've always been terrible at math, but mom wouldn't let me drop it. My teacher said Bobby was the best tutor in the tri-state area, so mom arranged a trial session. Quinn was so jealous.

"I almost flunked math on purpose just to qualify for his help. You wait, he looks *just* like he's in a boy band."

I thought Quinn was exaggerating but when I met Bobby in the library, I almost laughed. He had soulful brown eyes, big shoulders, and slightly stick-out ears. He was handsome in the friendliest possible way and I felt silly for liking that.

Bobby had worksheets arranged on the desk beside him, but before I could say 'hello' Kurt moved the sheets to the other side of the table. "Miss Whitehall will sit here."

I was so mortified, but Bobby smiled like it was totally normal to have pushy bodyguards. "No problem, January. Take a seat and tell me where you're having the most trouble with math."

We met three times a week after that, sitting opposite each other, going over my homework and practice exams.

"Don't call yourself stupid," he would say when I got frustrated. "You're not stupid, you're learning."

"Learning how stupid I am," I'd say, and he'd laugh.

He wore a rotation of dark blue sweaters and shirts. They always clung to his muscular chest, and he pushed up the sleeves so I could see his strong forearms. I used to fantasize about touching them. I knew if mom found out I had a crush on Bobby, she'd stop our tutoring sessions, so I never talked about him. The only time I ever said his name was during my confessions to Domenico.

Doc must have loved hearing my pathetic little fantasies and telling Bobby everything I said.

I press the pillow harder into my face trying to smother away the shame. He must see me as such a child.

A crushed-out schoolgirl telling her priest about her math tutor. So embarrassing.

Why do you care? a sharp voice in my head demands. *He killed Kurt.*

But it's hard to hold that knowledge in my brain. It doesn't feel real. Not real the way Bobby coming down the stairs was real. He was wearing a shirt I'd seen a million times at Trinity Grammar and all I could think was *'Oh my God, Bobby will save me!'*

But he looked different. At school he was always a little awkward, here he was agile and confident. And when he looked at me, his expression was hard.

Somewhere inside the basement, I hear water dripping. *Plink. Plink. Plink.* It's lucky I'm not the kind of person who gets stressed out by background noise. Mom would go crazy down here. Is she with the police? Or are she and Mr. Parker trying to handle this privately? I hope not. The men upstairs would tear anyone they'd send after me apart. Especially…

Adriano Rossi.

Ridiculously tall and even more tattooed than Doc. His light brown hair is so thick, it looks almost greasy. Long on top and shaved around the sides. He has a short scrubby beard and a proud nose all twisted from being broken. A gold tooth flashes when he talks. And those eyes, those Holographic green eyes. I should have recognized him at the cathedral. He was always waiting in reception at my ballet studio, staring so intently that for once I was glad Kurt and Theodore were with me. And when I started my lessons, he'd watch me dance through the windows of our classroom.

"He's a pervert," Nadia told anyone who would listen. "He's taking underwear out of lockers when we're not looking."

I used to think she was silly because he didn't watch in a gross way, staring at our legs and breasts. His eyes followed the movement, the way you're supposed to, and I felt bad for him because maybe he just liked ballet. Which proves what an idiot I am. I can still taste the barrel of the gun. See the bear-like shape of him above me, pumping it into my mouth. If someone takes my life in this house, it will be Adriano Rossi.

Unless it's the last one.

Elliot Morelli.

Even as I lie trapped in the dark, my insides glow at the thought of him. Eli Morelli ordered Kurt's death. He made Adriano put the gun in my mouth. He slapped me in the face. It shouldn't matter that he's handsome. I recall the feel of his shoe between my legs. The way he looked as he rubbed me. "Doesn't that feel nice?"

A fever breaks across my body. I refuse to touch the place where he violated me, but I know if I did, I'd be soaking. What is wrong with me?

I know the Morelli name. Their family is as prominent in New York as the Whitehalls. But I haven't heard of an 'Eli' or an 'Elliot.' That doesn't mean much. Mom doesn't like the Morellis. I think there's bad blood between our families. But if Eli is a Morelli, why is he a criminal? I'm not naïve, I know when the law prevents my uncles from doing what they like, they go around it, but abducting me and killing my bodyguard isn't bribing a city councilor to get a new skyscraper built.

"You are the property of Velvet House," Eli said as he stroked his shoe against me. But what is Velvet House? A gang? A business? He introduced himself as Elliot *Velluto* Morelli. Velluto means 'Velvet' in Italian. Whatever Velvet House is, he named it after himself.

A yawn stretches my jaw painfully wide and my vision swims. I want to stay awake for whatever happens next, but I'm so, so tired. I push Zia's medallion back into my bra and let my eyes close.

"*Bella.*"

Someone is shaking my shoulder. "Zia?"

"No, *bella.*"

I blink. My bedroom is cold. Strangely shaped. The truth rushes in like light under a door. Not my bedroom. Not my house. I'm kidnapped and a man is leaning over me, his smile like something out of a song.

"Mr. Morelli?"

"Yes." He examines me and his dark eyes gleam like amber in the lamplight. God he's pretty. I feel like I should apologize, though I have no idea what for. "Good morning…? Or good evening?"

He doesn't smile. "How are you feeling, Miss Whitehall?"

I'm exhausted. My face is grubby with old makeup and I'm worried I smell. And even though I know it's not true, it feels like at any moment, mom could come in and explode because I have a boy in my room. "I feel fine."

He smiles. His shirt is bright white, and the collar is open. I imagine burying my face in his golden chest.

"I'm glad to hear it, *bella*."

I wish he wouldn't call me that. I know he's not saying I'm beautiful. That it's an Italian pet name like 'sweetheart.' But the way it comes out in his accented voice sends butterflies fluttering through me.

Eli frowns, regal-looking lines appearing on his fore-head. "How old are you?"

I gnaw my lower lip. Why is he being so polite? Last night he struck me and acted like he hated me. Is he trying to find out more information to hurt Mr. Parker? "I turned eighteen last month."

"That's very young to be engaged."

"It, um, was an arrangement?"

Why am I saying it like it's a question?

Eli takes my left hand and examines my engagement ring. His touch sends shivers up my arm. His skin is soft, but I can feel the strength in his fingers. He could hurt me if he wanted to. He has.

He pulls the ring from my finger and holds it up to the lamplight. "This diamond, *bella*. It's very…" He gestures at me, demanding an answer.

"Big?" I suggest.

"Vulgar."

"Oh." The stone is four carats, so it wasn't cheap, but it does kind of look like a crystal microwave. Eli tucks the ring into his breast pocket. My stomach drops, but I know better than to ask for it back. What is he going to do with it? The obvious answer is 'sell it' but he doesn't seem like someone who needs money.

Eli smiles. His teeth are perfect. "Domenico tells me you speak Italian."

"I… Yes."

"Wonderful. It's not every day you meet an American girl who speaks Italian. *Sei mai stata in Italia?*" *Have you been to Italy?*

I hesitate. Zia Teresa and I only spoke Italian when my mom was away and it's easier to understand what people are saying than talk.

"No… *Non songa mai stata in Italia,*" I venture.

He nods. "Almost. *Non sono* mai *stata.*"

"Sorry," I whisper. "My Zia Teresa emigrated in the '60s and never learned modern Italian. She speaks dialect. So do I, I guess."

"I see." Eli shifts closer and I smell lavender cologne, fresh and achingly lovely. I wish I could have a shower.

"I have something for you, Miss Whitehall," he says.

"A change of clothes?"

He laughs. "Depending on how you receive my proposal, yes. And I might rethink my offer of yesterday and let you come upstairs. Would you like to sleep in a nice four-poster bed in a room with windows?"

The thought of escaping the cage makes my heart lift. "What would you like to give me?"

He looks me up and down. "All kinds of things, *bella.*"

My cheeks burn. I'm always doing this, setting people up to make jokes at my expense. In middle school, Ryan Wingfield said, 'If I told you that you had a beautiful body, would you hold it against me?' and I said yes. Everyone died laughing at me.

"Sorry," I mumble. "I'm kind of clueless."

"You're adorable. Here." Eli pulls something from his suit pocket. A small red apple. He holds it out to me. "Eat."

I take the apple as fast as I can without snatching. I already feel my teeth sinking into the skin between my teeth, the sweet juice crushing onto my tongue. But when the apple touches my lips, I pause. What if it's poisoned? I lower it to my lap.

Eli raises a brow. "You're not hungry?"

"I... Not right now."

"You're refusing me?"

My mouth goes dry. It's stupid to decline something from this man, even if it's poison. I give him my best silly smile. "Eating in front of people makes me nervous."

"Ah." A small smile curves his beautiful mouth. He takes my chin in his hand and my stomach turns over. "Would you like a gift, *bella*?"

"What about the apple?"

"That was a treat. This..." He reaches into his other pocket and pulls out a necklace. "... is a gift."

It's a short collar of diamonds set with fiery red stones. Even in the lamplight, it glitters like pirate treasure.

"It's so beautiful! Are they garnets?"

Eli brushes a finger over the center stone. "Rubies. My mother's family, the Vellutos have a passion for rubies."

"Oh."

"This..." He sways the necklace so that it shimmers. "... belonged to my mama. When she passed, it became mine."

"I'm so sorry."

He frowns. "You're sorry?"

"That your mom died. That's really sad."

A look passes over his handsome features. Then he

blinks and it's as though nothing happened. "As soon as I saw you, I thought of this necklace. Your red lips and pale skin. Nothing would bring out the beauty of these stones more."

"I… um, thank you?"

He smiles, but his eyes are all business. "Will you wear it for me?"

A rippling warmth spreads through my body. I ignore it, pulling the pillow into my chest. "Not if it's so important to your family. It wouldn't be right."

"I say what's right." His free hand caresses my wrist. "I'll have a dress made for you. Black velvet with a slit up the side. You'll be naked beneath it, my rubies at your throat, and every man who sees you will wish me dead."

He sounds pleased by the idea.

I can see it too. Us. Me in the velvet dress, my hair loose around my shoulders. Eli in a tuxedo, his arm at my waist. We're attending an event, the kind I used to go to with my mom, only this time I won't be hustled away at midnight. I'd be free to dance and drink and explore.

Eli's hand brushes my side, and I pull away. "I don't want… um…"

"You don't want my necklace? Or you don't want me?"

The weight of his questions rolls through my mind. I think I might want him but I don't want *this*. And why are we even talking about the future when I'm locked in his basement? "I thought I was here to punish Mr. Parker."

He smiles as if I'm missing something obvious. "You don't need to know the reason you're here, *bella*. You don't need to know anything at all."

I want that to be true almost as much as I want to put on his necklace and be whatever he wants me to be. But that's so pathetic. I look into his eyes. "Maybe. But I want to know."

"Why? You're a sweet little virgin and I've come offering rubies. Isn't that enough?"

I try to say no but he's already kissing me. I let him, warmth running from his lips to mine. My heart swells inside my chest. He's different from Doc. Softer and more complete. He groans into my mouth and the knowledge this perfect man wants me, sets my skin ablaze. I kiss him back, shame and sweetness battling inside me until Eli pulls away, rubbing a thumb over my lower lip. "Yes. You're everything a woman should be. You will be mine."

There's a rushing sound in my ears. "I'm already engaged."

He smiles "No, you're not."

"Mr. Parker—"

"Will soon be dead. After we've wrung enough misery out of him." He says it as though commenting on the weather.

"But you can't kill Mr. Parker!"

Eli's face contracts into a familiar expression. I'm annoying him, but I can't act like this makes sense. "Why do you all hate Mr. Parker so much?"

He looks at me like I'm a child wanting to know where the sun goes at night. He sighs. "He did wrong by the four of us a long time ago. Does that satisfy your curiosity?"

"Um…" That's not anything I couldn't have guessed. In fact, it would be weirder if Mr. Parker *didn't* do something to make them hate him. "What did he do?"

His face hardens. "Ask another question."

"Okay…" I cast my mind around for something I want to know. "Are you in the mafia?"

His lips press together. "If you ask that again, I will be forced to strike you. I'm a businessman. I have professional interests."

He sounds so disgusted, tears prickle at the corners of my eyes. "Sorry, Mr. Morelli."

"Ah, *bella*, do not cry." Eli throws an arm around my shoulders. I give in and collapse into his chest.

"It will be done," he mutters into my hair. "I will keep you."

I pull away. "You mean… marry me?"

For a second, he stares at me, and then he laughs. A rich, genuine laugh I haven't heard before.

"Sorry," I say again, wanting to disappear. "I shouldn't have... Sorry."

"Miss Whitehall, don't take this as a slight on your beauty, but the two of us are not a match."

I feel my face burn. If he's not attracted to me, why was he kissing me? "What do you mean?"

Eli picks up his necklace from my blankets. It must have slid there while we were kissing.

"It means, I can trace my bloodline back to the House of Savoy. You are from a wealthy family, but I would be marrying beneath my name."

"Oh." I look at the dark ceiling. It's not every day you're told you're not important enough to marry. Especially after everything with Mr. Parker.

He runs a finger along my jawline. "Do not mistake me, *bella*. You are a precious and beautiful thing and I intend to keep you as my own. We would have an arrangement."

My mind goes to designer handbags and tropical holidays. "You mean like a sugar baby?"

That gets another surprised burst of laugher out of Eli. "How does a girl whose internet use was monitored by her ex-fiancé know what a sugar baby is?"

I don't know what's stranger. Hearing him say 'ex-fiancé' as though it's all settled, or that he thinks Mr. Parker was spying on me. But of course he does, *he* was spying on me. Him and Bobby and Doc and Adriano.

"I'm waiting for an answer, Miss Whitehall?"

I swallow. "A girl at my school was on a sugar baby website. My friends and I talked about it sometimes."

"Ah. Well I suppose no amount of surveillance could stop teenage girls gossiping."

"Does that mean you *do* want me as your sugar baby?"

He looks amused. "You'd be my lover."

The word sends a shiver through me. "Oh."

"You'd have your own apartment. Your own car, your own money. We would see each other often. Go to dinner and to parties and on holidays. Everyone would know you were mine."

"And... what would I do when I don't see you?"

"Whatever you feel like, *bella*."

The scary thing is I already know what I would do. The same stuff I planned when I was going to be Mr. Parker's wife. I would cook, exercise, dance, watch true crime documentaries, hang out with Margot and Zia Teresa...

Zia Teresa. Her lined face appears in my mind as clearly as if I was looking at her. Zia disliked Italian men. "Arrogant," she said whenever some dark-haired boy whizzed past in a sportscar. "Mama's boys, every last one and that doesn't make them sweet. It makes them come home at four in the morning stinking of alcohol and another woman's perfume and lying through their teeth.

You'd be better off married to a kitchen sink."

I always thought she was being silly, but none of her daughters married Italians. What would Zia Teresa say about Eli Morelli?

"Look at this swaggering peacock, walking around like he's the king of the world. He's a criminale! You have a little think, January. Why is this mascalzone following you around offering rubies? What do you have that he wants?

I look across at Eli. "Why would you give me a necklace that's so important to your family?"

He turns his head to one side, as though trying to see where the question came from. "Because you will look beautiful in it."

"I think maybe you're not giving it to me. I think maybe it's a loan."

"A loan for what?"

"My body."

He rubs his jaw, but doesn't say anything.

"I don't think I should belong to you." The words fall from my lips before I can stop them.

He tucks the necklace back into his pocket with slow deliberate movements. "Is this about Doc? Would you prefer some tattooed *coglione* to be the first man to take you to bed?"

I remember my first kiss, that violent clash of mouths. "No. I just don't think I should be... um, seeing anyone right now."

It's such a stupid thing to say that I expect him to laugh again, but he just nods and moves closer to me on the bed. "What do they call a man who pays a sugar baby?"

I blink. "A sugar d—"

Before I can get the word out, he pulls me across his thighs. I struggle but he pins my hands together at the small of my back. He tugs my underwear down, exposing my backside. "I'm waiting, Miss Whitehall. A sugar what?"

My brain is numb, fifty thousand thoughts playing at a million volumes. "A sugar…"

His hand strikes my ass, making me cry out. "Yes?"

"… daddy," I gasp, my skin burning.

A huff of laugher. "Yes. A sugar daddy." He smacks me harder, the sensation like white fire across my cheeks.

"Did your father spank you when you were a little girl?"

I shake my head.

"That's not surprising. You need a man to teach you how to behave."

He smacks me again. I picture myself thrown over his lap with my wedding panties pulled down and heat pools between my legs. I look over my shoulder at him and a crazy part of me wishes he was my husband. That I had walked down the aisle yesterday and found Elliot Morelli at the end of it. My chest goes tight. "Please?"

"Please what?"

"Please let me go."

For a second, I think he won't, then I'm rolling off his lap, crashing onto the floor. Eli adjusts his cuffs as I crawl into a seated position.

"You will be mine," he says, calmly. "But you're not ready. You need time to understand your place in this world."

With a savage smile he reaches down and slides his hand into my corset, his fingers toying with my nipple.

I make a sound I've never heard before. A slutty sort of squeak.

Eli's smile fades. "I'll fuck your virgin cunt until you're melting in my bed, Miss Whitehall. Remember that."

His fingers bite down on my nipple and then he releases me, leaving through my cage door and vanishing into the darkness.

CHAPTER SEVEN

January Whitehall

I EAT ELI'S apple a few seconds after he leaves. I'm too hungry to care if it's poisoned. I wish I could say it was delicious, but I didn't taste a thing. My brain was fully occupied with his offer: '*You will be mine.*'

His proposal isn't so different from the deal my mother made with Mr. Parker. In fact, this one is more personal. Mr. Parker didn't want my body the way Eli does. He just wanted a Whitehall bride to make headway in New York society.

I'm not supposed to know why Mr. Parker wanted me. Mom never said. But when I was thirteen, I asked Zia Teresa why Mr. Parker was allowed to sit next to me when he came to dinner.

"Because he is," she told me.

"But no other boys are allowed to sit near me. If they even try, Kurt takes out his gun."

Zia avoided my gaze. "You ask too many questions, *bella*. A habit you should try to break."

I accepted her decision the way I accepted everything that happened to me but she knew if she didn't tell me the truth, no one would. Two days later she pulled me into my ensuite and ran the shower and bath at the same time.

"What are you doing, Zia?"

"Shh!" She drew me close, her voice barely audible over the pounding water. "You want to know why Mr. Parker sits beside you?"

I nodded.

"Mr. Parker is a billionaire. I don't know what he does, your stepmother says it's computers or something. Anyway, he met your father at a party we hosted for the mayor of New York. Mr. Parker and your father became friends. He was having trouble making connections. Your father told him he was 'new money' and he would have to wait to gain the kind of reputation he wanted."

"Was he angry?"

"Very. A month later he came back to the house and came back to marry into your family."

My eyes went wide. I was only eight when daddy died, so I must have been a baby when they were having these talks. "Mr. Parker wanted to marry me?"

"He wanted to marry your sister. Margot was fifteen, there would have been less time to wait—no, don't make noise, *bella*."

Zia pressed a hand over my pleading mouth, suppressing my moan of horror. Her eyes were fixed on mine. "Be quiet and let me finish. Your father didn't refuse Mr. Parker. But he didn't encourage him either. But then he died, God rest his soul." Zia whipped a quick sign of the cross.

"But Mr. Parker came back?" I pressed.

"He did, *bella*. He waited a year, then returned to negotiate with your stepmother. She offered Margot's hand in marriage, but Mr. Parker said she didn't have the right attitude for a wife. He knew Margot had just been suspended from school. I almost dropped the tray of roast potatoes I was carrying when he suggested you instead. I expected your stepmother to tell him to *di andare a fanculo* but she ordered me to bring you into the dining room. You probably don't remember. You were very young."

She looks at me hopefully and I shake my head. "I don't remember."

"Good." Zia shudders. "I woke you up and carried you to the dining room. I was hoping you would wet yourself in front of him. That you would fall down or beg for a glass of milk. I even pinched you, trying to make you cry, but when I put you down in front of Mr. Parker, you answered all his questions like a little lady in your nightdress and I saw there was nothing I could do.

He liked you. Your mother agreed to the marriage that night."

I could have asked why, but I already knew. Money.

The Whitehalls are seen as ultra, mega wealthy, but we're a large family and our fortune is spread between dozens.

"Asset rich," my Uncle Titus once said at a Christmas party. "But cash poor. That's half the Whitehall dregs these days."

Mom would sooner die than admit it, but we were once those dregs. After daddy died there was no one to work or negotiate our yearly share of the family fortune. We stopped going to our vacation homes. Zia Teresa became not just my nanny, but a cook and housekeeper. Mom and Harris constantly argued about his Audi, mom telling him he'd have to pay for gas and repairs out of his trust fund.

After mom promised me to Mr. Parker, everything changed. One minute mom was screaming we needed to sell our house in Big Bear, the next she had a silver Bugatti and there were four hundred people at my ninth birthday party. I didn't have to ask where the money was coming from. When I was ten, I heard mom asking our accountant "Is Zachery's quarterly payment here yet?" I just didn't know why he was giving us money. And then I did.

I don't blame mom. She was alone with three houses

and four children to take care of. She had a responsibility to look after our family and so did I. At least Mr. Parker wanted to make me a part of his family. All Eli Morelli offered was a ruby necklace on loan and a few nice outings.

And to be touched by him...

I shove the thought away. He kidnapped me, had my bodyguard killed, and locked me in this basement.

I get up and clean myself as best I can. I wash with water from the bathroom sink and rinse my wedding lingerie, leaving it on the towel rail to dry. I wrap the thin blanket around myself and return to the bed, putting my St. Christopher next to the lamp. My stomach rumbles. If I could only escape with Eli's necklace. I'd pawn it then go straight to the nearest deli and eat everything behind the counter. Then I'd book a hotel and take a bath. Call Zia and say, "I'm coming home!"

And then Mr. Parker would find me. And we would be getting married again.

My chest tightens. "Don't," I tell myself. "You would rather be his wife than stuck here."

A clattering scrape makes me jump. Extra light floods into the basement and footsteps clang on the metal stairs.

"Hello?" I call out, trying to sound strong. "Who is it?"

"What's up, Tesorina?"

My heart sinks as Doc emerges from the shadows. He's still barefoot and in ripped black jeans, but his T-shirt has changed. It's another sleeveless one that shows off his tattooed ribs. He must be very proud of the sides of his body. I wrap the blanket tighter around myself. "Hello, Mr. Valente."

"Oh, so well-mannered." He grips the bars of my cage and tilts himself backward. "You ready to chew through your own arm or what?"

I watch him swing himself back and forth. He's so manic, like if at any moment he'll do a backflip or walk on the ceiling. I move right up against the wall. "You never answered my question. Are you really a doctor?"

He grins. "I might be. Does that turn you on?"

I ignore the question. "What kind of doctor?"

"A gynecologist."

I frown. "What's a gynecologist?"

He stares at me for a moment then throws his head back and laughs. The sound bounces around the basement, and it's like a hundred blond Elvises are laughing at me.

My face burns. This isn't a new situation for me. Whatever a gynecologist is, I'm sure it's dirty. I wait for Doc to stop laughing. Eventually, he shakes his head and sighs. "Ah... You're worth every penny it costs to keep you down here, Tesorina."

"How much can one apple and a little water cost?"

"Don't go asking questions. It'll get you killed. Anyway, I didn't come down here to talk money. I've got something for you."

I remember Eli's rubies. Somehow, I don't think Doc's brought me jewelry. He reaches into his back pocket and pulls out an orange packet of Reece's Pieces. "You want?"

Reece's aren't my favorite, but my mouth waters at the thought of peanut butter and chocolate. "Yes please."

"What'll you give me for it?"

I feel like a TV camera is zooming out, showing me exactly how bizarre this is. I was supposed to be married and now I'm considering begging for candy in a basement. "I... I don't know. Just, please?"

With a look that says I've ruined his fun, he tosses the package through the bars, landing it in my lap. I pick up the candy. It's warm and probably half melted from Doc's body heat.

"It's sealed, Tits. Untampered."

I don't know if that's true but just like with the apple, I'm too hungry to care. I tear the packet open and pour the chocolate into my mouth. I chew and swallow it before licking every trace from my teeth and cheeks, avoiding Doc's gaze.

"Want more?" he asks.

Agreeing would be playing into his hands, and even though I'm starving, I don't want to give him that. I look at him, taking in his thick blond hair and bright blue eyes. "You're very fair for an Italian."

He returns to pulling himself back and forth on the bars like he's doing vertical push-ups. I try not to stare at his arms.

"I might not be Italian. I could just speak it."

"Okay."

"You don't believe me?"

I shake my head. It's in the way he moves. That swagger as though the world is secretly his and he's waiting for everyone else to notice.

"I'm northern," Doc says finally. "My mom's family came from Milan. Dad from Vercelli. Or that's what mom said, I never met the prick."

He gives me a look, as though daring me to ask about his absent father. "What about the others? Where are they from?"

"Basher's from Dovadola, the Morellis are from Naples and Adri's a mixed bag. Roman dad. Ukrainian mom."

For some reason, I can picture Adriano's mother, green-eyed and pretty. You can see her in him. The beauty mixed in with that swarthy, scarred face.

"You pissed Morelli off, asking if he's a mafioso." Doc smirks at me as though we planned this together.

"I wasn't trying to be rude."

"Morelli's Nonno on his mom's side was mobbed up.

The old guy wanted to give Eli the empire when he died, but he couldn't."

"Why?"

"Can't pass a dynasty down the maternal line. Not when you've got a son. Morelli's cousin Giovanni's a dipshit, but he's blood, so whaddya gonna do?"

I think of my stepmom. Her Bugatti. Her Chanel suits. Offering Margot to Mr. Parker and settling on me. *Whaddya gonna do?*

"So Eli is a Morelli, like the big New York Morelli family?"

Doc gives me a sly smile. "Yeah, but he's not a big dick player where they're concerned. His old man's the third son."

Just like me.

So even if he's Italian royalty on his mother's side, Eli Morelli is just a third son's son. Maybe that's why he called his business Velvet House, he's leaning into his mother's fancier name.

I feel Doc watching me like he can taste my thoughts. "Not as goofy as you come off, huh?"

"I'm not goofy. I just wasn't very good at school."

"You got that right. You don't have the grades to shill essential oils, but you still got into Fine Arts at Colombia."

I look down at my lap. I never should have gotten into Colombia, but mom and Mr. Parker wanted me to go to college. They said it would make me a more accomplished wife.

"I don't want to get a degree."

"And you think that makes it better? Pushing out someone who did want to be there?"

"I didn't have a choice!"

Doc and I glare at each other, and I half expect him to leave. He jumps off the bars and there's a jangle of keys. "Coming in, Tits."

My cell seems infinitely smaller with Doc pacing inside. I can smell him, that sharp boozy cologne, fresh soap, and clean skin.

He pauses. "You done being a virgin?"

I say nothing. If this is his pitch, it's awful. At least Eli brought rubies.

"… because if you are done being a virgin, we can wrap it up right here, right now."

I picture him on top of me, all that wiry aggression forced down onto my body, and my pussy flutters to life. How long does it take to get Stockholm syndrome?

"What? You want Morelli to bust you open with his golden dick instead?"

Elliot asked me the same thing about Doc. Maybe they have some kind of problem with each other? That could come in handy, although I don't see how.

Doc clicks his fingers. "Hey, I'm talking to you."

"Why would I sleep with any of you? You're holding

me *hostage*."

Doc's eyes narrow. "Do you want nice baby Bobby to get in first?"

"No, I said I don't want *any* of you."

He swaggers closer to the bed, lip curled in a sneer. "If Basher's the one you want, that's okay with me. I'm happy to play second string. In fact, I prefer it."

My brain melts a little. He can't be telling the truth. Guys don't like it when you've slept with anyone, even I know that.

"Or maybe it's not Bobby," Doc says slowly. "Maybe you want it to be Adri?"

I pull my knees into my chest. "Go away."

"I heard your confession, remember?" He clasps his hands to his chest. "I should be kinder to the man who cleans my dance studios. I should say hello to him even though I'm *so* scared."

He gives a loud echoing laugh. "Did you imagine him following you down some dark hallway and making you sit on his big, tattooed cock?"

I want to grab Doc by his pretty blond hair and scream in his face. But if I touch him, he'll be free to touch me, and then I really might lose my virginity in this basement. I think of Zia Teresa. She saved me from Eli. How would she deal with Doc? The answer is obvious. But I don't have a spatula to hit him with.

"Hello? Earth to virgin?"

I meet Doc's eyes and channel every ounce of my inner, disapproving Zia. "Domenico, if I have to be trapped in here, could you maybe, *maybe*, not be so gross?"

He snorts. "You didn't answer my question, *January*. You wanna get fucked by a tattooed murderer?"

"Do you mean Adriano? Or you?"

He smirks. "That's pretty good, Tesorina. Live and you might develop a personality after all. But enough fucking around. You want to die?"

"Excuse me?"

He drops onto the end of the bed, making the thin mattress bounce. A swatch of his thick hair falls into his eyes. It's not fair that someone so insane should be so good-looking. Eli is gorgeous but he's also elegant and can pretend to be nice. Everything about Doc says he'd kill you for dropping a coffee cup.

"Have you realized you're never gonna see your family again?"

All the air rushes out of my lungs. I've avoided thinking about what might happen to me because I thought it meant dying. But Doc's right. Even if I can leave the basement, why would they let me go home and risk telling everyone who abducted me?

A warmth falls on my hand and Doc pushes his fingers through mine. I should pull away, but the feel of another person's touch is too nice to refuse.

"You need to let this all sink in," he says roughly. "But once it does and you're ready to leave the basement, I think you should come dance in my clubs."

"I… what clubs?"

He raises his blond brows.

"Strip clubs?" I ask, my heart sinking.

"Yeah. Good money. Safe as fuck."

I imagine Doc surrounded by beautiful naked women and prickly feelings mix into my panic. I bet he sleeps with the dancers. I bet he flirts with them all psychotically. I bet they like it.

"I'll put you in white lingerie just like your wedding shit. Get you some angel wings and tell the clients you're a virgin. They'll go fucking crazy."

I listen with the same disbelief as when Anita told me I could model. I can't be a stripper. I've never worn a miniskirt before. And will I even be a virgin by the time I leave this cage?

Doc reads my mind. "I don't know if I should fuck you or not. The smart thing would be to keep you pure. Let you work the pole, then auction you off. That way we'd pay for your kidnapping four times over."

I try to pull my hand from him, but Doc holds me fast.

"Tempting," he mutters. "Too fucking tempting. I've never been into virgins, but you…"

Without warning, he kisses me. Hard. My brain

blurs as our mouths move together with far too much familiarity. The fluttering in my pussy becomes a throb.

Doc releases me. "You're just a horny little hand grenade, aren't you?"

"You're disgusting."

His teeth flash in the semi-darkness. "You're like one of those Disney Channel girls, kept squeaky clean for way too long."

His hand slides across my shoulders, making my skin spark. "I think the pendulum's ready to swing the other way, don't you?"

I open my mouth and he cuts me off with another kiss. This one is deeper, his tongue flashing expertly over mine as he shoves the blanket down, exposing my breasts. He palms them, rubbing roughly. "Fuck you've got great tits."

"No…"

"Yes. Now, shhh." He moves closer, his lips brushing my cheek. "I know you, Tesorina. Better than you know yourself. You want freedom."

I struggle sideways. "I do *not*—"

"You were jealous of your friends for going on dates. Jealous of your sister for wearing clothes not made by grandmas. You wanted to be them so badly it cut you up inside."

My protests die in my throat. I confessed to him. He already knows my darkest secrets.

He cups my breast, pressing them together. "Pretty little January stuck at home, engaged to some limp dick old man. Never getting to have fun. Never going out. It was so fucking unfair, wasn't it, Tesorina?"

His words scratch some long-hidden itch in my brain. It feels good to hear someone say it out loud.

Doc rubs his stubble against my cheek. "Give yourself to me and you can do whatever you want. Wear whatever you want. You can get on stage and watch men bankrupt themselves just to look at you. Wouldn't that be fun?"

I swallow. "If I did what you wanted, I'd still be trapped. I'd belong to you."

Doc grips my arms, lifting me onto his lap. "You don't want to be mine?"

We're practically nose to nose and I'm topless. Bottomless, if he decides to tug away the last of the blanket. I stare at him, breathing hard. He gives me a strange look. Is he about to tell me I'm beautiful? That he's fallen for me?

Doc frowns. "I'm not the jealous type. You can fuck whoever you want. Experiment. As long as you're bringing in money, I don't give a shit."

I flinch. Does he really mean that? I try to imagine sleeping with people from his clubs. The men who pay me. My stomach drops to my feet. "I don't want that."

"Liar." Doc bends forward and captures one of my

nipples in his mouth. Wet heat pulses through me and I throw my head back.

"See," he says, releasing my nipple. "Do the Catholic schoolgirl thing all you want, but you're aching."

"No, I—"

"Spare me. I'm not Morelli." He turns us onto the bed, his body arching over mine like a tattooed cage. I screw up my eyes and try to ignore the glow between my legs.

"Tell me you don't want me?"

It should be easy. Just four little words. But I've never been a good liar and as much as I hate this man, the words won't come.

Doc's hands return to my breasts, and he lowers his mouth to my other nipple, drawing on it and making my whole body jerk.

"Doc!"

His tongue circles my sensitive peak. "Say my real name."

"D-Domenico." He sucks me until I see stars. "Please don't do this."

He grinds his hips into mine and I can feel the hard length of him behind his jeans. "It's okay, Tesorina, I'll make it gentle. It's been a long time since I took someone's cherry, but I can do it again."

I hate him. I hate the thought of him with other virgins. I grab his hair and pull as hard as I can.

He looks up at me mildly. "Ow...?"

"You can't sleep with me. Eli promised... he wants..."

Doc's eyes go dark. "Morelli can go fuck himself."

Before I can say anything, his tattooed arm is between my legs, fingers brushing at my thighs. His hands are practiced, surer than sure. I hold my breath as he feels my wetness and grins from ear to ear. "You're soaking, Tesorina."

I screw my eyes shut. "Domenico."

"Yeah, say my fucking name." He runs a thumb over my waxed outer lips, and a moan escapes me.

Doc lets out a low laugh. "You want to get fiddled, baby? You want to come?"

He makes it sound revolting, cheap, and ugly. The way I'll be if I let him do this. I push his chest. "I don't want this."

"Oh yeah, what do you want?"

"I want to go home!" It bursts out of me, tearful and pathetic, and something in me shifts. "Get off me! I want to go home!"

Doc bares his teeth and I'm sure he's going to slap me. Then the pressure on my lower body vanishes. He stands beside me, looming over the bed. "You're pathetic."

I yank the blanket up, covering myself. "I want to go home."

"Home to what? Being trapped and controlled? Having your mom cash checks on your pussy?"

My chest contracts. "Don't talk about my mom!"

"You mean your pimp?"

"Shut up!"

He gives a mean jagged laugh. "If some trailer park bitch did what she did, the cops'd throw her in jail. Your mom sells you to the highest bidder and the Governor comes to the wedding."

Tears burn in my eyes. There's nothing nice about these truths. Nothing exhilarating. They're ugly and even though I want to, I can't dispute them.

"When are you gonna get it, moron? You were already for sale. Now you don't have to sit around crying about it. You've got a choice."

"By working for you?" I sob.

Doc thumps a fist into his chest. "Yes! Freedom. Money. Self-respect. Whoever you want to fuck whenever you want to fuck them."

My stomach churns so hard I almost throw up. Has it really come to this? All my ballet lessons and body-guards. My wedding plans and my acceptance into Colombia. Is my only real chance for freedom to be Eli's sugar baby or a stripper? My gaze falls on the tiny gold pendant on my dresser. Protection for whenever you journey from home. I meet Doc's gaze. "No. I won't work for you."

"Because you're a weak little girl?"

I move so fast I don't feel myself do it. One minute I'm on the bed, the next I have a finger in Doc's face. "Because you don't deserve me!"

He takes a step back. I move with him, pressing my finger into his chest. "Maybe my mom sold me. Maybe I was always going to be someone's property, but at least Mr. Parker was respectful! At least Eli tried to make being with him sound nice! You come down here with Reece's Pieces, telling me you couldn't care less who I sleep with and that I'm stupid and you expect me to want to be with you?"

Doc grabs my finger and reels me in like a fish. "I could make you want it. I could make you so desperate you'd fuck me on the cathedral altar in front of your whole family."

My bravery vanishes in the blink of an eye. "What do you—"

His hand closes around my throat. "You want me to show you? Take the choice right out of your hands?"

I sense a genuine question and while I have no idea how he could take my choice away, the last thing I want is less choice. I shake my head.

"Fine." Doc releases my throat and heads for the cage door, pulling his keys from his pocket. "You've got three options. You can strip in my clubs, you can eat a bullet, or you can get sold to the Bratva. Know what that is?"

"No."

He shoves the key in the lock and wrenches it open. "Russian mafia. You'll earn on your back. Get fucked two dozen times a day. Come on so many strangers' cocks you won't walk a block without seeing someone who's railed you."

He moves through the cage door and slams the bars between us. My heart shrinks in my chest. Despite everything, I don't want to be alone again. I put my arms through the cage. "Doc?"

He doesn't look back. There's still a card I can play. Maybe the only one I have left. "Who's Alessia Valente?"

He stops, his whole body tensing. Instantly I know I've made a mistake. "Sorry, I didn't—"

A hand grabs me through the bars, pulling me into the cold metal. The blanket falls to my feet and I'm naked. The point of Doc's butterfly knife is at my throat.

"How," he rasps, "the fuck do you know that name?"

I try not to scream. "You said it at the cathedral. To Mr. Parker before you spat on him. And your last name's Valente so I thought Alessia might be your mom or your sister?"

Doc doesn't move. "You have no idea. None. Because you're a stupid bitch with no sense. Isn't that right?"

I nod frantically.

"So let me help you out." He runs the flat of the

blade along my cheek. "Say my sister's name again and I'll cut you from ear to ear then fuck you with the knife."

His eyes are hollow points of light. Headlamps in the dark. You could disappear into them without a trace. He's telling the truth. He could cut me. He could kill me without a second thought.

"I won't say it again," I tell him. "I'm sorry. I'm *so* sorry."

He pushes me backward and I fall to the ground, relief blaring through me. Doc's cheeks hollow and something wet runs down my face.

"Oh my God, you spat on me!"

For a moment we stare at each other and it's crazy, but I want to laugh. I'm pretty sure Doc does too.

"Sorry," I say in a rush. "Doc, I mean it. I'm sorry."

His face works furiously but he turns, storming away without another word.

I lie motionless on the ground. I was right. Alessia is his sister.

CHAPTER EIGHT

January Whitehall

"**G**ET UP," A voice barks, and I jerk awake. I cried for so long after Doc left that I must have dozed off.

"I said, get up." I jump to my feet like I'm in the army and turn to the voice. It's a man I haven't seen before. He must be at least sixty with a grey mustache and unfriendly expression.

He throws a cloth bag through the bars. "Put this on."

I don't move.

"Do it or you won't get to wash."

Wash? Like take a shower? I grab the bag off the floor and ram it over my head. Even if he's lying, I'm willing to take the risk if it means feeling clean again.

I hear the cage unlock. The man takes my elbow and guides me forward. I'm unsteady on my feet, but his touch is light as if he doesn't really want to come near me. His directions are clipped as he leads me up flights of stairs and around corners.

"You've got fifteen minutes," he finally says, dropping his hold and pulling the bag from my head.

"What—" I say, but he's already closing the door behind him.

I blink, readjusting my eyes to the bright lights of the room before letting out a shaky laugh. He was telling the truth. I'm standing in a beautiful white marble bathroom. There are stacks of fluffy towels, shelves heaving with body wash and shampoo and moisturizer, and toothbrushes still in their packaging.

I grab a strawberry body wash and a coconut shampoo and conditioner and strip out of my underwear in a second, practically running into the big rainforest shower. I let the hot water pound on me for minutes before scrubbing myself with a loofa. The thick white bubbles slide over my skin and it's like a religious experience.

Mindful of the time limit, I finish quickly and step out of the shower and wrap myself in a towel, feeling five pounds lighter.

Beside the towels is a small pile of clothes. A pink T-shirt, white cotton shorts, white socks, and pink panties. A little girlie but much better than what I expected—I'm sure Doc would want me in a dog collar and a leather thong or something.

I brush my teeth, moisturize my face, comb my hair, and roll deodorant under my arms in a state of rapture. After being trapped in the dark, I'm beginning to feel almost normal again. The clothes fit snugly but there's no bra or pockets for me to put my St. Christopher in and you can see my nipples through the T-shirt. I pull the socks on and look around for shoes. I knock on the inside of the door. "Hi, are there any shoes?"

"No."

"Oh, but my socks will be ruined on the floor?"

An irritated grunt. "Are you dressed?"

"Yes."

"Then put the bag back on your head."

I do it, and hold my St. Christopher in my fist. The door unlocks and the man takes my arm again. When he next takes off the bag we're in a small room, empty except for a table and chair. On the table is a bowl of tomato soup and a grilled cheese. My heart leaps. "Is that for me?"

"Yes. Sit."

"Thank you! Thank you so much! Mr…?"

He looks at me with his flinty grey eyes. "Gretzky."

"Thank you, Mr. Gretzky."

I eat fast, burning the roof of my mouth, but I don't care. In seconds the plate and bowl are empty.

Mr. Gretzky scowls. "Done?"

I nod. "Everything was delicious."

"I didn't make the food." He hands me back the bag.

I hesitate. "Does anyone want to see me? Mr. Morelli, maybe?"

"No."

With a sigh I lower the bag onto my head. Mr. Gretzky leads me back down the house until I hear the now-familiar creak of the basement door. My chest hollows out. It'll be better to be clean and fed in my cage but it's so lonely in the dark. Maybe that's Eli and Doc's plan? To melt my sense of perspective and force me to choose one of their proposals out of sheer boredom.

Or they've forgotten about me.

"Lift your feet so you don't hit the grate," Mr. Gretzky says.

I do as I'm told before I pull the bag off my head. "Thank you for helping me—Ahhh!"

Bobby rises from my bed, his hands up. "Sorry! Sorry, January, I didn't mean to scare you!"

He's wearing chinos and a navy sweater with the sleeves pushed up. He looks like a TV boyfriend. "What are you doing here?"

"I wanted to talk to you."

The basement door slams. Mr. Gretzky must have left. Which means Bobby and I are alone.

He moves to one side, gesturing at the bed. "Come sit down."

Unsure what else to do, I sit, tucking my feet underneath me. I'm super aware of my damp hair and scrubbed face, my nipples brushing against my T-shirt. I fold my arms across my chest. "Um, so why are you here?"

Bobby scrubs a hand through his short hair. "Do you feel better after your shower?"

"Yeah totally."

"That's… good."

He's not acting cool and confident anymore. He's more like he was when he was tutoring me, nice but awkward. I try not to smile. Bobby's not insanely beautiful like Eli, or dangerously pretty like Doc. He's more practical. More American. The kind of guy who sends roses on Valentine's Day and your family likes—if your family was normal.

"So, I uh…" He gestures to my side table. "Got you some stuff."

I turn. Beside the lamp is a small bunch of pink flowers in a plastic cup and a thin gold necklace.

"I saw you've got that St. Christopher. I thought you might wanna put it on a chain."

I throw my arms around Bobby's neck. "Oh my God, thank you, thank you, *thank you*!"

He makes a strangled sound but his arms close around me. His sweater is cashmere and I rub my face against it, inhaling his sweet, wood smoke scent. Bobby's so strong, he's so—

Cold expands in my core as I remember him approaching Kurt, his face steady and sure. The man holding me raised the gun that killed my bodyguard. I saw it. Saw Kurt lying on the ground, gaping red where his face used to be.

I push myself away. "I… um…"

Bobby's jaw sets, his brown eyes fixing on me. "Give me your St. Christopher. I'll put it on the chain."

I open my fist and stare at the little gold circle. A part of me wants to give it to him, but a much bigger part of me wishes he hadn't killed Kurt. As lovely as it would be to wear the medallion around my neck, I can't have Zia Theresa's precious St. Christopher attached to something so compromised.

"Or not," Bobby says, his face bright red.

"I'm sorry Bobby, I just—wait, what are you doing?"

He drops to one knee in front of me. "January, I need to say something. I want you out of this basement. I want you safe and happy again."

There's a throb in his voice, as though my pain has been hurting him too.

"Can I talk to my Zia Teresa or my mom?"

"Not yet. But we can make other arrangements."

"What kind of arrangements?"

He reaches out a hand to mine. Sparks tingle up my arm and as much as I want to pull away, I don't.

"JJ." His soulful brown eyes lock on mine. "You're the most incredible woman I've ever met."

My heart slams against my chest. "But I don't know how to do anything. I don't know what seven times nine is."

"That doesn't matter. I waited my whole life to find someone like you."

My head is pounding. I want so much to ask what he means if he's saying what I think he is, but this isn't the Trinity Grammar library. And in a corner of my mind, Kurt is begging for his life as Bobby walks toward him, holding Eli's gun.

I imagine Zia Teresa smoking under the rangehood of my stepmom's oven. *Wake up, bella. You're being lied to again.*

I look down at my clean, tight shorts. "Did you make it so I could go upstairs and wash and eat?"

"I… yeah."

"How come you didn't take me yourself? You got Mr. Gretzky to do it?"

I try to sound sweet, non-threatening, but Bobby's eyes narrow. "I'm not trying to manipulate you."

"Of course not," I say. But I know he is. He wanted me to be clean and comfortable, but he didn't want to bag my head and steer me around Velvet House like a crash test dummy. He still wants me to see him as a sweet, gentle guy. My math tutor. My high school crush.

The thought is more painful than Eli's threats, Adriano's gun in my mouth, Doc's knife against my neck.

"January? What's wrong?"

I pick up my pillow and hug it to my chest. "Um, like, everything?"

The corner of his mouth kicks up. "Yeah, I guess that's about right, but we can make things better."

I look away. Part of me wants to tell him anything is better than being locked in a basement, but I don't want to waste Bobby's niceness by making him mad. "Thank you for letting me wash and giving me food."

"JJ… I'm still the guy who taught you trigonometry."

I know what he really means. You can still like me. I'm still safe. But one thing might not be true and the other definitely isn't.

"I know."

There's a long painful silence.

"How did you even become my math tutor?" I ask, needing to say something.

"It wasn't too hard. I've got a master's degree in computer science."

"Oh." I assumed he'd blackmailed his way into Trinity Grammar, like Doc posing as the priest or Adriano pretending to be a janitor. But then again Bobby did tutor people with math. People who weren't me. "Do you… work in computer science?"

"Velvet provides surveillance services. I run our operations. They're some of the best in the country."

I hear a note of pride in his voice and my stomach knots. "Surveillance services for criminals?"

He traces his tongue over his lower lip. "Yes. But also, corporations and hotels and families like yours."

"Like mine?"

"Wealthy people with a lot of assets." He shifts on his knee. "I know the impression we must have given you, but Velvet House isn't a gang. It's a business."

"I don't think a lot of businesses kill people on their carpet. Or kidnap brides."

He lets out a slow breath. "There are some complicated sides. But what's happening with you, it isn't standard practice. Parker is… different."

It's so strange to hear him say Mr. Parker's name. I thought my math tutor and the man I was supposed to marry were separate parts of my life. Turns out they were actually joined long before I showed up.

"How does Mr. Parker fit into your business?"

Bobby's face shifts. He becomes the man who killed Kurt again. I wriggle backward. "Sorry, I shouldn't have asked."

"No, you shouldn't have. But take my word for it. Parker isn't who you think he is. He's dangerous."

I picture Mr. Parker's round face and baby blue eyes. "I've seen more dangerous cavoodles being walked through Central Park."

Bobby doesn't smile. "He's a bad man. Take it from me."

"But he's always been so nice!"

Bobby surges to his feet, his face tight. "He was biding his time until you married him. How can you not see that?"

"Mr. Parker had plenty of time to be mean to me, but he never even touched me."

A low growl rumbles in Bobby's chest. "I never touched you either."

"You weren't supposed to be my husband."

Bobby's jaw juts out. "So you wanted to marry him? You wanted his filthy hands all over your body?"

"No, but I wanted to do right by my family. And I *didn't* want to be locked in a cage."

Bright red spreads down Bobby's cheeks and into his neck like melted raspberry gelato. "You're right. But that's what I'm here to talk to you about—the other arrangements. You'll need to stay here for a while longer. But once this has blown over, I think it could be a good idea, if you want, and *you* think it's a good idea for us, for you and me. For us… Not that there's any pressure. There's no pressure. It's up to you, JJ…"

His words sound like anagrams. Like there's a message in there but I can't figure out what it is without a roll of paper and tri-color pens. "Bobby, what are you saying?"

He clears his throat, so red I can almost feel the heat coming off him. "We can get married. For your protection."

Somewhere in the basement, water drips.

I want to ask if he's joking, but I'm pretty sure he'll die of embarrassment. "Um, how will being married protect me from Mr. Parker? Aren't you guys planning to kill him?"

"I… yeah." Bobby's gaze slides sideways. "It's more of a… future type… thing."

I get it. He doesn't mean 'protect me' from Mr. Parker. He means 'protect me' from his friends. From stripping and becoming a sugar baby and whatever Adriano Rossi wants to do to me. I gnaw at my thumbnail.

"January?"

I can't meet his eyes. "Yeah?"

Bobby drops back onto his knee. Getting the news out seems to have relieved some of his internal pressure. "I know this is a lot to take, but it wouldn't be a marriage like you had with Parker. I don't want to control you. Once you're under my protection, you can do whatever you like."

Except go home. And I can't imagine Doc, the man who just held a knife to my throat, letting me go skipping into the sunset with Bobby. "Will the others…

um, be okay with us getting married?"

"They won't like it. But if it's what you choose, I'll put my foot down and they'll have to respect it."

I believe him. My heart jolts. Could I marry Bobby? It would be better than stripping or being sold to the Russian Mafia. But even as I consider what saying yes would mean, my insides twist. I'm trapped behind dirty glass. I can only see pieces of what's happening or why. I want to wipe it clean and see the whole thing. "I thought I wasn't fancy enough to marry?"

"That's Eli. I'm no Italian prince. You'll be punching a few belts below your weight with me."

There's a smile in his voice. Without thinking I look right into Bobby's face and his loveliness overwhelms me. His brown eyes are welcoming, and I imagine walking down the aisle toward him. Sleeping in his big, muscly arms. My mind tries to dream up what he looks like naked, and I turn away.

Bobby takes my hand again, folding it in his. "Just because I'm not a Velluto doesn't mean I can't take care of you. What I do pays better than Wall Street. You can have everything you had at your mom's house. More."

The gooshy romantic feelings vanish. "Is that what you think of me? That I'm a gold digger who wants diamond spoons and Amex black cards?"

"No! I just want you to know the world is open to you. That if you marry me, I'll work my ass off to make your life beautiful. I'll buy us a house anywhere you like, and you can go to college or start your own business or dance or take singing lessons or just... be my wife."

Bobby sounds exactly the way I wanted a man to sound when he talked about marrying me. He even looks exactly the way I dreamed my husband might look. But from the corner of my mind, Zia Teresa speaks. *If you marry this man, you'll be a murderers' wife.*

"... and we can get a dog or a cat or—"

I lean forward and press a finger to Bobby's lips. "Are you asking me to marry you or are you *saying* that's what's going to happen?"

His eyes widen. "I'm asking. I'd never... I'm *asking,* January."

"Then my answer is no."

Bobby's face falls. "Is this because you want to be with Eli?"

Oh my God, not this again. "No."

His mouth becomes a hard line. "Doc?"

I tear my hand from his. "What is your problem? You and the others all asking, 'Is it him instead of me?' I don't want any of you! Why is that so hard to understand? I just want to go back to the way things were!"

Bobby's mouth softens. "JJ..."

"Only my family calls me JJ! You can't call me JJ!"

He stands, his jaw working. He wants to be kind and soft, but I can feel his anger burning beneath the surface.

"You can't go back. And you don't want to. You don't want to be Parker's wife."

"How do you know? You won't even tell me what he did to make you angry."

Bobby shakes his hands in frustration. "Okay," he says. "When did your dancing lessons start?"

"I… when I was little?"

"When you were nine," Bobby corrects. "Because Parker has a thing for ballerinas."

"How do you…?"

"I run professional surveillance for a living. Parker made you start dancing and he's the reason you weren't allowed to give it up when you were in high school."

My stomach swoops. When I was fifteen, my ballet instructor, Madame Blanchet, told me it was time to consider dance styles 'more suited to my figure.' I wasn't too heartbroken. I was already a head taller and two cup sizes bigger than every girl in my class. But when I took Madame Blanchet's letter to my mom, she threw it in the trash. "You're staying at New York Academy. It's important for young women to have poise."

I shake my head like a dog trying to get rid of water. "*Mom* wanted me to be a ballerina."

"And what about your weight? Did your mom want you to weigh exactly one hundred and twenty-one pounds?"

Every muscle in my body goes stiff.

"Again, Parker. He wanted you that way."

The room starts spinning. I try to find Bobby in the blur of lamplight. "Mom weighed me. She changed my food if I wasn't at one-twenty-one."

"And did she do that with your sister? Or just you?"

A million terrifying thoughts zap through me and then everything blows out. My mind goes blank, my body slumps onto the covers, heavy as cement.

An arm wraps around my shoulders. Bobby, engulfing me in cashmere and his sweet smoky smell. He presses his mouth to my hair. "I'm sorry. I'm so fucking sorry. You deserved better."

Energy surges back through me and I turn and half climb into his lap. Bobby goes stiff as a board "JJ... baby... what are you doing?"

"I just need to be closer. Is that okay?"

He twists his knees away. "Ah, maybe not right now..."

For a second, I'm stung, then I see it. The thick ridge along his hip. "You've got a... I gave you a...?"

Bobby's face is scarlet. "Sorry, you're just so beautiful and—"

I move without thinking, shifting myself fully onto his lap. Bobby makes a noise of protest but when I kiss him, he kisses me back.

It isn't like with Doc or Eli. It isn't like anything I've ever felt. It's golden and delicate as a spring morning. A first kiss. A real first kiss. The start of something precious.

We break apart, grinning like idiots. Bobby presses his forehead to mine. "I can't tell you how long I wanted to do that."

"Me too. I never thought…"

"I know."

We kiss again, slower this time, and the feel of Bobby pressed against my shorts makes heat lick between my thighs.

"JJ." Bobby's hands are on my hips and he grinds against me. "You're so gorgeous."

It's wrong, rocking against Bobby's erection. Even wronger than Doc sucking my nipples. Doc made me feel trapped, forced to feel things. Being with Bobby is a choice. But I don't stop and neither does he. He's rougher than I thought he would be and I like it. We kiss until I'm out of breath. Until everything between my legs is tight and soaking.

Bobby's hands brush the bottom of my T-shirt. "Can I?"

I swallow. "I don't know. I'm so confused."

"That's okay." Bobby ducks his head. "You know when I knew I had feelings for you?"

I beam at him like a dork. "Tell me?"

"It was hearing you sing Rex Orange County. That 'Loving is Easy' song. You were smiling and tapping your feet and I just…" He presses a hand to his heart. "Melted."

I laugh, embarrassed and delighted. "I can do better songs."

"Impossible." He kisses my cheek. "I don't want to rush you, but if we get married, I can make everything right."

The glow in my chest evaporates. "Bobby…"

"I know. I know it's a lot of pressure, but we can make it work." His face is earnest and boyish. I open my mouth to ask how old he is exactly and then the thought clicks, as though it was always there. "Bobby? Did you hear me sing Rex Orange County at school?"

His dark eyes flick to the left and then back again. "Yeah."

The taste of cheese and tomato rise in my mouth. "I never sang at school, even to myself. I would have been too embarrassed."

He doesn't say anything but a blush creeps down his neck again. I slide off Bobby's lap and walk to the side of the cage, as far away as I can get. "You were spying on me, weren't you? At home or at my singing lessons or somewhere."

He lowers his head. "I'm sorry."

"I guess you are really good at surveillance."

He huffs out a humorless laugh.

"And you've killed other people, haven't you? Kurt

wasn't the first."

"No."

I nod, feeling calmer than I should. "I think maybe you should go."

"Yeah." Bobby gets to his feet and walks away slowly as though trying to think of some reason to stay. I'm thinking hard too, but there's nothing there. The basement door swings open and then he's gone, just like the other two.

His gold chain is still sitting on my dresser. I don't check if it's fine enough to hold the medallion. I don't touch it at all.

CHAPTER NINE

January Whitehall

PEOPLE HAVE ALWAYS thought I was stupid. I'm the baby of my family. I couldn't say 'spaghetti' properly until I was twelve. My grades have always been terrible, and I believed *everything* people told me. Santa's real. Swallowed gum stays inside you for seven years. Storks deliver babies. Margot and Lachlan made sure kids were never mean to me, but they still laughed when I didn't know what a 'sausage party' was or what '420' meant. I read the wrong parts of the book out loud in English class. Bradley Fox made up a song about me in seventh grade. I still know all the words.

January White,
Can't read or write.
She's too dumb to play,
And eats dirt all day.

People have always thought I'm stupid, but after Bobby left my cage, I *felt* stupid. Bone-deep, soul-piercingly stupid.

I don't have to question what Bobby told me. Mr. Parker is a bad man. The truth is like a spotlight, shining on years of evidence. Mr. Parker watching me carefully while I ate. Mr. Parker always asking about ballet. Mr. Parker begging mom to watch my classes. But more than that, I remember the fearful look in Zia Teresa's eyes when she saw me in my wedding dress. Her St. Christopher medallion. A last-ditch attempt to protect me from an impossible situation.

I don't know if Mr. Parker is a bad man the way the four men in this house are bad men. But he's not who I thought he was. The marriage I imagined having with him, friendly and respectful if not romantic, was a fantasy. He made me do ballet. He controlled my weight through mom. Who knows what else he wanted to do?

I am exactly what Doc told me I was when I first woke up in this house. A stupid girl who can't see what's in front of her face.

Bobby's visit drains the life out of me. I climb back into bed and doze until Mr. Gretzky appears again, banging on my cage door. "Do you want to wash and eat?"

I don't want to go anywhere but I know I'll feel better once I've had some food. "Sure."

He throws me the cloth bag and I cover my face and allow Mr. Gretzky to lead me back upstairs to the bathroom. I have another shower and try not to think about the look on Bobby's face when I told him I can't be his wife.

There's a new outfit beside the shower, a red sundress and black leather flats. Shoes that are barely shoes. What do they think I'd do with sneakers? Hit Mr. Gretzky on the head and try to escape? And where are these outfits coming from? Did Eli do a clothing haul when I got here or something?

The dress feels too small. It isn't but my breasts are pushing over of the top and the waist is tight. I half expect Mr. Gretzky to tell me to change back into my T-shirt and shorts, but he barely looks at me before throwing the bag over my head and leading me to the food room. Scrambled eggs and buttered toast are waiting for me. At home I was never allowed bread unless Mom was away and even then, Zia Teresa bought expensive sourdough. My toast is plain old sandwich bread. The kind that comes in a bag. It's incredible.

"Who cooks my food?" I ask Mr. Gretzky. "Can I thank them?"

He ignores me. Five minutes later I'm back in the cage. A week ago, if you'd told me my biggest issue with being kidnapped would be the boredom, I would have said you were crazy. But it is. With nothing to do, my problems cluster around me like mean birds, pecking and squawking.

"Zia," I whisper. "Please help?"

I'm scared she won't answer, that her voice has abandoned me like everything else, but then it comes.

Get up, bella.

I get to my feet, feeling clumsy and overexposed in my red dress. "What should I do?"

What do you usually do when you're bored?

I smile. I know exactly what to do. I'm amazed I didn't think of it before.

It takes twenty minutes to run through my warm-up scales and then I sing. I sing Adele. I sing The Beatles. I sing Kate Bush. I sing Edith Pilaf. I sing sitting down. I sing pacing the cage. I sing until my voice goes husky and then I keep going. As the hours pass, the sensation of being watched grows stronger, but I don't care.

Singing is easier than talking. I find strength in the repetition of it, the rise and fall of my voice. The pull of my abdomen. The emotions you can pour into lyrics and behind them. Singing is the easiest way to be me.

Eventually my voice gives out, but it's okay. I already know what to do next. I take off my flat shoes and practice ballet. There isn't enough room to dance but using the cage bars as a handrail, I move from position to position, humming Swan Lake. Soon my skin is glowing, and my mind is blissfully empty. When bad thoughts push in, I push them back, re-focusing on the positions. Mr. Parker might have forced me into it, and I might have the wrong body and be stupid, but ballet has made me strong. I'm going to dance every day I'm down here.

I'm practicing dégagé combinations when the basement door bangs open. I freeze in place, one hand on the bars holding me prisoner. It's not Mr. Gretzky. The silhouette in the doorway is too large.

A thrill runs down my spine. I know who it is. The only person I want to see even less than I want to be held in captivity. Boots pound on the metal stairs and the basement door melts back into darkness. His voice scrapes out from the shadows. "Keep going."

I freeze. I didn't realize I'd stopped dancing. I try to start again but my legs are melting into the floor, and I can taste my own teeth.

He moves closer to my bubble of light, poison green eyes shining.

"Hello, Mr. Rossi," I say.

His footsteps are slow and heavy. "Keep. Dancing."

I move jerkily into fifth position, raising my hands over my head. Adriano comes forward, materializing out of nothing. He's so much bigger than the others. His head reaches the basement ceiling. I think of the half-bull man we studied in Greek Mythology. The one who killed people for fun. I lower my arms into demi-seconde and see the gun strapped to his side. My skin goes ice cold. I hold the pose out of pure muscle memory, my insides trembling. I want to collapse.

Zia! I scream in my mind. *Zia!*

The voice comes again, slow and calm. *Dance, bella. Just keep moving.*

I do little girl positions. First, second, plié, pirouette.

Seconds scrape past like hours, my arms and legs vibrating with fear. *Please just go away, please just let me live*, I repeat to myself.

I cycle through the same poses until my legs are shaking. He knows I can do more, but he doesn't say anything, just watches until my body goes rubbery and I collapse to my knees.

"Did I say you could stop?"

I try desperately not to cry. "No."

"Look at me."

I lift my gaze to his. Adriano's scar gleams in the lamplight, silver against his olive cheek. He must have got it in a fight but all I can picture is him deep in a forest battling a bear. Him, shirtless and holding a sword, and the bear with a snowy muzzle, swiping at his face. The animal gets a single slash before Adriano seizes his throat, tearing it open with his teeth.

"Mr. Rossi, is there something you want to ask…?"

A beat. "You think something about you interests me?"

The words come before I can think. "My dancing."

"Your dancing?"

I shake my head, tears prickling at my eyes. "You… watch me dance. You always have."

Adriano's huge, tattooed hand drifts toward his gun and he eases it from its holster. My insides flicker like water and I fight not to scream.

He takes a step toward the bars, swallowing the ground between us. "I watch you dance?"

"Yes. I mean no. Never."

He points the barrel at me. "You think *anything* about you is interesting?"

"No, of course not."

"You're right. The most interesting thing you could do for me is die."

"No." The whisper forces its way past my lips. I press my trembling hands to my mouth. The gun hole stares at me.

"No?" Adriano repeats. "You don't want to die?"

Death is so close I can taste it, cold metal with an edge of relief—the taste of *his* gun in my mouth. I screw my eyes shut and say goodbye to Zia Teresa and Margot, to Lachlan and Penelope and—

"Kneel."

I open my eyes. "P-Pardon?"

"Get up on your knees."

Adrenaline pulses through me like rusty nails. Is this what executioners make you do? I push myself into a kneeling position and try not to stare at his heavy canvas pants. There is something besides killing me that could be done while I'm on my knees. Is that what he wants? I don't know what to hope for.

"Open your mouth."

My jaw drops before my soul can protest.

Adriano's lips twist. "You little whore." His tattooed hand moves to his zipper and my heart thumps so hard I taste blood. I'm going to see a man for the first time. Taste him. Unless I pass out before it even starts and then he shoots me.

Cold drops into my cleavage. Adriano is rubbing the gun barrel against my breasts.

"The others think you're innocent." His voice rumbles in the dark, deep and inhuman. What was the bull-man from Greek Mythology called?

The gun comes back up my collarbone, the metal warmed from my body heat. My jaw is aching from being open and my tongue feels furry with fear. I don't want to give him a blowjob, but I wish anything else was happening.

"Are you a good little whore?"

Should I agree? Disagree? I decide to go with the truth. "No?"

He presses the barrel hard against my temple. "Did I tell you to close your mouth?"

I'm petrified, but I still know that was a dirty trick.

My breath catches and though I want to beg I know it won't work. Nothing will. I let my jaw hang.

He grips the side of my neck. "That's it, little whore. Now suck."

A split second of panic before he slides his gun into my mouth. I try to pull away, but his big hand claps the back of my head, holding me in place.

"I said 'suck.'"

Whimpering, I close my lips around the barrel tasting the now familiar oil and metal. I move back and forth, tears leaking from my eyes. I feel a hot surge of unreality and know I'm going to pass out. Maybe Adriano knows it too because he fists my hair. "Suck harder. Tight and fast."

It isn't like last time. Last time I was in a chair with Adriano above me. He was shoving the gun into my mouth while I tried to keep my teeth out of the way. It was violent. Forced. Almost staged. This is different. I'm on my knees and Adriano's pumping the gun slowly, working it in and out of my mouth. It feels more like doing *that* than sucking a gun. My eyes lock on his canvas pants. The front is thick and distorted. He has a… but he's making me suck his gun instead. Doc was right. He is a big freak. I sputter a laugh against the barrel. Adriano's hand tightens in my hair. "Something funny?"

My insides swoop. I suck the gun deeper making

myself gag.

He smiles, his lips twisting to reveal his gold tooth. "Use your tongue on the underside."

I flick my tongue against the metal and his smile grows wider. "Good girl."

How does he know? He can't feel it. Or maybe he can. Maybe he's some kind of cyborg.

He moves his free hand from my head and rubs a palm across his zipper. I imagine him hard and thick as a python and an unwelcome burr goes through me like static.

Some girls like that, Doc whispers in my mind. *Some girls want to be fucked by a big freak.*

But not me. I can't want that. Because if I did want to sleep with Adriano, it would mean I'm broken inside. A shattered doll.

He grips my chin through the bars. "I want you gone, little whore."

I choke, accidentally biting down on the gun. Adriano glares at me. "Do better."

I open my mouth wide and try to suck softly.

"That's it." He smooths a hand through my sweaty hair. "Did you already know I want to kill you?"

Yes. I knew it when he first pushed Eli's gun into my throat. The hatred in his eyes said he was dying to shoot me and pile my body on top of Kurt's.

"All those times you thought I was watching you

dance, I was wishing I could choke you to death."

I sputter. Spit spills from my lips, down my chin.

Adriano sneers. "You're drooling on yourself like a toothless old woman."

I tighten my lips around the barrel and try to swallow the spit but more dribbles out and I feel it reach my chest.

"You're a disgusting little girl, aren't you?"

I nod, tears leaking from my eyes.

He jerks his head at the basement door. "I've watched you manipulate them. Try to win them over with your crying and pretty smiles. You're pathetic."

The gun goes deeper, and I choke.

Adriano's gold tooth flashes at me. "Keep going."

My jaw aches, but I suck faster, wanting to be good. To please him. It occurs to me that if he really was forcing himself into my mouth, I'd act the same way. A bolt of sick heat goes through me. Do I wish it was his cock? Do I want him to want me even as he does this?

Adriano's hand moves from my hair to my neck, his fingers locking around my throat. "If you try blowing Bobby, or Eli or Doc, if you try and get what you want out of them by being a little whore, I'll kill you before their cum is halfway down your throat."

Light pops in front of my eyes but still, I keep sucking.

"Got that?"

I moan around the barrel.

"The fuck was that?"

"Erg Ungersturghhh."

"Good. Squeeze your tits."

I hesitate.

"Put your fucking hands on your tits and play with them or I'll blow your head apart."

Minotaur.

The word spits out of the back of my brain as I cup my breasts through my dress. Minotaur. The cursed son of a goddess and a bull, charging around a dark maze and killing for fun. I suck hard, suck until my cheeks are scraped and my mouth is full of cuts and blood and my brain is a white blur.

"You're almost done," Adriano snarls. "Make my Glock cum in your mouth."

Does he mean he's going to shoot me? Fear fuzzes my mind but my mouth keeps moving, sucking, and swallowing.

"Enough."

He's barely got the word out before I'm pushed backward and I crumple on the floor.

"You're an embarrassment." Adriano wipes his gun on his pants and returns it to the holster. "You try to con your way out of here, I'll do worse than kill you. You'll find yourself in a dirty hole, pissing into a bucket. I've got a tattoo machine. I'll mark you up. Your face. Your tits. I'll put my name all over you. Pierce your nipples, cut your skin and then, if you're lucky, I'll kill you."

I gag, tasting bile and cheese and eggs. Adriano smiles like it's the sweetest thing he's ever seen.

"You want to know why you're still alive? Because my brothers want your pussy. But as soon as they're done with you, I'll end your life and I won't bother fucking you first."

I nod, but I can see the front of his pants is still swollen. He doesn't think I'm ugly. Or if he does, he still liked doing that to me.

"You think I want your worthless cunt?" He says it so quietly he might be talking to himself.

"No," I whisper.

He presses his face between the bars, his eyes cold as outer space. "Let's be clear, little girl. You're not worth raping."

The words ring in my mind like broken bells, shattering my insides. I'm too scared to cry, too hurt to breathe.

He turns his back on me. "Enjoy the last days of your life, Pryntsesa."

I lie in the dark, listening to the water drip from the ceiling. I count three thousand nine hundred and thirty-three drops.

Money.
Freedom.

Marriage.

Death.

These are the four choices my future holds. The only paths I can hope to walk.

CHAPTER TEN

Elliot Morelli

THE TRUTH OF being a boss means waking up every morning to maintain a thousand-part machine that despite constant upkeep is one mistake from exploding. I should be happy. I should be fucking ecstatic. Everything following the cathedral has gone perfectly. Minimal underworld complaints, minimal police interference, enough journalists greased to keep a pretty debutante's disappearance out of the news. I expected trouble from the outside—Parker's supporters, rival families, the Whitehalls funneling money into ex-Mossad agents. Instead, the chaos is coming from inside Velvet House.

I thought January would break like a wave on the shore. She was to be a pleasurable inconvenience. A way to torment Parker before we ended him in fair retribution for what he did to us seventeen years ago. But every day I hold the girl in my basement, she becomes a larger thorn in my side.

She should be begging to leave the cage by any means necessary but she's eating and sleeping well and her moods are stable. Meanwhile, my brothers, the men I need focused on and in fighting form, are tearing each other apart. Day and night they argue about what to do with January Whitehall. Twice, Adriano physically separated Bobby and Doc. Three times Bobby's headed Adriano away from the basement, sure—as I am—he was planning to kill the girl. And on four separate occasions, Adriano has hauled Doc away from the security monitors where he's passed out drunk, watching her. The last time he had a lit cigarette between his fingers. The fucking idiot could have burned Velvet House to the ground.

It's enough to drive a man insane. But if I mention how irrational and idiotic they're being, all I hear is that I'm pissed off January didn't choose me. Which I am. If the little brat had taken my rubies and agreed to be my mistress, we wouldn't be in this mess.

I never should have given her a choice. Doing so rendered her off limits, while we awaited her decision—a decision she'll never make. We abducted January to send Parker footage of her getting passed between the four of us like a bachelor party hooker. Now none of us knows how to proceed. Not when what we desire is in complete conflict. Who has the right to get what they want? The four of us have never competed over anything more serious than poker, let alone a girl. But now we are. And I fear what each of us is capable of.

Ten days after January arrived, I find my friends in the dining room, a live feed of her cage playing on a nearby screen.

"Even if she decides to marry you," Doc is telling Bobby. "I'll fuck it up."

Bobby lays his hands on the table. "If she chooses to marry me, you have to back off. It's what we all agreed."

Doc blows into the barrel of the revolver he's cleaning. "I didn't agree to that shit. I want to fuck her. And I get what I want."

Bobby's eyes narrow. "Not this time."

Adriano lifts his gaze from his phone. "I can make it so no one has her."

Doc points the gun at him. "You stamp out that pussy before I've had a taste, you'll get a knife through the ear."

I clear my throat. "Nice to see this is still going on."

My friends don't even glance at me.

"You screwed up everything between me and January," Bobby tells Adriano. "If it wasn't for you making me kill her bodyguard—"

"You're not the little whore's math tutor," Adriano snarls. "You wanna delude yourself, that's your business. But you're not pretending in front of me."

My gaze falls on the monitor. January is sitting on

her bed in a white dress, her hair loose around her shoulders. She's grown thinner in the days since she arrived, but it's only sharpened her beauty. Her mouth opens in a red 'O' and I realize she's singing. I watch her croon with her eyes closed and it seems to me she is drawing strength from us like a flower absorbing sunshine.

"I should have killed her at the altar," Adriano says. "Slit her throat in front of her family."

Doc slaps the clip into his revolver. "Bullshit."

"What did you say?"

"I said bullshit," Doc spins the colt on his finger like a gunslinger. "You want to stick your cock in her. Maybe you want to do it *while* you kill her, but don't act like you're above it. Even once we had enough info from her studio, you were back there every week. Watching her."

Adriano lunges across the table and Doc pulls away laughing. "What? You gonna kill me like your little Pryntsesa?"

Adriano stands, shoving his chair back. Doc will be lucky to come away whole from this one. And the two of them are the oldest friends of the four of us, neighbors from when they were six or seven.

A memory comes to me. Mama breaking up a fight between my brother Kit and I on Christmas morning. We were wrestling over a water pistol, and she snatched it away and slapped both of us. *"I hope you're happy.*

Now, no one gets to have it."

I know what I have to do. Truthfully, a part of me has known since I left the basement with my necklace still in my pocket.

Adriano advances on Doc, his massive hands balled into fists. Doc throws the revolver onto the table and takes out his butterfly knife, shifting his weight from foot to foot. Bobby hovers like a nervous cop, unsure who to hurt or protect.

I move to stand between them. "That's enough."

Doc shows his teeth. "Can we have *one* fistfight around here?"

"You're holding a knife," I snarl. "But shut your fucking mouth and listen to me."

To Doc's credit, he doesn't respond. I take a step backward so I can see all three of my brothers. "I hope you're happy," I tell them, looking from face to sulking face. "Now, no one gets to have it."

Doc frowns. "The fuck are you talking about, Morelli?"

"This January Whitehall situation. It ends. Tonight."

"What do you mean?" Bobby asks, going white.

"I'm sending her away. And you know why? Because you egotistical bastards don't know how to compromise."

Doc points his knife at me. "*I* don't know how to compromise?"

"Put that away, you blond asshole. I haven't forgotten about you almost burning us alive."

Doc shakes his head, but I can tell he's trying not to grin.

I expect further argument, but the stinging silence says the others understand what I'm doing. Maybe even hoped for it. The relief of a decision made, and a problem solved.

"Sit down," I say. "I'll get us all drinks and we can talk."

As they take their seats I head to the bar and open a bottle of Bowmore. By the time I'm finished pouring drinks, the fight's forgotten and they're already discussing a married bouncer who got one of Doc's strippers pregnant. Doc found him threatening the girl in the ladies' bathroom.

"I gave her five grand, told her to go back to Dallas, but it's not over. The prick'll get at her again. He knows where her parents live."

"Is this Revesby?" Adriano asks. "The Latvian?"

"That's the one."

"He fucked up a drop last year. Seems like the asshole's more valuable dead than alive."

"Yeah, but he's with Enzo's crew. We don't need the drama."

Bobby pulls out his phone and checks something. "He's got a few days off next week. Marco could take him to Atlantic City. Accidental overdose."

"Could work," Doc muses. "He's coked to the eye-balls most days. I could mix him a bad batch."

As my brothers hammer out the details of dispatching this useless man, I grow more convinced of my own plan. For almost two decades the four of us have solved problems and respected each other's opinions. We've built something that's equal to any of the old families. It will not be compromised by one little virgin.

I take my seat at the head of the table. "As soon as we can arrange a passport, the girl goes to Naples. My cousin Gio will find her a place in his house."

Doc downs half his scotch. "So, you're gonna let your cousin earn on her after all our hard work?"

"She won't be whoring. She's a pretty girl from a rich family and she speaks Italian. She can be married to one of his caporegime."

Doc's mouth opens, but Bobby speaks first. "You'll force January to marry someone else?"

"No. Gio will. But that's none of your business. You offered her your hand and she didn't take it."

Bobby's eyes go dark. "You—"

"Stop. Roberto, we're family. Are you going to burn that down for a girl you barely know?"

"You don't understand."

"I understand better than you do. You're in love with her and you want her to be your wife. She doesn't want to be your wife. So you want to keep her around until she changes her mind. I say she goes to Italy before she completely fucks up your head."

His hand tightens on his glass. "She's our responsibility. You can't just get rid of her because she's not doing what you wanted."

Doc raps the table. "I want to say something."

I glare at him.

"I want to say something to Bobby," he clarifies, turning to him. "I love you."

Bobby's eyes nearly fall out of his head. "What?"

"I love you," Doc says lightly. "I always have, but you can't be stupid about January. If she wanted to marry you, she'd have said yes. She's that kind of girl."

Bobby's expression doesn't change but his shoulders slump. "She's scared. She just needs time."

"You're wrong. More time and Adri'll kill her."

Bobby looks at Adriano, who shrugs.

"I might."

Bobby gives a humourless laugh. "So, we send January to a foreign country to be forced into marriage?"

Doc shakes his head. "You want to marry for love, Bash. You're never gonna be happy with a wife you backed into it. So let this girl go. She's not the one."

Bobby looks to me, his oldest friend. I raise my scotch. "He's right for once. She's not the girl you marry."

He makes a helpless sound somewhere between a laugh and a groan. "All our plans, years of surveillance, and nothing good has come of it. We're just going to let her go."

I swirl the liquor around my glass. "Oh, I wouldn't say that."

"What do you mean?" Doc says.

I choose my words carefully. Just because this situation has a silver lining, I can't have anyone thinking they're going to get their way. "I said we send the girl to Italy. I didn't say what condition her pussy has to be in when she gets there."

Adriano lifts his nose like a predator scenting blood.

"Hang on," Bobby says. "Your cousin, if we tell him January's a virgin and she doesn't bleed…"

"Most girls don't bleed," Doc snaps. "Not if you can get them wet. Someone was gonna have to tell January to shove a needle in her finger on her wedding night. I'm happy for that to be me."

"But the risk—"

"Are we Velvet House?" I ask Bobby. "Or some weak collection of assholes? I want to fuck Parker's fiancée. And I don't give a shit if we send some mafioso a wife who's been screwed a couple of times. They should be grateful they're getting Miss Whitehall for longer than I do."

Doc's eyes widen in mock surprise. "Elliot, that

might be the most romantic thing I've ever heard."

I scowl. He knows I hate being called Elliot. I look to Bobby, expecting revulsion, but the corner of his mouth has kicked up. I can almost see the wheels in his mind turning. *If I can't marry her, at least it'll be something.*

Across from him, Adriano flicks his glass, making the crystal chime. "Who gets to go first?"

A new tension crackles through the room.

Bobby looks me dead in the eyes. "You pulling rank again?"

I could. It's tempting. I turn to the monitors. Miss Whitehall is still singing in her white dress. She looks like an angel. I could tie her to my bed, lick her little cunt and take her as a man should. Keep her a few hours, then hand her over, soaking and fuck-drunk and thoroughly broken in. Then let the others do what they will, knowing I was her first.

But it won't work. Resentment is already brewing in my brothers and resentment breeds incompetence. If I claim Miss Whitehall's virginity, getting rid of her won't help. I'd still be the captain of a ship falling apart under pressure.

I shrug in as bored a manner as possible. "No. I don't need to go first."

Bobby sits up straighter. "Then how?"

He's got me there. I have no idea. And I need one fast before more petty bickering breaks out.

Doc snaps his fingers. "What if she still gets to decide?"

"She's had ten fucking days to decide," Adriano growls.

"Ah, but she won't be deciding on her own. We'd be giving her a little help."

I stare at Doc. "Do you mean…?"

"I do." Doc grins. "Gimmie an hour and I'll knock some up."

Orchard.

The reason we're all here. If I close my eyes, I can still see Doc swaggering up to my school gate, hair tucked behind his ears like Kurt Cobain. The girls at Trinity weren't supposed to like a lowlife like him, but whenever he showed up selling, he walked away with a dozen numbers. Adriano was there too, glaring over Doc's shoulder. Two years older and already hitched to a psycho with more brains than sense. They ran everything alone. No cartels, no bosses, just the pills Doc mixed in his basement and Adriano kicking the shit out of anyone trying to steal from them.

"You need money to expand," I told Doc. "And you need leadership. Someone with the foresight to protect you."

I was an arrogant shit. They did need a leader, but to think that at seventeen *I* was that leader… Ridiculous. I take a deep swallow of scotch.

"Fine," I tell Doc. "Mix it up. We'll give it to her."

"Ell…" Bobby's face is tight. "I don't know if I can do this."

I could command him upstairs. Tell him to go pray a rosary without us if it'll make him feel better. But I know Bobby. As a teenager, Doc got Adriano laid by giving girls free weed. I got Bobby laid by inviting our class-mates back to my father's Manhattan apartment. The leggy, dark-haired girls Bobby could barely speak in front of. They'd show up all shy, saying they only wanted to watch a movie and a few hours later they'd be getting fucked at both ends and screaming for more. Bobby always went to church afterward, but he never told me to stop. He's scared of his dark side. Scared of what he likes. But I know how to push him to happiness.

"You want to be with January," I remind him. "You want her as badly as any of us do. Maybe more."

"Then can you see why I have a problem with this?"

I smile. "You're supposed to. That's the point. None of us get what we want. All our plans with January Whitehall end tonight. And believe me, twenty years from now you'll regret not having her more than you'll regret joining in."

Bobby lets out a long, slow breath, and I can tell his resistance is waning.

Doc claps him on the shoulder. "Don't worry, Bash. You'll feel better about all this shit once you give the girl a good old-fashioned fucking. So where should we dose her? In the cage? See who she tries to fuck through the bars?"

I shake my head. January's shown too much cheek in her cage already. I want her rattled. Off balance. "We'll bring her to the sitting room. Put her in lingerie in front of the fire and watch the show."

"Fuck yeah," Doc grins around at us. "Ten grand says she begs me to break her open."

Bobby downs the rest of his scotch. "We'll see."

I laugh, mostly in relief that he's accepting our plan.

"What do you mean, 'we'll see?'" Doc demands.

"January had a crush on me before all of this started. You give her Orchard, and you think she won't come for me?"

Doc scoffs. "I've kissed her."

"*I've* kissed her," Bobby shoots back. "And unlike you, she wanted me to."

This time my laughter is real. "Sorry to tell you both, but Miss Whitehall can barely look at me without blushing. She's as good as mine."

"We'll fucking see," Doc mutters.

"What about you?" I ask Adriano. "Are you in?"

He shrugs, but there's a smile playing on his lips.

Doc points his drink at Adriano. "You'll get fucked by climate change before you get fucked by January Whitehall. She's terrified of you."

Adriano's smile gets a little wider.

"He thinks that'll help," Bobby says shrewdly. "Don't you?"

"Maybe…" Adriano says. "Wouldn't be the first girl to try to fuck her way out of dying."

"Do we want to put money on it?" I ask the table.

Doc narrows his eyes. "What kind of money?"

"What you said. Ten grand. Unless you think you won't win?"

Doc scowls. "Fine."

"Fine," Bobby says.

Adriano grunts which I take as a yes.

"Then it's a deal. We give her Orchard and the first one to fuck her virgin pussy, wins."

Everyone nods and relief pulses through me like novocaine. We'll have a night of debauchery that Miss Whitehall will enjoy as much as we will, and then we'll send her off on an Italian adventure. She'll be married to some wealthy, well-connected man and it will be everything she was promised by her stepmother with the added benefit of not having to fuck Zachery Parker.

An image comes to me, January, barefoot in the water at Mappatella beach, her belly heavy with another man's child. My chest pangs but I ignore it and return my attention to my brothers. "About tonight, we need some ground rules."

Doc rolls his eyes. "You take the fun out of everything."

"What rules?" Bobby asks.

"Rule one," I say holding up a finger. "No one is allowed to touch her before she touches them."

"That's fair," Doc admits.

"The second is no fighting. Any of you throw hands and *you'll* get locked in the basement while I take Miss Whitehall upstairs and fuck her until she moans."

"Also fair," Doc says. "Anything else or can I go make Orchard now?"

"One second." I raise my glass and wait for the others to do the same. When they've all followed suit, I smile. "To a problem solved."

We drink as beneath us January Whitehall sings. Oblivious, in her little white dress.

CHAPTER ELEVEN

January Whitehall

I FALL SILENT as I hear someone on the stairs. I ate and washed hours ago and I usually sleep before I see Mr. Gretzky again. But here he is. "What's going on, Sir?"

"Get up, Miss Whitehall," he says, unlocking the cage.

I stand. "Am I going to see Mr. Morelli and the others?"

Mr. Gretzky beckons me forward.

I must be seeing them. Maybe they're bringing me upstairs to find out who I've chosen? Unless I'm out of time and they're going to kill me and that's why Mr. Gretzky hasn't put the bag over my head. The idea should scare me, but aside from a souring in my mouth, I'm a little excited. After days that bleed together at least this is something new.

The bright downlights hurt my eyes as I walk into a

wide hallway with walls that are half polished wood, half cream.

"This way." Mr. Gretzky leads me past dusty China vases and statues on little wooden stands. On the cream parts of the walls hang oil paintings of cows and knights and pretty olive-skinned women. The thick carpet I've felt beneath my feet a dozen times is blood red. I don't see or hear another soul as we make our way through an unending labyrinth of staircases and hallways. Velvet House is empty.

Eventually, Mr. Gretzky pauses at a wooden door with a gold handle. "Go inside. Wash and dress."

I wait, but he doesn't give a time limit the way he usually does. "How long should I take?"

A pained expression crosses his face. "As long as you need."

Maybe I'm having dinner with the four of them? A last meal before Adriano strangles me with a long string or whatever it was in that movie Lachlan used to love. I open the door and walk into the familiar bathroom. Lingerie is waiting where my clothes usually are. A sparkly pink bra, matching thong and garter belt, black stockings, and a pair of shiny black pumps.

"Oh," I whisper. "Oh… *shit.*"

I approach the lingerie with the tiniest of steps. I lift the panties. They're so small, they can't even be called underwear. "F-Fuck."

Thoughts twist through me like fire. Adriano might not murder me in lingerie, but I don't think my virginity isn't going to last the night.

Are they still going to make me choose between them? Who should I pick? I've had days to think about their offers and I still don't know. Eli will get bored of me in a month, and I obviously won't pick Adriano killing me. The smartest choice would be to marry Bobby, but he killed Kurt. If he did worse things once I was his wife, I'd only have myself to blame. Choosing Doc and working in his strip clubs seems like the easiest way to find or buy a phone and call my family. But it also seems like the fastest way to spend time with Doc who is the meanest *and* carries a knife *and* spat in my face—

There's a loud knock on the door. "Miss Whitehall. Shower."

I jump. "Yes, sorry."

My hands shake under the hot water. I don't want to lose my virginity. Without it, the force field against the men who brought me here will be gone. I won't be worth protecting. And Adriano told me that once his brothers slept with me, he'd kill me.

Actually, he said once they're bored with me, he'd kill me. Maybe I can entertain them? But how am I supposed to entertain three dangerous men, one of whom owns strip clubs? I don't know anything about sex. And once the novelty of being my first is gone…

Then I can't lose my virginity. I'll just have to do whatever it takes to stay untouched.

Another knock on the door. "Get moving, Miss Whitehall."

I frown. For saying I could take all the time I needed, Mr. Gretzky seems impatient. I turn off the shower and wrap a big towel around myself. There are more things in the bathroom cabinet than usual, a tiny bottle of vanilla perfume, a row of Dior lipsticks, and a Yves Saint Laurent eye shadow palette.

I knock on the door. "Mr. Gretzky… am I supposed to put on makeup?"

There is a pause and I'm sure I hear him swear. "Yes, Miss Whitehall."

I feel bad for him. Whatever his normal job is, he really hates dealing with me. I learned a lot about that from Theodore and Kurt.

Kurt… I picture his body, blank-faced and bloody on the plastic tarp. Whatever happens, I will not lose my virginity to Bobby. It doesn't matter that Kurt was creepy and bad at his job and sold me out to Eli. He didn't deserve to die. But then I think of Bobby kissing me in my cage, his arms around me. I think of the way he looked at me when he talked about us living together. "Stop it," I tell myself. "Just stop."

I'm not very good at makeup. I wasn't allowed to

wear any to school, and it was done for me when our family went to events. I also have no idea who I'm dressing up for and I'm sure they'd all like something different. Bobby definitely likes the 'girl next door' look. Doc would want glossy lips and contouring. Eli seems like a guy who'd appreciate glamor—red lips, and fake lashes. Adriano…

I remember him staring at me through my cage, the lamplight carving shadows into his scarred face. *You're not worth raping.* The mascara I'm holding skitters out of my hand and onto the tiles.

"Miss Whitehall?"

"Coming," I yell, my voice much higher than usual.

I try for subtle, tiny dabs of foundation and peachy eye shadow like I had at my wedding. At the last minute, I add glossy lips and lots of mascara. I don't know if it looks good or like a little girl raided her mom's makeup bag, but you can tell I tried.

I walk over to the lingerie. I've been avoiding looking at it until now. I pull everything on with my back to the mirror. It takes ages to attach the straps hanging from the pink belt to my stockings. As soon as I get one on, another pops off.

Mr. Gretzky knocks on the door. "We need to get moving."

I manage to attach the last clip then glance at the mirror. My mouth falls open. I look… I don't know *how*

I look. The bright pink bra and panties bring out the ivory notes of my skin. You can see my nipples through the sheer material and the line of my… down there. But it doesn't look tacky, it looks subtle and kind of pretty.

Whoever picked out the underwear has great taste.

I pile my hair onto my head and turn, studying the lines of my body. Grown-up. That's how I look. Grown-up and sexy. I shake my ass in the mirror and smile. What are the guys going to say when they…

I wince. What is wrong with me? This isn't a game. This is my life. What happens when I leave this room decides my future and I'm prancing around in my underwear like a moron. Doc's right. I'm like a Disney girl, rebelling against her stage mom. I release my hair and vow to stay focused.

My St. Christopher medallion is beside the sink. I pick it up, ready to slide it into my bra cup but realize everyone will be able to see it. I can't leave it here and I wouldn't put it on Bobby's chain even if I had it on me.

A hard rap on the door. "Miss Whitehall, we're done."

I look at the medallion and for a crazy second, I think about swallowing it. Then I shove it into the side of my bra. There's a risk whoever I'm meeting will see it and take it from me, but I'm not going anywhere without it. "Coming!"

I wrap my arms around my body to try and cover

myself from Mr. Gretzky.

He barely glances at me. "About time." He grabs my elbow and leads me to another set of hardwood stairs.

"Where are we going?" I ask, trying not to trip in my heels.

"Sitting room."

My pulse jumps. Am I going to be touched or killed? Allowed to choose my future or given to someone for reasons I don't understand? Or am I wrong about everything? Am I about be used and sent back to the basement?

We move through a dark set of double doors into a room where the only light is coming from a roaring fire. It splashes orange over leather couches. I see the backs of four men. One blond, one glossy black, one boyishly brown, one with shaved sides. My mouth dries over. They're all here.

The hand on my elbow tightens and Mr. Gretzky drags me toward the fire. I keep my eyes on the carpet as heat washes over my body.

"Good evening, Miss Whitehall," Eli drawls.

I know better than not to respond. "Good evening, Mr. Morelli."

"Look at us."

My head feels like it's made of concrete, but I meet his gaze. He and Adriano sit in winged armchairs, Doc and Bobby are at opposite ends of a couch. The air seems to thicken around me and my chest heaves as though I've been running.

Eli is wearing a dark blue suit and his pristine white shirt is open at his throat. He looks like a magazine spread. Why does he have to be a murderer?

He raises his tumbler to me. "We have news for you, *bella*. Your time at Velvet House is almost over."

My heart stops. "Are you going to kill me?"

He smiles indulgently. "No. But you've been in that basement long enough. We're sending you to Naples."

My legs wobble as if the floor beneath me is moving. "Naples?"

"Yes. My cousin Gio lives there. He can find you a job and a safe new home. Would you like that, *bella*?"

"Of course," I say automatically. What happened to my choices? Is this part of the plan to mess with Mr. Parker? Will any of them go with me? Or are they lying, and I really am about to be strangled with string after all?

I look across to Bobby. My insides squirm. He's wearing a black T-shirt and I can see a big tattoo inked into his right bicep. He looks different tonight. Older, I guess. I didn't know he had tattoos. God, why does *he* have to be a murderer?

Elliot smiles. "Have you been missing Bobby? Were you hoping he'd come visit you again?"

I drop my gaze to my hands. I did think he would visit me again. I thought they all would, but aside from

Mr. Gretzky, I've been alone for days.

Doc shifts on the couch. "She's disappointed, Morelli. She doesn't wanna leave."

I glance up at him. His blond hair is falling into his pretty blue eyes as usual. I remember his tattooed body arched over me, his mouth drawing on my nipple and a surge rolls through my body. His lip curls and I'm sure I know what he's thinking. *Should have chosen me, Tesorina.*

Maybe I should have. Stripping can't be scarier than going to Italy alone to live with Eli's mafia cousins. Why does Doc have to be a murderer? And a psychopath? And a jerk?

"Don't be disappointed, *bella*," Eli says. "Just because you haven't chosen any of us, doesn't mean we're angry. We're … Doc? How would you put it?"

Doc's eyes are bright and cold as a dying star. "Proud of you."

"Yes," Eli agrees. "Proud of you. In fact, *bella,* we're so proud of you, we'd like to give you a goodbye present."

My heart pounds so hard I'm sure it's about to come crashing through my ribs. "What… what kind of present?"

Adriano shifts in his chair. I refuse to look at him. Wherever I'm going, be it Naples or into the ground, at least he won't be there.

"On her knees," Eli says lazily, and Gretzky pushes my shoulder making me tumble to the floor.

Eli waves a hand at him. "Thank you, Gretzky, that will be all."

He leaves and then we're alone. The four of them and me. The only sound is the hiss and crackle of the fire. I look to Bobby for reassurance, but his face is set. My stomach tightens. Sex or death. I can't be here in my underwear for anything else. But surely, they won't make me… in front of the others. That would be gross. It would be wrong.

Elliot clears his throat. "Domenico, show Miss Whitehall the Orchard."

Doc puts his glass on the table beside the couch and stands. His tattooed feet are bare, and his black jeans are ripped at the knees. He pulls something from his pocket, smirking as though this is all a big joke. "Know what this is?"

I look at his hand. It's a tiny plastic fish. The kind that has soy sauce in them at sushi places. Only the liquid in this one is clear. "Is it poison?"

Doc laughs. "I fucking wish."

Elliot stretches his arms along the back of his chair. "Why would we poison you, *bella*? What a waste that would be."

"So, what is it…?"

Elliot's eyes are liquid black in the firelight. He's

189

trying to look relaxed, but his muscles are coiled, like a big cat about to pounce. "It's something that'll make you feel very excited about the idea of getting to know us better."

Heat licks up my neck and hands. I'm half certain the fire is spilling out of the grate all over me. I look at Doc and his smile is hard as diamonds. "What do you say, Tesorina? Want to get high?"

I stare at the fish. "Is it… MDMA?"

Elliot and Doc laugh and even Bobby smiles.

"No, *bella*," Eli says. "It's something special. Something just for you."

I swallow, my throat contracting around a lump. "Is this so you can film me for Mr. Parker?"

From the darkest corner of the room, Adriano growls.

"Do not say that name in front of us," Eli says lightly. "Not if you want to go to Italy."

"I'm sorry."

Eli's face cracks into a handsome smile. "You're sweet, Miss Whitehall. Isn't she sweet, Bobby?"

"Yeah, she's sweet." Bobby drawls, and I wonder if he's drunk. He sounds drunk.

Doc takes a step toward me. "Morelli. Give the word."

"What's your rush, Domenico? *Bella*, would you like a drink?"

"Um, I'm okay." One of my heels has slipped between my legs and I realize I'm leaning against it, rubbing myself on it. I make myself go still. "Could I maybe just go back to my cage, please?"

Doc's hand shoots out, fastening around my neck. "That's enough talking, Tits. Morelli, make the call."

I sputter with indignation, but everyone ignores me.

"What do you think, Bobby?" Eli says in his slow, melodic voice. "Should we give her the Orchard?"

I look to Bobby, my eyes wide, pleading. He can still save me. Protect me.

He drains his drink. "Do it."

My heart falls as Eli smiles. "Okay. Domenico, go ahead."

Doc shoves the tip of the fish in his mouth and bites off the red cap. "Open up."

I press my lips together and shake my head.

Doc's thumb brushes my cheek. "Come on, baby. Don't make me force your pretty jaw open."

I can smell something coming from the capless little fish. Something sweet and weirdly familiar.

Doc looks at Eli. "Permission to hurt her?"

The scent grows stronger, and it clicks. Jolly Ranchers. That's what it smells like. Green apple candy. 'Orchard', Eli called the drug. That must be why. Because it smells like apples. But what does it do?

"Tits," Doc's voice is irritable. "Here's the deal. You

wanna speak to your Zia Teresa?"

I gasp. "Seriously—"

He hooks a finger into my cheek and before I can blink, liquid splashes down my throat. I try to spit, to bite, to pull away, but it's already gone. I've swallowed it. Doc removes his finger and tucks the empty fish into his pocket. "Done."

Eli laughs. "Underhanded."

"Effective." Doc's eyes glitter. "No going back, Tesorina."

My mouth is slick with the sweetish aftermath of whatever was in the fish. "What... what's going to happen to me?"

"That's the fucking question, isn't it?" Doc throws himself back onto the couch beside Bobby. "Shouldn't be long."

Eli drums his fingers against the arm of his chair. "Estimate?"

"Fifteen minutes. Maybe less. She hasn't eaten for a while."

All four sets of eyes turn to me. In the firelight, they seem like gods deciding my fate. I should probably do something, convince them not to do whatever it is they're planning, but there's a golden glow in my stomach and it's spreading through my veins like honey. I feel good. I feel very, very good. And though it's impossible, I'm almost sure I've felt this way before.

CHAPTER TWELVE

Elliot Morelli

JANUARY KEEPS REARRANGING herself. She crosses and uncrosses her legs as though trying to fold herself into the smallest possible piece. Her nipples are like hard candy beneath her sheer bra, and she keeps tossing her hair and arching her back. Doc's put on some Russian hardbass, and you can tell she's trying not to writhe to the beat.

She's adorable. When the Orchard hits her fully, she won't be able to keep her hands off her virgin pussy. Or she'll climb on my face and beg me to slide my tongue inside her. I'm feeling generous enough that I probably will.

"Mmm." January turns sideways, stretching out her long legs and we all glimpse the sheer pink material covering her cunt.

Bobby suppresses a groan. "How long?"

"Shut the fuck up," Doc mutters, his voice rough as if he were already inside her.

He's gone over this girl. This man who never puts his dick in the same stripper twice, has spent the last week ignoring his responsibilities to get drunk in front of the security monitors and watch January sing. It just proves I made the right choice to send her to Naples. Whatever happens, I will not entertain regrets.

The room is still heavy with the scent of sugary green apples. Doc doesn't know what makes Orchard smell that way. That's the problem with savants, they can't do the working out. Not that anyone else can either. Seventeen years and God knows how much money I've put into research and we're no closer to answers.

January gives a soft moan. Her pupils have dilated.

"Fuck yes," Doc mutters. "Here we go."

All of us sit up straighter.

"What's happening to me?" she whimpers.

"What does it feel like?" I ask.

"Like… pink fire is running through me." She trails her hands up her arms and shivers. "Like electricity."

I smile. This demure little virgin is going to spread herself wide and we're going to plunder her body like the perfect fuckdoll she is. I turn to check the camera light is blinking. Even if we don't send this to Parker, I want a copy of it.

"Domenico…" The way she purrs his name makes

my cock ache. "What is Orchard?"

Doc looks at me. "Should I tell her?"

I watch January rock back and forth like she's riding an invisible pony. "I don't see why not."

"Orchard is something I invented while I was mixing up pills."

January's pretty face is quizzical.

Doc gives a cackling laugh. "Here you are thinking I was some kind of pharmacist. I dealt drugs, Tesorina."

Her mouth falls open and Adriano snorts. She spares him a single glance before returning her gaze to Doc. "Oh…"

"Judging me?" He demands.

"No."

"Liar. Sorry I didn't come out of some millionaire's ballsack and I had to make my own way in the world."

January doesn't seem to be listening, just nibbling on her lower lip.

Doc's face softens. "Do you wanna know what's happening in your body, Tesorina?"

She releases her lip, trying to focus on his face. "Yes?"

"Your blood is thinning. Your heart is racing and your pussy is pulsing like a strobe light. You're thinking about how empty you are. About how nice it would feel to have something thick push inside you. Soon you won't be able to stop thinking about it. You'll feel so empty, you'll scream."

I adjust myself through my suit pants.

"No," January whispers. "I won't."

"It's not up to you, Tesorina. That's what Orchard does. Pretty soon you'll crawl over broken glass to taste my cock."

I laugh as she presses her face into her hands. "Don't worry, *bella*. It doesn't have to be Domenico. You can come here to me. No broken glass involved."

Doc shoots me a nasty look. "Fuck off, Morelli."

January's hands fall from her face and she lightly brushes her palms over her nipples. "Mr. Morelli?"

"Yes, *bella*?"

Color floods her cheeks and she squeezes her tits through her bra. "I… I feel strange."

"Come sit on my lap and talk to me about it."

"Fucks' sake…" Doc snarls. "Stop talking to her."

I raise my glass to the others. "Nice dealing with you, gentlemen. I'll expect the money on the dining table at breakfast."

"Bet's not over," Bobby says.

"Bet?" January looks from me to him. "What bet?"

I smile. "Thirty grand to whoever fucks you first. Now, come here and make it me."

January's gaze is on Bobby. "You're not…?"

"You don't think I would?" Bobby asks in a hard voice. "Or you're hoping?"

Her face falls, the truth sinking in. Even her math

tutor isn't her savior anymore.

Doc cackles. "It's fun when Basher stops pretending that he's nice."

Bobby ignores him and refills his scotch. He's been drinking steadily since dinner and from the way he's looking at her, still absently massaging her tits, he's going to fuck her nine times before he's had his fill.

"You're all here…" January's voice is a husky moan. "You can't *all* be here."

Doc smirks. "How else will we know who you want to fuck first?"

"But if you're all here…?"

"It's a good thing," I tell her. "Once I've deflowered you, you'll still be hungry. Then my brothers will step in and help."

January realizes she's touching herself and pins her hands to her sides. "Please don't make me do that."

"I won't make you do anything, *bella*. You'll be insatiable. Four men might not be enough."

"No…." Her voice is a breathy moan. She sounds like she already has a tongue between her legs.

My cock is hard as a spike. How much longer will it be before I can take her?

Doc puts his drink on the carpet. "Do your nipples hurt, Tesorina? Do you want me to suck them again?"

Longing pierces January's face like the sun through a cloud.

Doc smiles, the hard, intense smile that broke a hundred schoolgirl hearts. "Come here, baby. I'll make it all better."

She shifts on her heels and for a moment I freeze, sure she's about to go to him. But then she whips her head from side to side. "No. I can't... Not my first time. Not with... all of you."

She's not denying it'll happen. She must already feel it. Already know it's too late. When I rubbed my shoe against her pussy she wanted to be fucked then and there. But she's been raised a good girl and it's hard for her to admit she wants sex, even to herself. Now her first time will be with four men, and she'll love every second of it even if she hates herself afterward. But then if she wanted to be with one man, she should have chosen me.

"Yes, with all of us," I say. "But don't worry, *bella*. When we parcel you off to Naples, I'll tell my cousin you're as pure as snow. Your future husband will—"

Doc shoots me a furious look. "Shut the fuck up, Morelli."

He has a point. Why overload her pretty, overstimulated mind? I smile at January. "Focus on how you feel. Embrace it."

She closes her eyes, her pouty lips parting in a silent plea.

I stare between her legs. A dark patch is spreading across the material. I can only imagine how soft and swollen her cunt is. I've taken Orchard, but the effect on men is a faint hum of what it does to women. A chromosomal thing, Doc thinks, but that's another guess.

"Oh my gossssssh," January whimpers, her palms working up and down her thighs.

She's so beautiful, writhing golden in the firelight. A million perfect photographs in motion. But still she doesn't come for any of us.

Doc rolls his head back along the couch. "Fucking hell this is taking forever."

I clear my throat to make sure I don't sound like a gasping idiot. "She's stronger than I gave her credit for."

"We should have taken bets on how long she'll take to crack."

"There's still time." I check my watch. "A thousand says she doesn't last another five minutes."

Doc picks up his vodka and finishes it. "Eight. She's got nothing left in the tank. What about you, Basher?"

"Six."

I smile. "Always splitting the difference. Rossi?"

Adriano face is half-hidden in shadow. "Twenty minutes."

Doc snorts. "Twenty? Have you hit your head and forgotten how Orchard works?"

"She'll fight it with everything she has. And she has a lot."

I laugh. Doc going soft on a girl is one thing. But Adriano? "That almost sounds like a compliment. Are you changing your mind about the girl?"

A growl. "Twenty minutes."

"It's your money. So, it's settled, five minutes, six, eight and twenty. May the best man win."

"You won't win." January's eyes are still closed. She's shifted into a cross-legged yoga position, her hands resting on her stockinged knees.

"What was that, *bella*?"

"You won't win. None of you." Her voice is stronger the second time.

Doc laughs. "Tesorina, haven't you been listening? You won't be able to resist. No one can. You're going to get railed like a filthy whore."

Her eyes fly open, cool and clear as a forest lake. "I won't."

I study her. She's found some well of resistance inside herself. Fuck that. She can't go to Gio a defiant little brat. If it were just the two of us, I'd spank her backside raw. But we're not allowed to touch her. I'll need another way to discipline her.

"Okay, *bella*," I say. "A new deal. If you can resist the Orchard and keep your virginity, you can leave your cage."

Her mouth parts. "Really?"

"Really. You can move upstairs and sleep in a beautiful wing all by yourself."

"Ell…" Adriano warns.

I wave a hand at him. Her defeat will be all the more humbling this way. Getting fucked knowing she'll have to go back to her cage a horny, broken girl. "Do you agree, Miss Whitehall?"

"Yes," January says. "I can do it."

"Of course, you can." I pour myself more scotch. "Now close your eyes and try not to think about me bending you over this armchair and fucking you like the good little girl you are."

Her cheeks burn and she closes her eyes again.

"Just wait," Doc mutters. "Eight minutes."

"Five," I say.

But five minutes pass and January doesn't move. Another minute and Bobby loses the bet. Two minutes later so does Doc. Furious, he collects a bottle of JB from the bar and swigs from the neck. "This shouldn't be happening."

"Maybe the dose—"

"The dose would turn Mother Teresa into a porn star. There's nothing wrong with the dose. There's something wrong with *her*."

January sits serenely. A smile is curling the corners of her mouth.

Bobby presses a palm to the front of his jeans. "I can't take this."

I don't say anything, but I have no idea what to do. Doc's right, this isn't supposed to be happening. We've tested Orchard dozens of times, mostly on girls from Doc's clubs. With their consent we lock them in an observation room. When the drug hits, they pound on the two-way mirror, begging whoever's watching to fuck them. All of them masturbate, some of them hump the corners of the table, they're so desperate for stimulation. How is she not already on top of us? Or at least touching herself? But as we watch, her movements grow subtler. Quieter. She's breathing rhythmically, her thick hair covering her breasts. She looks supernatural, kneeling peacefully in her lingerie like a little goddess.

"For fuck's sake, this doesn't make any sense." Doc slurs.

She's humiliating us. We were supposed to be controlling her, corrupting her. Reminding her there's nothing she can refuse that we can't take. Now we're circled around her, staring at her. Worshiping her almost. This girl who declined to be my mistress, to work for Doc, to marry Bobby or to beg Adriano for her life. This girl…

Doc blows out a hard breath. "If she takes much longer, I'm jacking off."

"Coming on her counts as touching," I warn.

"Fucking fascist."

"Why don't we just touch her?" Bobby suggests.

"Not a proper touch. Just, like, a massage or—"

"Fuck this," Doc pulls his T-shirt over his head. "Hey, Tesorina? Over here."

I expect her to ignore him, but her eyes widen as she takes in his bare chest.

"Yeah, you see this?" Doc runs a hand down his tattooed abdomen. "All yours. Come get it."

"Idiota," I mutter, but January's tongue flashes out, wetting her swollen lips.

"Yeah, you like that, Tits? You wanna get fucked into a screaming mess?"

January's expression is tortured. "Stop calling me that!"

"No." Doc grips his cock through his jeans. "Come on, you know you want to."

Her face goes scarlet. Is this going to work? Should I take my clothes off?

Doc undoes the top button of his jeans and Bobby recoils. "No getting it out near me!"

"Or me," Adriano rumbles.

"Yeah, like you scumbags haven't already seen it." Doc pulls open his zipper and works himself into his palm. "Like it, Tesorina?"

January's gaze is fixed, hypnotized. Has she seen a hard cock before? Is she imagining how it feels?

Doc pumps himself. "Yeah, nice and big, isn't it? Wanna come sit on it?"

At the other end of the couch, Bobby drains his glass. "January?"

"Fuck off," Doc snaps but he's already lost January's attention.

When she looks at Bobby, her green eyes mellow and I feel a rush of jealousy. She's never looked at me like that. Never come close. All Bobby's coolness has vanished. His cheeks are red as he swipes a hand across his mouth. "JJ, if you come here, I'll… I'll…"

"What?" Doc sneers. "You'll stutter at her?"

"… I'll lick your pussy."

Silence greets the end of Bobby's sentence until Doc's laughter breaks it. "Smooth, man. Very cool."

January's face goes even redder, but she doesn't break eye contact with Bobby.

Looking mortified but determined, he leans forward. "January, I swear to God, you don't have to do anything to me. I won't take your virginity. I'll just take care of you. Touch you. I'll use my hands. My mouth."

Her lower lip trembles.

"I've dreamed about you for so long, JJ. I've fantasized about what you taste like. That's all I want, to lick you until you come."

I watch the idea of giving in flash across January's face.

"Don't listen to him, Tesorina," Doc calls. "The minute you let this nice guy asshole near you, your virginity's gone."

She frowns.

"Ignore him, JJ. He'll say anything he needs to win."

Doc laughs. "I will, Tesorina, because I'm an asshole and I don't lie about it. But what about Bobby? He lies about who *he* is. He pretended to be your friend then he wasted your bodyguard right in front of you, remember?"

January gasps.

"Jesus," I hiss. "Is that necessary?"

Bobby turns to Doc, fist raised. "Fucking—"

"Asshole? Sorry, Bash. All's fair in love and war."

Bobby opens his mouth, but I get in first. "Anyone who violates rule two is out."

Doc turns back to January and pats his thighs. "Come on, honey. I'll pound you like your pussy's the only thing keeping me alive."

Bobby swears under his breath. "January, Doc's killed about a million people, and I never meant to lie to you. I—"

"Just stop talking, please?" January looks like she's about to faint.

"You idiots are both fucking this up," I say.

Doc glares at me. "Let's see you do better."

"Fine." I shift in my seat. "Miss Whitehall, *guardami*." *Look at me.*

January's eyes find mine.

"*Brava bambina*," I say. "*Stai andando così bene.*"

Good little girl. You're doing so well.

Doc laughs as he tucks his cock back into his jeans. "Breaking out the Italian, are you? We can all do that."

I ignore him. January's green eyes are already following me like I'm performing a magic trick.

"When you first saw me, you could barely look at me, *bella*." I flick my right sleeve over. "That was appropriate. You're a shy, respectful girl and you were engaged to another man."

Her throat contracts. I'm going to clamp a hand around it while I make her ride me. I reach for my left sleeve. "But it's not inappropriate for you to want me now. I can kiss you. Touch you. Look you right in the eyes while I slide my cock into your beautiful cunt."

She lets out a helpless little whimper. "Mr. Morelli…"

"Yes, *bella*," I say quietly. "I know it hurts. Come to me and I will take care of you like the precious little girl you are."

She jerks forward and Bobby groans. "How is this happening?"

"Fucking forearms," Doc mutters. "Women and shirts and fucking forearms."

I keep rolling up my sleeve, nice and slow. "Come on, *bella*. Come to daddy and he'll make everything better."

She puts a nervous hand on the carpet then sits back,

her face red with embarrassment. I hold her gaze and let her drink me in, knowing she can't resi—

A whistle cuts through the air, making all of us jump.

Adriano lowers his tattooed fingers from his mouth, ugly as one of Goya's demons.

Doc rubs his chest. "You scared me, you giant fuck."

Adriano doesn't acknowledge him. He and January are staring at each other, green eyes into green eyes. He points to the floor at his feet. "Here."

January cringes away.

I force myself to laugh, my heart still racing too hard. "Nice try, Rossi."

Adriano taps a boot against the carpet. "Now."

A split-second later January crawls toward him. She moves slowly, one hand after another like a great weight is tied to her legs. My stomach sinks.

Doc lets out a wild drunken laugh. "Fuck me, talk about a dark horse."

I grit my teeth. Adriano's greedy. If she chooses him, the rest of us are going to be waiting hours.

"*Bella*?" I prompt but she doesn't look my way.

"Still time to change your mind," Doc calls, but he's just glad she's giving in. He and Adriano go back a long time. He has the best chance at getting in on the action with him.

January is inches from Adriano. Even from this distance, I can see she's crying. Rossi won't like that. He likes causing pain, but he can't stand tears. His usual solution is to wrap a T-shirt around the girl's face then fuck her from behind. I imagine him gripping her pale hips in his tattooed hands. Manipulating her beautiful body with his scarred one. Sometimes I like seeing beautiful things get broken, but I don't know if I'll be able to put my bitterness to one side and enjoy the show.

"January…" Bobby's voice is low, imploring. "January, he wants to kill you."

She freezes. Adriano makes a noise like an angry bull.

I bite back a laugh. *Yes. Ruin this, you clever little fuck.*

"If it weren't for us, he'd have killed you already," Bobby says so quietly his voice is barely audible over the music. "He's wanted you dead the moment he saw you. Don't let him win."

January sits back, her chest heaving.

"You fucking moron," Doc snaps. "We were *this* fucking close."

"All's fair in love and war."

"You'll pay for that, Bassilotta," Adriano says quietly.

I glare at him. "Do not threaten Bobby in front of me."

"Fuck this." Adriano gets to his feet, looking as unsteady as I feel.

"You leave, you can't come back," I remind him.

"It doesn't matter. She's done. No one wins."

January looks up at Adriano. "Sorry, Mr. Rossi."

He gives her a look of utter loathing. "Remember what I told you, Bambi."

I frown. "Bambi?"

Adriano turns his crazy green eyes on me. "The dead deer."

"Bambi's mom dies, you idiot," Doc mutters but his gaze is still locked on January. "How are you doing this, Tits?"

She smiles at him. "Maybe your drug isn't very good?"

I almost laugh but catch myself at the last second. Bobby can't hold back, he doubles over, cackling. Adriano leaves, his tread heavy even on the carpet. Doc stares mutinously into space. I know that mood, but before I can say anything, Doc paces to the nearby wall and puts his fist through it, plaster dust scattering the carpet. He storms out of the room slamming the door behind him.

"Idiot," I mutter, though I'm relieved he didn't take a swing at Bobby or throw one of the paintings in the fire.

"Does this mean I've won?" January's voice is small but steady.

Bobby looks at her and I see him realize he'll never get to touch her.

"Go," I tell him. "I'll deal with the girl. Get out of

here."

"You sure?"

"Yes. I'll escort her to the east wing. Go."

He leaves the room as quickly as he can without running. Probably to fuck his fist somewhere.

January's fight with the Orchard has drained her. Curled up on the carpet, she seems smaller and even more delicate.

"The competition is over," I tell her. "You keep your virginity."

Her mouth puckers like a little rosebud. "Oh... I'm sorry, I guess."

"So am I, *bella*. I've never been a good loser. Come here a second. Sit with me."

She doesn't move. I roll my eyes. "I'm a man of my word. I won't touch you. Sit on Doc and Bobby's couch, if you like."

She still looks nervous, but she does as she's told, wrapping herself into a ball on the leather. I can smell the warm heaven of her cunt. I want to peel off her soaked panties, stuff them in her mouth then shove my cock deep inside her.

Instead, I head for the bar. If anything calls for a martini, it's this evening. I pour gin into the cocktail shaker. "Doc is too proud to ask, *bella*, so I will. How did you resist the Orchard?"

"Um, I think ballet, maybe. Learning how to hold

uncomfortable positions for a really long time."

So, Parker is to blame for all of this. Fucking asshole. I remember the video recording. I'll have to make sure Bobby deletes the footage. I never want to relive this experience.

"Mr. Morelli…?"

I drop three ice cubes into the cocktail shaker. "Yes?"

Her cheeks burn red. "That wasn't the first time I've felt that way."

I smile. "Wet and horny?"

"No." She gnaws at her puffy lower lip. "I… I think I've been given Orchard before."

"That's impossible."

"It's true. When I was fifteen, I was at a ball, and I got…. *sick* the exact same way."

I put down the cocktail shaker. Her expression is steady, her eyes clear. She's not lying. My stomach knots. "Parker. Was Parker there?"

"I… Yes."

In two strides I'm beside her, pulling her to her feet. "Bobby?"

"What?" A strained voice calls from down the hall. He's probably in the bathroom masturbating into the sink.

"Get Doc and Adriano and meet me in the east wing. We have a problem."

CHAPTER THIRTEEN

Bobby Bassilotta

V ELVET HOUSE ISN'T an easy place to navigate drunk. Brass busts and stupid vases lurch out of the darkness at me and I'm so full of booze and horniness and second-hand panic, it's like the place is on a tilt. I find Doc in the kitchen, an unlit cigarette between his teeth, pulling a six-pack from the fridge.

"We need to go to the east wing," I tell him.

He doesn't turn around. "No."

"Eli needs us."

Doc's back stiffens. The two of them are always sniping at each other, but Doc knows Eli doesn't overreact. He slams the fridge door shut. "I'm bringing the beers."

"Whatever. We need to get Adriano."

Doc takes the cigarette from his mouth and tucks it behind his ear. "He's gonna be pissed."

Adriano lives in the south wing. No one is allowed to go near his floor. Not even the cleaning ladies. Doc and I head there in silence and I try not to think about January. Her kissable mouth, her shiny hair. The way she looked at me when I talked about going down on her. She still wants me—to save her and to touch her. Tonight was a shitshow, but at least it proved that.

We arrive at Adriano's door. "What do you think he has in there?" Doc asks.

"Goat heads? A bunch of pictures connected with red string?"

Doc buzzes the intercom. "Lurch, get the fuck out here."

"Do you have to call him that?"

"Fuck off, altar boy."

Adriano opens the door shirtless. I've seen his bare chest a million times, but it always makes me kind of sick. There are bullet scars and cuts across his shoulders, ugly tattoos over everything else. He looks from Doc to me. "What?"

"Ell needs us in the east wing,' I say.

"The girl?"

"Yeah."

Adriano starts to close the door, but I shove my foot through it. "It's important."

"And if it's not, you can kill her," Doc adds. "And Morelli."

There's a pause.

"Lemme get a shirt."

The east wing is where guests stay, not that we have many of those. It's on the fourth floor and a bitch to get to. My cock strains against my jeans as the three of us make our way there. I can't stop picturing January writhing on the carpet. She was so close to giving in.

"I need pussy," Doc mutters. "I can't fucking concentrate."

I stay quiet, but I feel the same way. Only, the thought of being with anyone but January makes my stomach churn. I just want her. Why the fuck has everything turned out this way?

The outer door to the east wing is open. We head for the bedroom and find Eli in a velvet-backed chair beside the four-poster bed. January is asleep under the covers. My heart flips at the sight of her. She looks so tiny among all the pillows and blankets. I want to climb in beside her and hold her close. Promise her everything will be okay.

Eli takes us in. "Thanks for coming."

Doc takes the cigarette from behind his ear. "This better be good."

"Smoke that in here and I'll gut you," Eli says lightly.

January gives a soft moan, turning her head from side to side.

"God she's beautiful," I say, because I'm drunk, and I

can't not say it.

Ell looks at me. "I didn't bring you here to watch her sleep."

He reaches across the bed, shaking January's shoulder. "Wake up, *bella*. We need to talk to you."

January's eyes flutter open and she pulls the sheets to her nose. "What's going on?"

"Don't panic," Eli says. "Tell them what you told me."

January lowers the blanket. "I… um, I've been given that drug before."

"No, you haven't," Doc mutters around his unlit cigarette.

"But… um?" She looks to Eli who raises a hand.

"Just keep going."

"It was at a charity ball," January whispers. "I went cold, then hot, and I couldn't stop thinking about…" She breaks off, flushing scarlet.

"So, you got horny," Doc snarls. "That's not the same thing as having O."

"Let her speak." Eli lays a palm on the covers, where January's thigh must be. "Finish, *bella*."

For the millionth time, I wish I was Eli Morelli. It isn't a new feeling, being jealous of him. But he could marry January if he wanted and that burns.

"After the ball, I was sick for days," she says. "I couldn't get out of bed, and I kept—"

"Fucking yourself." Doc looks at Eli. "This horny schoolgirl shit doesn't mean anything."

"Because you're not listening," Eli says testily. "January, who gave you a drink that night?"

"Mr. Parker."

The cigarette tumbles from between Doc's teeth. "What?"

"Mr. Parker," she repeats. "He was sitting at my family's table, but I'm not sure he was the one—"

"Shut the fuck up. What drink did he give you?"

"Um, a mocktail. It was blue with glittery syrup."

"What did it taste like?"

"Sweet but, um, funny. I thought he'd maybe got a normal cocktail by mistake."

My muscles go weak. *He drugged her.* I know what Parker is capable of, but he was supposed to leave her alone until he married her.

"Say the last part," Eli orders. "What happened next?

"I started to… feel the way I felt tonight." January's voice is barely a whisper. "Only it was worse."

"Speak up," Doc barks. "How was it worse?"

"I couldn't concentrate. My head was spinning. I told Margot I needed to leave. I was trying to find somewhere private because…" She looks down at her hands and a twisted pang goes through me. Because she was trying to find somewhere to touch herself.

"Mr. Parker followed me. He said he knew a place

where I could sit. He took me to a side room and gave me a glass of water. I remember because he was so careful not to touch me and I…" her voice cracks. "I… wanted him to touch me."

My hands ball into fists. I want to kill Parker. Go back in time and murder him when I was seventeen. All this time planning and fucking around. Meanwhile, he stole our drug and used it on the girl I love.

"What happened next?" Doc asks. His voice is sharp, but I can hear something else creeping in at the edges. Fear or maybe just softness.

"I felt sick. I was so scared I was going to ruin my dress."

"You mean you wanted to puke?"

She nods, her eyes huge in the semi-darkness.

"Did you?"

"No, my mom found us and got really angry. She and Mr. Parker went somewhere else, and then she came back and told me we were going home."

"What happened when you got home?"

January looks away, gnawing her lower lip.

"I don't give a shit how embarrassed you are, Tesorina. What happened next?"

She cringes and I shove Doc's shoulder. "Watch how you talk to her."

He rounds on me, eyes narrowed. "Or what?"

I square my shoulders. Doc's vicious in a fight, and

not above hair-pulling and groin-punching, but I'm bigger and he knows it. Adri's always been his muscle. Question is would he step in if we fought now? I glance at Adriano, and he stares back, blank as a statue.

"Enough," Eli says. "The two of you are acting like fools."

"*Basher's* acting like a fool," Doc snarls. "Tell him to go pull his dick and come back with a clear head."

"Go fuck your—"

"I touched myself," January blurts out. "When I got home."

Doc and I turn back to her. She's flushing. "I touched myself, then I threw up. I was up all night doing it."

The corner of Doc's mouth kicks up. "Puking or touching yourself?"

"Both." She shakes her head as though trying to dislodge the memories. "Zia Teresa wanted me to go to the hospital, but mom wouldn't let her take me. She said I had food poisoning. I was so scared because all the while they were talking by my bed, I couldn't stop… you know." Her eyes grow bright with tears. "… I was under the covers, and I don't think they saw me, but it was humiliating. I didn't know what was happening."

I tense my arm, ready to punch Doc for laughing, but for once he looks as horrified as I feel.

"Go on," Eli prompts.

January draws in a shaking breath. "Eventually I stopped being sick and... you know... but I was exhausted. I didn't feel better for almost a week."

"Did you throw up the next day?" Doc asks.

"No, but I felt like I had the flu."

"And your mood? Were you depressed? Did you have trouble sleeping?"

It's been a long time since I've seen him like this. Professional. Take away the tattoos and the cigarette and he could be a doctor doing hospital rounds.

"Um, just tired I think." January seems a new kind of nervous as though Doc asking sensible questions is more disturbing than him taking his cock out. "Do you think Mr. Parker gave me Orchard?"

Doc looks out the dark rain-flecked window. "Did your mom talk to you about what happened?"

"No."

There's a heart-breaking tremor in her voice. I can't fucking stand it. "Your mom might not have understood. She might have really thought you got food poisoning or something."

January gives me a soft smile. "My stepmom is pretty smart. I don't think she misses much."

There isn't anything I can say to that.

"Thanks for telling us what happened," Doc says quietly. "How you feeling now?"

"Um, good?"

She's lying. Her voice is shaking, and her eyes are bright with tears. Again, I look at Doc, ready to chew him out if he mocks her, but his face is tight with worry. I remember him looking that way back when everything first started. Before Alessia, before Orchard, he used to have normal human emotions. But somewhere along the way, the laughing mask became his face.

"Enough." Eli's voice is cold. "Outside. We need to talk."

"Should I come with you?" January mumbles.

"No, *bella*, you be a good girl and sleep. In an hour I'll have Gretzky bring up some food."

She nods, her eyes already closing. The urge to climb into bed beside her returns. I hang back as the others file out of the room. "Are you okay? Do you need anything?"

Her cheeks go pink. "Could you maybe… stay with me for a bit?"

Something in her eyes makes my cock harden. I think of the Orchard still swimming in her blood, my offer to make her come without taking her virginity. "I… what do you—"

Ell whistles. "Bobby. Now."

I bite back a sigh. "Sorry JJ. Sleep well."

She lowers her head. "Goodbye, Bobby."

"Simp," Doc says, as soon as I'm out the door. I glare at him but what am I supposed to say? That I'm not completely stupid for January Whitehall? That I don't want to be whatever she needs?

Ell locks the door behind me, giving me a look as he puts the keys in his pocket. "Don't even think about it."

I expect him to lead us to the dining room, but he heads for the nearest balcony.

"I want a cigarette," Eli says. "Do you have your pack, Domenico?"

"Don't call me that," Doc mutters but he pulls his battered Marlboro lights from his jeans.

It's freezing cold outside, rain falling off the roof in a steady stream. Doc hands Eli and Adriano a cigarette then looks at me. "Want one?"

I never smoke unless I'm so wasted, I don't remember doing it. I shake my head, the icy wind whipping at my face. It must be below freezing but Doc's barefoot and in a T-shirt. Still, I know better than to suggest he put shoes on. Doc's the sulking big brother I never asked for.

"What do you think?" Eli asks.

Doc lights his cigarette, a flicker in the dark. "He gave her O."

"How?"

"Parker must have stolen some."

Ell exhales a stream of white smoke. "Did he steal it? Or did he replicate it?"

Doc draws hard on his cigarette. "He'd need a sample to replicate it, so either way he must have stolen some. But he gave her some of ours."

"What makes you think that?" Eli asks.

"Because she threw up a bunch of times."

Adriano flicks his cigarette, creating a shower of sparks. "Could have been the alcohol."

"One cocktail she barely drank?" Doc shakes his head. "Orchard isn't shelf stable. Longest I kept a dose was six months and when I gave it to Mel—no, Meg—she said she felt sick after. She didn't puke, but it was the first time anyone's said that. If Parker's been making his own gear, then the puking's a new feature. If he's kept what he stole, it oxidized. My money's on that."

"I'm surprised he didn't kill her," Eli says darkly.

Doc lights a second cigarette off the tip of his first. "If she'd drunk the whole cocktail, he probably would have."

We stand there for a long time, our breath and cigarette smoke mixing with the wet air. I imagine the girl tucked into the bed not two rooms away, dead at a charity gala. I want to go to her and give her anything, everything, to make her feel better.

"Risky," Adriano says. "Doping her in front of her family."

"Fucking pig," Doc mutters. I remember watching him pace the hospital after Alessia was attacked and my gut knots.

"Did he want her gone?" Eli asks. "Was he trying to

kill her?"

Doc snorts. "No fucking way."

"Then what...?"

"The motherless cunt got sick of waiting. He had a room all picked out to take her to, didn't he? If her mom hadn't come after her..."

A horrible thought comes to me. "Did January say how old she was when it happened?"

"Fifteen," Eli replies.

I'm expecting anger, and it's there, but mostly I feel miserable. January's sweeter than anyone I've ever met. How has this been her life?

"Why would he throw everything away like that?" Eli asks. "Paying January's mother for years, not even letting himself hold her hand. Why would he give that all up just to dose her at a gala where there's every chance he'd get caught?"

"Because he snapped." Adriano grinds his cigarette end under his boot. "You know what he's like."

We do. Better than anyone. But I learned a long time ago that revisiting those memories is asking nightmares to take up permanent residency in my head.

"*Porca miseria*," Eli mutters. "What a fucking mess."

Doc blows smoke toward the sky. "You got that right."

"We can't send January away. Not until we know whether Parker's making Orchard," Eli says.

I try not to let my expression change. "Do you want her back in the cage?"

"No. She can stay in the east wing. Actually, she can walk the house for all I care. It's not like she's a danger to anyone."

Adriano turns away.

"Fine by me," Doc says. "I need to ask her about the O. Maybe run some tests—"

"You won't be doing that," Eli interrupts. "Parker still needs dealing with. We have a job to do and limited time."

Doc looks mutinous but he doesn't say anything.

"That goes for all of you," Eli adds. "Stay away from the girl. We have bigger fish to fry."

He holds my gaze until I nod. "Okay."

"Good." He rounds on Adriano. "I'm warning you, Rossi. She dies and you are in the shit."

Adriano inclines his head.

Eli rubs his brow. "I need to call Peirce. He hasn't mentioned Parker has access to a drug that works on women, but he didn't know that's information we're interested in. Get some sleep. Tomorrow, we go to work."

He leaves, taking the key to January's door with him.

Adriano grunts and disappears after him. I feel a stab of panic and remember that if I'm locked out of January's room, so is Rossi.

Doc pulls another cigarette from his pack. "Big night."

"Yeah," I say. Should I follow Adriano? Make sure he doesn't go after January?

"Another girl doped because of me."

There's a beat and I realize Doc's being serious. Misery lines every inch of his face. I grab his arm, his skin is cold as a corpse. "You're not responsible for what Parker did."

He doesn't look at me. "She could have died."

Again, that twist in his voice, fear and softness together. I tighten my grip on Doc's arm. "You weren't trying to hurt her. You couldn't have known."

"That's what you said about Alessia."

It's been years since I heard him say her name. I squeeze harder. "You're not a bad man."

He snorts. "Then how did we end up here?"

We're skating dangerously close to the thing none of us wants to talk about.

"Things happened the way they did. You're still not responsible for Parker."

A smile quirks Doc's mouth and he lifts a frozen hand to mine. "Thanks."

"Anytime." I clear my throat. "You need to put some fucking shoes on."

Doc laughs. "This is why all the ladies love you, Bobby. You're so sincere."

I shake my head but I'm grinning. "Let's go get some sleep."

"Wait a moment." He fumbles with his lighter, igniting his fresh cigarette. "You want a hand? I can use my powers for good and evil, you know?"

"The fuck are you talking about?"

"January. I saw the way she was looking at you before Morelli made you leave."

I roll my eyes. "Don't butter me up just because you feel bad."

"I've never buttered anyone up for anything. The girl's been alone for days, she's probably dying to be touched. And as much as I hate to admit it, you got the closest with her tonight. She still trusts you."

"She hates me for killing her bodyguard."

"She's confused and horny. She wants you to comfort her."

"But she won't marry me."

Doc chokes on his cigarette. "Fuck, Basher. You don't want much, do you?"

I fail to suppress a smile. "Whatever you're thinking, it won't work anyway. Eli locked her in."

"Did he?" Doc pulls Eli's keychain from his pocket. "Should we go pay her a visit?"

I hesitate. The four of us are close but there's always been divisions. Doc and Adriano on one side, me and Elliot on the other. I owe Eli my loyalty. But he was going to send her away and he wasn't going to ask my opinion about it.

Doc flicks his cigarette and heads for the door. "Come on, Basher."

I stare into the rain. "She's supposed to go to Eli's cousin."

"That's later. Now is now."

And then I'm behind him, walking back to January's door. The bedroom is warm and already smells like her. I inhale. I'm dizzy and drunk yet all too aware of my surroundings.

Doc pads to her bedside table, flicks on a lamp. "Hey, Tesorina."

She is lying on her back. Looking at her makes me wish I wrote music. Her green eyes flick open and she looks from Doc to me. "Hi...?"

Doc sits on her bed. "Basher and I thought you might want some company."

"Oh." She places a tentative hand on Doc's arm. "You're freezing."

He grins. "Yeah. Can we share your blankets?"

January's chin dips into her chest, but she smiles. "Maybe."

My heart is going like a freight train. Doc's right. She's scared and horny and craving comfort. This might actually happen.

January moves across the bed, making space for Doc.

"Thanks, baby." He climbs in beside her and beckons me forward.

For a million reasons I want to tell him to stop—Elliot, the Orchard, his dirty feet.

Instead, I watch as the smartest, most irritating man I know snuggles into the woman I love. My cold hands are burning, my heart is still going too fast.

"Bobby?" January's voice is shy. "Are you…? Do you need to get warm too?"

I do, but I can't move. I can't even speak.

"He'll come, Tesorina. Just give him a moment." He grins at her, bright and wide, and she smiles back.

She's nervous, but you can tell she's glad he's there. A tight feeling hooks behind my navel and pulls hard. This isn't the first time, me, Doc, and a girl. But it's always some dancer at one of his clubs. Someone who knows the score and wants nothing but sex. This is January and January is everything.

Doc strokes her hair out of her eyes. He makes it look natural. Like he's done it a million times. "You won, Tesorina. You beat me."

I move toward the foot of the bed until the covers brush my knees.

"What do you mean?" January asks.

"You beat me," Doc repeats. "You withstood the O and made fools out of all of us."

January smiles. "Sorry."

"Never be sorry for winning." Doc runs his finger down her cheek to the nape of her neck. "Would you like a reward for being such a good girl?"

She shivers so hard it makes her curls tremble. "What do you mean?"

Doc leans closer his nose an inch from hers. "You want to get your little pussy licked?"

January's eyes go wide and I see the same fear and longing that's burning inside me. "I don't know…"

The blanket has tumbled down her shoulders. She's still in her pink lingerie. Slowly, easily, Doc moves an arm around her. "Basher just wants to do what he said before, Tesorina. He wants to tongue your virgin pussy until you come. Don't you want to let him?"

She bites her lip. "I shouldn't."

"Shouldn't is a stupid word." Doc's hand moves lower, caressing her through her bra. January's eyes roll in pleasure before she pulls away, staring at me with enough shame to torch a nun.

"I'm sorry, I can't do this with both of you."

"What do you mean, both of us?" Doc says in mock puzzlement. "I'm touching you and Bobby's not doing anything."

"But you can't both be here when…"

"Why not?" He moves his palm across her breasts in a slow circular rhythm. "Don't you want your first orgasm to be special?"

"I don't know." She closes her eyes, her breathing hard. "But won't you want me to... do something back?"

No, I think. *It can be just for you, January. Of course, it can.*

Doc laughs quietly. "Don't worry about us, Tesorina. We're big boys. We can control ourselves."

He pinches her nipple and she gasps. "Then I guess... I think... but I really shouldn't..."

Doc gives me a hard stare. *Move. Now.*

I lift the covers from the mattress and duck under, feeling completely disconnected from my body. Am I really about to do this? And in front of Doc? But January's feet curl above my head, her smooth soles and cherry-painted toenails. I can smell her already, sweet as apple pie.

"Are you excited, Tesorina?" Doc asks, somewhere above me.

"I shouldn't... I'm supposed to stay a virgin."

"And you will."

I grab January's ankles and ease them apart. She gives a high, breathy moan. "Bobby..."

"Shhh," Doc's voice is low. "It doesn't count, baby. It's just the three of us in your little bed, playing together. No one needs to know. Just let Basher make you feel good."

She says something I can't hear, but her scent grows stronger. I slide my hands up her calves. Her skin is soft and smooth, long muscles twitch beneath my fingers.

"Bobby, are you sure?"

"He's exactly where he wants to be," Doc says. "Why don't you just lie back and let me…"

There's a sound of material shifting, and January gives a sharp moan. My cock pulses against my stomach. He must be sucking her nipples, the way he did in the cage. I watched him do it on the monitors. Jerked off about it later. Not that I'd ever admit that.

I slide my hands to the top of January's thighs, brushing my thumbs over the sheer pink thong Eli chose for her. She's soaked through, wet as the rain outside. My mouth fills with saliva. All I want to do is to make her come with my tongue. With a single fingertip, I move the sodden panties to one side and my vision swims. She's small and pink and soft and perfect.

And then her hands are cupping my head. "Bobby, you don't have to…"

I pause, tongue already extended. I'll die if I have to stop, but I'd die for January anyway.

"Tesorina," Doc croons. "You're a big girl and you won your bet. If you don't want Basher's mouth on you while I suck on your tits, you can say no."

"I can say no," she repeats, her voice thick with lust. I hover, tongue quaking, praying Doc knows what he's doing.

"That's right." There's a soft sucking noise. "But you want some relief, don't you, baby? You've been aching for it all night, all your life, you just want a man to make you come."

"Yes," she breathes. "Yes… I want to come."

That's all I need. I lean forward and give her a long, slow lick. She gasps and her thighs close around my head, locking me in. Half-convinced this is a dream, I go to work, licking her pussy the way I'd like to kiss her perfect pouty lips.

"You greedy little girl," Doc mutters. "You like Bobby's tongue nice and soft in your cunt while I play with your tits?"

January bucks hard against my face. The noises she makes are like razor wire going through my brain. I press my aching cock against the mattress and wish it was her pussy.

Light makes me look upward. Doc's lifted the sheets, checking out the action. Fucking pervert. I smirk into January's folds and go back to work. She whines and a surge of silky girl juice floods my mouth.

She's close, I want to tell Doc. Real fucking close.

But he already seems to know. The light vanishes and I hear him suck her nipples again. I draw soft circles with my tongue and January's hips shudder. She says something I can't hear.

"I can't kiss you, baby," Doc says. "I've been smoking."

"I don't care. Please, Domenico?"

The way she says his name… It hurts. It hurts and feels good and fucked up. Tangled the way it always is when I get talked into screwing a girl with Doc or Eli, only a million times worse. A million times better.

Doc chuckles. "You want two tongues in you, Tesorina?"

"Yes," January sighs.

I can't help myself. I rut against the mattress. I was hoping I'd be able to make it to my bedroom to jack off. But fuck it, if this is the closest I'll ever get to January, I might as well come while I eat her out.

"Kiss me," January whispers and I know she's talking to both of us. I lap at her slow and steady and feel her come as she and Doc make out. The sound of them kissing goes through me like bullets. I've always liked watching, liked threesomes, but something about Doc kissing January while she comes on my face just makes me lose it. I moan into her pussy as liquid pumps out of me.

I keep licking until January pushes my forehead away. I want to crawl up and hold her, but Doc's already sliding out of the bed. I move out from the blankets the way I came in, blinking in the golden lamplight. I feel disgusting, but you can't see anything. No one has to know. She looks up at me flushed and so gorgeous it hurts. "Um, thank you, Bobby."

I can't talk, I can't even smile. I can still feel her legs wrapped around me, smell her everywhere.

"Basher'll do that any time you like, Tesorina." Doc backs away from the bed. "We're gonna go before

Gretzky shows up with pizza rolls for you."

January's smile dims, then she tilts her head to the side. "Do people call you Doc because of the pills?"

"Huh?"

"Your nickname. Is it because you were a drug dealer?"

A beat and then a half smile. "Yeah."

"I thought so." Her voice is soft. "I'm not always stupid."

I reach down, finding her foot through the covers, and give it a gentle squeeze. "You're never stupid."

"Bobby..." she mumbles.

Doc catches my eyes and taps his wrist.

I let go of January's foot. "Bye JJ."

"No," she says, all sweet like a little girl.

Doc leans forward and gives her a swift kiss on the forehead. "Sleep, Tesorina." He jerks his head at me. "Let's go."

Back in my wing of Velvet House I strip off and shower. Put on my pajama bottoms, brush my teeth. As I do it, I replay the kiss Doc gave January. Not the mind-bending one while I was going down on her, the fast one on the head as we left.

That kiss worries me. I know I love January and Eli wants her, and Adriano hates her. But as of fifteen minutes ago, I have no idea what my psychotic, chain-smoking, drug-inventing friend feels about her.

CHAPTER FOURTEEN

January Whitehall

BOBBY IS BETWEEN my legs, licking me softly. I tilt my hips and pleasure washes over me like a wave. I shouldn't let him do this but it's so good. His brown eyes find mine, warm and kind. "Touch me, JJ."

I reach down and brush my fingers through his hair and it becomes long and blond. Doc grins. "You gonna come on my face, Tits?"

"Don't call me that!"

"Ah relax, little *bella*." Eli is sitting in a chair beside me. He leans forward, brushing a hand over my breasts. "Domenico's only complimenting you. You have perfect tits."

The tongue between my legs moves faster, fluttering over my swollen clit. I scream as my orgasm surges closer.

"Stop! Please? Let me go?"

Elliot fastens his ruby necklace around my throat.

"Too late for that, Pryntsesa."

I look down and it isn't Doc licking me, it's a man with shaggy brown hair with shaved sides. His mouth is hot as steam and he digs at me, deep and hard with his teeth. I try to yell but no sound comes out. He looks at me, green eyes glowing like twin traffic lights. "Come and I'll kill you."

He lowers his head and his tongue slicks through me. He's good at this. Too good. I'm going to come, but then so is death. I need to scream—

"Miss?"

"No!"

"Miss Whitehall?"

I jolt upright. I'm not where I was.

A man stands in front of me. A stranger. He's wearing the same grey uniform as Mr. Gretzky but he's white-haired with a long Santa beard. He raises the bundle in his arms. "Sorry for disturbing you, Miss"

I pull the blankets up to my chin, my heart racing. "I… That's okay."

The older man smiles. "I'm Harvey. I'm here to bring you fresh clothes and take you down to the dining room for breakfast."

It's been so long since someone talked to me in a normal way, I'm a little blindsided. "Breakfast?"

"Of course. Although it's almost lunchtime." He lays the bundle on my bed with a toothy grin. "The ensuite is through to your left if you haven't already seen it. I'll wait outside."

He leaves, closing the door behind him.

I was too stressed to pay attention to the room last night, but it's pretty. There are leaf mouldings across the roof and a small grate for a fire. I crawl out of bed and wander to the huge window. Outside is a white fountain and what looks like a tennis court. Beyond that are rolling green grounds as far as I can see.

The ensuite is just as pretty as the rest of the room. Vowing to use the claw-foot bath later, I run the shower as hot as I can and get in. As I move the loofa across my skin, arousal pulses through me. This was where Bobby's mouth was. This is where Doc's hands were. That was no dream. I let a man go down on me while another man and I kissed. "Oh God…"

The night we met, Eli told me my morals were un-tested. I want to say I'm a good person and I know what's wrong and right, but do I? I was excited to be put in front of them in my underwear and relieved to have a reason to be attracted to them. I know Bobby killed Kurt and Eli ordered it and Doc would have happily done it instead, but I still let them touch me last night. And I wanted them to touch me more. All of them, even—my stomach contracts as I think it—Adriano.

I shake my head, sending water everywhere. "But I'm still a virgin," I tell myself. Even I hear the hollowness in my voice. It doesn't feel like much of a consolation. What would mom say if she knew? What would Zia Teresa say?

I imagine her sitting on the edge of the bath, playing slot machine games on her phone.

"Zia, do you think I'm disgusting?"

She looks up at me, her expression mild. "I think you should get out of the shower, *bella*."

I do as I'm told, drying myself and examining the clothes Harvey brought me. Yellow cotton panties, a blue sundress and ballet flats.

As usual, the dress I've been given fits perfectly but snugly. I look at myself in the full-length mirror and sigh. No wonder Doc keeps calling me 'Tits.'

There's a light knock on the door. "You ready to go, Miss?"

I put on my best 'meeting new people' smile. "I'll be right out."

Harvey leads me from my wing down another red carpeted hallway. The house is even prettier by daylight, but it's dirty. There's an inch of dust on every surface and cobwebs across the gorgeous stained-glass windows. Beyond them, I can see the edge of a thick green forest. We seem to be miles away from anywhere.

"Excuse me, Harvey?" I ask, trying to sound innocent. "Where are we?"

"Albany."

Relief floods through me. Upstate New York. Not too far from home.

"And what is this place? It's so beautiful."

"Isn't it? Velvet House belongs to Mr. Morelli now, but it was built by Wallace McKenna in 1869. He was a financier and a Governor of New York…"

As we walk down wooden bannisters and past huge bedrooms, Harvey keeps up his tour guide-y speech. He tells me when the conservatory was built and how old certain paintings are and the important people who were married in the gardens. I smile and nod, but my mind keeps dragging me back to last night. Kneeling in front of the fire as Doc took off his shirt; Eli murmuring to me in Italian….

Slut, my mind whispers. If I'd let them have me last night, I'd probably be on a plane to Italy right now. Is Eli still going to send me away? The floor seems to skid beneath me and I halt, one hand over my eyes.

"Miss? Are you okay?"

"Just a bit dizzy." I try and smile at Harvey. "Is, um, Mr. Morelli or any of the others around…?"

His expression is a little too sympathetic. "Mr. Morelli and Mr. Bassilotta have gone to New York and Mr. Rossi and Mr. Valente have business elsewhere today."

"Oh." I suppose it was the same while I was in the cage and I just had no idea, but it's strange they've gone and left me here. Like all five of us should be in the same space.

"Mr. Morelli told me you're free to explore the house," Harvey says. "There's a library and gym. Or you can visit the family gallery on the third floor or watch a movie in the cinema. Or I'd be happy to take you for a walk around the grounds?"

My head swims. I just want to go somewhere quiet and sit down. "That all sounds really lovely but could I maybe have breakfast before I decide please?"

"Of course."

We continue on our way, Harvey talking about the history of Velvet House at the top of his voice, and I wonder if he was involved in getting rid of Kurt's body. He seems like such a nice man. Is he some kind of psychopath? But then who am I to judge? I let Kurt's murderer go down on me. And I came while he did it. I could blame the Orchard, but I'd be lying.

Your morals are untested.

It's another couple of minutes of winding staircases and same-y hallways before we enter a marble-floored area. Harvey pushes open a metal door. "This is the kitchen."

I have to bite my tongue to keep from crying out. It's gigantic, even bigger than the cafeteria at school, and it's *filthy*. Every surface is covered in grease or dirty cups and plates, and it smells like old vegetables that have been left in the sun. If Zia Teresa saw this place, she would faint.

Harvey clears his throat. "It's a little... We haven't had a cleaner in a while. Or a chef. Let's not stay here. Your breakfast is this way."

He leads me out through another door to a beautiful dining room that is also filthy. The massive table is heaving with boxes and paper and takeout containers and more dirty plates. There's so much garbage that most of the velvet-backed chairs have been stacked high too.

Harvey points to where a small space has been cleared for me. A box of cornflakes waits patiently next to a bottle of milk and a single bowl and spoon. "There you go, Miss"

"Thank you, Harvey." Inside, I'm screaming. How do these men live like this? I know they're murderers but messing up this gorgeous old house is a different kind of crime.

I take my seat and pour the cereal. Harvey hovers with grandfatherly concern. "Would you like some coffee?"

"Only if you're getting some for yourself," I say, and a thought occurs to me. "Mr. Harvey—"

"Just Harvey."

"Sorry, Harvey, how many people work at Velvet House?"

I expect him to become cagy, but he keeps smiling at me. "There's a rotating staff of thirty, and five of us live on site. Gretzky and myself you've already met, but there's also Dolmio, Jackie Schnee and my son, Sal."

"Your son?" I say. "You live here together?"

"We do. It's been great for Sal since his divorce." Harvey glances at the door then gives me a big grin. "Would you like to meet him and the others?"

The idea of meeting more men is a little scary but Harvey's excitement is cute. "That would be lovely."

He leaves by the door we came through and I add milk to my cereal and try not to think about how dirty my bowl might be. You can tell this is a house only men live in. Aside from the mess, it's freezing cold. Maybe this is why Adriano is in such a bad mood all the time.

I'm scraping up the last of my cereal when there's a knock at the door. Harvey reappears with a bald-headed man and a middle-aged guy with droopy eyelids.

"Dolmio and Schnee," he says. "Sal's napping and I couldn't get that grumpy bastard Gretzky to come see you. Oops. Apologies for swearing."

"That's completely fine." I stand, extending my hand to the middle-aged guy. "Hi, I'm January."

"I know," he says, rubbing his nose. We shake hands. Mr. Schnee's touch is as limp as wet noodles.

The younger guy, Dolmio, grins at me. "You're eighteen."

"I am." I hold out my right hand. "How old are you?"

"Thirty-nine." He holds out his left hand and the

two of us stare at each other. But when I withdraw my right hand and hold out my left, he changes hands too, leaving us unable to shake again.

"Christ," Harvey mutters, elbowing Dolmio to one side. "Just go back to the security room, okay?"

"Okay," Dolmio agrees. He leaves the room, whacking his shoulder on the doorframe.

"Sorry," Harvey says to me. "He's a family friend and he's still in training."

"It's fine. He seems nice."

"Hmm. Anyway, have you decided what you'd like to do today?"

"Could I maybe... call my sister?"

Schnee's heavy eyebrows lift. "No."

"Okay, well..." I mentally scan the options Harvey suggested but I don't feel like doing any of them. My gaze falls on a velvet chair stacked high with pizza boxes. "Could I maybe... clean up?"

The men exchange uncomfortable looks.

"That's sweet of you, Miss," Harvey says slowly. "But I'm sure that's not what Mr. Morelli had in mind."

"I know, but I'd like to feel useful." And if it convinces the others to be nicer to me and possibly not kill me or send me to Italy, that would be a bonus.

Harvey looks at Schnee who shrugs, wiping his nose again. I really wish we hadn't shaken hands.

"I suppose there's no harm...?" He tells Harvey.

I beam at them. "Amazing! Do you have any cleaning supplies?"

Schnee shows me to a small closet full of rubber gloves and leaking bottles of cream cleanser.

"Do you… want a hand?" he asks.

"Not at all."

"Great, I'm allergic to dust." He swipes a hand over his runny nose. "Okay, well there's an intercom in every room. Press the middle if you need us."

"Sure."

He's halfway out the door when he turns. "If any of the bosses ask why you're cleaning, make sure you tell them it was your idea."

I frown. "I don't think any of them care what I do."

Schnee gives me a long look. "You're wrong."

Before I can ask what he means, he vanishes.

The kitchen is gross, but it's also empty. There's nothing on the shelves or in the industrial refrigerators except wine, condiments, and a six-pack of orange soda.

Glad I don't have to throw anything out, I pile all the dishes from the kitchen and dining room next to the sink and fill it with hot soapy water. As I scrub, I run through my scales, up and down and back again. I like cleaning. I always tried to help Zia Teresa at home, but she didn't want to look lazy in front of mom. And if I so much as took an empty carton to the recycling bin, mom would scold me.

Here I can take as long as I want and focus on getting the—peanut butter?—stains off the plates. When the dishes are done, I wipe down the stainless-steel counter tops, until they gleam silver again. I sing Dolly Parton as I go. I'm digging the ancient mop and bucket out of the closet when Harvey sticks his head through the door. "Are you hungry, Miss? I can run out and get you something? Anything you'd like."

I wipe the hair out of my eyes with my bicep. "If it's not too much trouble, could you please go to a grocery store for me?"

"Of course," he says, surprised. "What would you like?"

"Well, I was thinking I could cook you dinner to say thank you for being so kind to me."

A flush spreads over his cheeks. "That's not necessary."

"But I'm cleaning up the kitchen. It would be a shame not to use it."

Harvey's expression is pained. "I'm sorry, Miss Whitehall, but Mr. Morelli is due back this evening and I'm worried he'll think… well I don't know what he'll think. But I know he wouldn't want you cooking for me."

I remember the way Eli looked in the firelight, slowly rolling up his shirtsleeves. My pelvic muscles clench. If I belonged to Mr. Morelli, he probably wouldn't want me cooking for another man. But I don't. So why would it be a problem?

I smile at Harvey. "Mr. Morelli would love for me to cook for you. He told me to make myself useful."

Harvey's brow smooths. "Did he?"

Last night Eli told me to 'be a good girl.' Surely cooking and cleaning is being a good girl? I cross my fingers behind my back, just in case. "He did. And I can make enough food for everyone. You and Mr. Gretzky and Mr. Schnee and Dolmio and Sal…"

Harvey gives me a rueful smile. "It has been weeks since I've had a home-cooked meal…"

I try not to look too excited. "Wonderful. Could I maybe write you a list of ingredients?"

"Of course. What are you going to make?"

The food to cure all sadness. The one thing I feel like eating whenever I'm low. "An old family recipe."

Harvey finds me a pen and paper and I note down everything I need. When he leaves, I mop the kitchen floors until they're sparkling clean. As they dry, I move back into the dining room and stuff all the dirty containers and paper into trash bags. Everything that looks useful goes into a big box in the corner of the room. Once the junk is cleared, I polish the dining table and sideboards and push all the chairs back into place. The carpet is still dusty but everything else looks a hundred times better.

Feeling stupidly proud of myself, I go back into the kitchen and get an orange soda. I sit on the clean counter and drink it like I'm the queen of the world.

My whole life I've just *been there*, like a candy cane on a Christmas tree. Zia Teresa did my chores. My teachers and Bobby made excuses for my homework. I was good at singing and ballet, but I didn't help anyone with it, just like I wouldn't have helped anyone if I studied Fine Arts at Colombia. No one even needed me to marry Mr. Parker. Mom needed money and Mr. Parker needed a wife with an important last name, but no one needed January Whitehall.

Yet this kitchen used to be dirty and now it's clean because of me. For the first time in my life, I've done something useful. Mom would be furious to see me acting like a servant but what's so bad about cleaning? Everyone likes when things are clean. I look around at the sparkling surfaces. Maybe I could ask Eli if I could be his housemaid?

It sounds crazy, even in my own mind, but they definitely need somebody and I'd like being a housemaid a lot more than I'd like being shipped off to Italy. Plus, it might be safer if Eli and the others saw me as a servant. I don't want to be their sugar babies or wives, their strippers or murder victims. I want to be too unimportant to proposition or kill. I want to melt into the walls of this beautiful house the way Zia Teresa did at my place. As a maid, I'd be nobody. And I could be happy being nobody.

"Afternoon!" Harvey bursts into the kitchen, arms laden with groceries. "Everything looks wonderful."

"Thanks," I say, sliding off the counter. "How did it go at the store?"

"It took a while, but I found it all."

Harvey bought three times as many ingredients as I need. I decide to make everything at once, that way all the staff can eat and they can have leftovers. I've already found a big pot for the meat, so I set the chicken and beef to simmer in salted water as I carefully shred the skin off the carrot and potato.

I shouldn't know how to cook. Mom didn't like my interest in food any more than she liked me singing, but whenever she was gone, I hung around Zia Teresa in the kitchen. Zia could make any cuisine under the sun, but when it was just the two of us, we only cooked Italian. The meals she grew up with and loved. Zia showed me how to cut spaghetti and fettuccini, to roll gnocchi, to fold ravioli parcels full of parsley and fresh ricotta. We made alfredo and carbonara and cannelloni though most of the dishes didn't have real names.

"What do you call this?" I would ask of a thick soup of spinach and rice.

"It's spinach and rice," Zia would say.

"But what is it in Italian?"

She would roll her eyes. "Spinaci e riso."

While mom was away getting her eyelids done, Zia Teresa focused my studies on desserts, tiramisu and profiteroles and continental cake. When mom returned and I was back on a diet of kale and grilled chicken, I dreamed about mascarpone cream.

In the eighth grade I wanted to run away and become a chef. As I got older, I imagined cooking for Mr. Parker, making him so happy with my food he would let Zia Teresa move in with us. Then she and I could hang out in my kitchen and we could talk and make trays of lasagne and sugar-dusted biscotti. As I skim the fat from the surface of my broth, I hope with all my heart Zia Teresa knows I'm alive and well and making brodo.

"Hey, Tits."

I jolt, my spatula flying out of my hand. Doc leans against the clean counter, smirking at me.

"Doc! You scared me."

"Sorry," he says, then looks around the spotless kitchen. "What's with the cleaning? Are you broken?"

His T-shirt is baby blue today. The color makes his eyes a million times prettier. I wipe my hands on my dress. All day I've tried not to ruin it, but I'm already covered in grime and my hair is a mess.

That doesn't matter, I remind myself. You want to be a servant.

Doc folds his tattooed arms across his chest. "Is there

a reason you're playing housewife?"

"I just felt like doing something."

"I don't know if anyone told you, rich girl, but we have a gym. We have a pool. You don't have to do Mrs. Hughes' cosplay."

I don't know who that is, but I can tell Doc's making fun of me. That even after last night, he still hates me. "I can't help being a Whitehall any more than you can help being where you're from. And I'm not trying to suck up to you guys, I just like cleaning."

Doc hauls himself onto the counter. "Fair enough, Tits." He looks me up and down. "You know, if you want to be our little maid, I can get you a uniform."

I know he means a frilly apron and high heels. Stripper clothes. "No thank you." I pick up my vegetable knife and return to my carrots. "How was your day?"

"Why?"

God, what is his problem? "I'm just trying to talk to you."

"Oh yeah?" He shifts closer to me. "How about we talk about what me and Bobby did to you last night?"

I shave a tiny piece of skin off a carrot, refusing to look at him.

"You sigh, you know," he says conversationally. "Whenever anyone kisses you. At first, I thought you were putting it on, but you're just that horny, aren't you?"

I ignore him, peeling another strip of skin from my carrot.

He shifts closer again. "Remember, Tesorina? Remember how I kissed you?"

All too well. His mouth soft and lazy on mine, the taste of liquor and rain and fresh cigarettes.

"It was a good kiss," Doc says with a grin. "Don't you agree?"

I bend my head, letting my sweaty hair swing between us. It was a perfect kiss, but that doesn't make it any easier to peel vegetables. Doc has probably kissed a thousand girls. He doesn't care about me.

"Gonna ignore me, Tits? After that nice orgasm I gave you?"

I carefully slice a potato into halves. We both know it was Bobby who gave me the orgasm. He just wants me to talk to him and I won't.

Doc swings his long legs against the counter. "You gonna stay and cook once Morelli's wife moves in?"

My mouth falls open. "Mr. Morelli's *married*?"

Doc laughs. "What's wrong, Tits? Jealous Prince Elliot's already taken?"

I drop my gaze to the potatoes, furious at myself for talking.

"Don't worry. He's not married yet. But he needs pure-blooded Italian babies to inherit his eighteenth-century wine glasses or whatever the fuck. He'll have a wife by summer."

I try to focus on cutting vegetables, but I can't stop picturing an Italian goddess with golden skin and liquid brown eyes. Eli's rubies around her neck. My plans to be a housemaid go up in smoke. There would be nothing more humiliating than waiting on Mr. and Mrs. Morelli.

"What are you making?" Doc asks. "Harvey said it was an 'old family recipe' but judging by what's going on here, that's bullshit. Unless you're doing mayonnaise salad."

I can't help but smile. "I never said it was *my* family recipe."

"Very clever, Tesorina. Another gift from your Zia Teresa?"

He remembered her name. A silly little thrill goes through me. "It is actually. Brodo is Zia's favourite. And mine."

"Right." Doc's gaze lingers on the simmering pot.

"Did your mom make brodo?"

He snorts. "My mom was a pillhead, Tits. Kraft mac and cheese was the only pasta I got growing up."

Before I can think of what to say to this, Bobby wanders in. "What's going on? Why can I smell—"

He sees me and does a double take. Doc laughs. "Here's a boy whose mama made pasta, Tesorina. Basher's nearly as bad as Morelli. Won't go to Italian restaurants because it doesn't taste enough like home."

"Hi," I say, avoiding eye contact. "Welcome back."

"Hey." Bobby's wearing a cable knit sweater and looks every bit my former math tutor. "Are you... good?"

I think of his stubbled cheeks brushing my thighs, the soft swipes of his tongue, the tattoo of a swordfish on his heavy bicep... I stare down at the cutting board. I know people hook up with people and then talk to them again. Why can't I?

Doc cackles into the awkward silence. "Hey, you know what actually tastes like home to Basher, Tits?"

"Shut the fuck up," Bobby snarls.

I manage to smile at him. "Thanks."

"Anytime."

"Aww lovers reunion," Doc mumbles, shoving a cigarette between his teeth. He pulls a lighter from his pocket and snaps it so a tiny flame appears.

I almost have a heart attack. "You can't smoke in here!"

Doc raises his blond brows. "Pardon?"

"I just cleaned! Can't you go outside?"

He scowls, and for a moment I'm sure he's going to light it just to spite me. But then the cigarette and lighter vanish. "If I behave, can I kiss you again?"

I remember those slow, confident laps of his tongue and my face becomes unbearably hot. "I... No. You can just have healthier lungs."

Doc rolls his eyes and I'm reminded so forcibly of Zia Teresa I almost burst into tears. Maybe it's fate. No matter where I go, some grumpy Italian will refuse to quit smoking around me. I pick up the cutting board and slide the chopped vegetables into the pot.

"How about I give you another kiss anyway?" Doc says. "Just because you like it so much?"

I glance over my shoulder and Doc laughs. "Worried Basher'll get jealous? Don't. He likes sharing. Remember last night?"

Bobby's cheeks go scarlet, but he doesn't look angry. My insides tighten. I have no idea what I want to happen.

Doc slides off the bench and takes the cutting board out of my hands. "One kiss, Tesorina. That's all."

"Doc…"

"Domenico," he corrects. "Whenever we do this, you call me by my real name."

I look away. It wasn't supposed to go like this. I was supposed to be a servant. To fade into the background.

Doc's finger lifts my chin. "Just one little kiss."

My eyes flick to Bobby. He's watching the two of us with a strange expression on his face.

Doc bends down and nuzzles my neck. "Don't be shy, baby. Basher knows how much you like kissing. He could taste it."

I swallow, my mouth dry as toast. Doc smells like

cigarettes and liquor, cologne and sweat. I know I should pull away, but I close my eyes instead.

"One kiss," he says, so close I taste his words. "One kiss for me, then one kiss for Basher."

"No," I whisper.

"Yes. A kiss for both of us and then—"

"The fuck is happening here?"

I jump like someone fired a gun. Doc sighs, lowering his finger from my chin. "Perfect timing, Morelli."

Elliot stands in the doorway in a dark suit and red tie. As always, his angular beauty hits like a brick. I tuck my hair behind my ear. I felt untidy in front of Doc and Bobby. I feel disgusting in front of Eli.

"So this is where you've been all day, Domenico? Making Miss Whitehall clean the kitchen?"

Doc snorts. "I've been dealing with Romanov. The girl cleaned on her own."

Elliot gives him a skeptical look.

"Believe me. If it was my call, she'd be upstairs polishing something else."

Elliot glances at me. "Was the cleaning your idea, *bella*?"

I wish I'd done anything else today. Gone to the gym. Walked in the grounds. Even read a book. "Yes, um, it was."

"I already offered her a maid outfit," Doc says. "Want to kick in? Buy her a feather duster?"

Elliot ignores him. He walks to the stovetop where the brodo is beginning to smell like heaven. He turns to me. "You can cook?"

"I… Yes?"

He walks closer, shiny shoes clicking on the newly washed floor. "You didn't tell me you could cook."

"I, um, didn't think you'd want to know?"

He jerks a thumb behind him. "Is that Pastina di Pollo?"

"I don't know. It's… my Zia Teresa calls it brodo."

"I see." Eli's expression is mild. Maybe my dinner is so inauthentic, he's going to pour the entire pot down the sink.

"You don't have to eat it," I say quickly. "I just thought Harvey and the others would like it and *I* like it and I really wasn't trying to… do anything…"

Eli's gaze falls on the plastic-wrapped parmesan sitting beside the grater. His face darkens. "*Cos'è questa merda disgustosa?*" *What is this disgusting shit?*

I wince. "Harvey brought it back."

I feel bad throwing Harvey under the bus, but he's way less likely to get locked in a cage if Mr. Morelli hates store-bought Parmesan as much as Zia Teresa.

"Put it in the trash," Eli snaps. "Harvey can drive to the deli for parmigiano."

He pulls out his phone and taps a message. A text to Adriano ordering him to strangle me for insulting their heritage? What possessed me to make Italian food in the house of an Italian prince? Why didn't I just ask Harvey for a burger?

Eli shoves his phone back into his suit jacket and looks me over. "You're filthy. And your dress is ruined."

"I know. I'm sorry but—"

"Can your meal wait another hour?"

I blink. "Um, of course. It gets better the longer it simmers."

"Good. Go clean yourself up. I'll bring you a new dress and we'll eat at seven."

"You mean me and the guards?"

His mouth curves upward. "I mean all of us. There are things the five of us need to discuss."

My stomach twists. Five means Adriano. I don't know his opinions on Italian food, but I really don't want to offend him. "Maybe you can eat without me? Or I can serve you and eat in the kitchen?"

Doc laughs. "See? Told you she wants to be our maid."

Elliot raises a brow. "Is that true, *bella*? Do you want to serve us?"

It's my moment to say yes. To take the first step into becoming a useful, invisible nobody. But as I look into Eli's amber eyes, I think of the rubies he once offered me. The ones I would see around the neck of his Italian wife.

"Um, no. Not really. I mean, not like that."

"I see."

"Pricktease," Doc says. "I wanted that uniform."

Eli points to the kitchen door. "Leave now, Miss Whitehall. Go make yourself pretty for us."

The sentence echoes in my head as I wander the halls trying to find my way back to my bedroom. 'Go make yourself pretty for us.'

Us, as in all of them. Does that mean Eli knows about me and Doc and Bobby? He didn't seem upset to find Doc about to kiss me. Could they have already told him what we'd done? That seems impossible, but they did plan on sleeping with me in front of each other last night. They had bets on who would go first. The skin on the back of my neck tightens. Is this a thing men do? Share one woman between them? I imagine asking Zia Teresa and all I see is her taking off her slipper and whacking me with it. I could ask Margot or Penelope maybe if they were here, and we'd all been drinking.

"Oof!"

I've walked right into a wall. I look up grinning to find Adriano Rossi glaring down at me. I open my mouth to apologize but before I can speak, his tattooed hand shoots out and closes around my throat. He pins me against the paneled wall.

"Help," I gasp.

He leans in, his beard rough against my cheek.

"Heard you came very close to getting fucked last night, little girl."

I want to scream but my body is frozen. I remember my dream, those electric green eyes burning bright as his tongue delved deep inside me. "Please…"

"The second they're done with you, you're gone."

He lets go of my throat and I crumple to the dusty carpet. He steps over me and keeps walking.

"Mr. Morelli said you're not allowed to hurt me," I whisper.

Adriano turns, gold tooth flashing. "Accidents happen, Pryntsesa."

I watch as he disappears around a corner, every fiber of my body humming with fear.

CHAPTER FIFTEEN

Elliot Morelli

"I'M SORRY, MR. Morelli." Harvey lays the freshly grated parmigiano, warm bread and salted butter on the dining room table in front of me, his face flushed with embarrassment.

I offer a small nod. "It won't happen again?"

"Of course not."

"Good. Take everything into the kitchen then go fetch a few bottles of the Montalcino."

The old man dashes away and I wonder if January knew she was being held next to a few million dollars' worth of wine. Probably not. She strikes me as a delightfully unobservant girl. Not simple but focused only on the things that interest her. I Inhale the aroma of her cooking. If it tastes half as good as it smells, she's very talented. A beautiful little virgin who speaks Italian and cooks. Am I really going to give a girl like that to Gio?

Adriano wanders past, his face buried in his phone.

"Coming to dinner?" I call.

"I wasn't planning on it."

"It's not a suggestion. We need to discuss things with the girl."

"I've got nothing to say to her."

"And what about us? Your brothers?"

A look crosses his face. Weariness. Or maybe just plain old tiredness. "Do you have any idea what you're doing with this girl?"

"Don't be melodramatic. She'll be out of your hair soon enough."

His eyes narrow.

My temper, held back through endless meetings with paranoid associates of Parker, rises. "If you've got something to say, say it."

"Parker pissed away millions keeping that pussy on hold. You sure you're not doing the same thing?"

It's a question I've asked myself many times today, as I ignored Gio's calls confirming January's place in his house. But I'll be damned if I'll tell Adriano that. "We took her for the right reasons."

He looks pointedly at the glossy carrier bags on the chair beside me. "You sure it's not something else?"

"Are *you* questioning my judgment?"

"No," he says flatly. "But you need to be careful. Doc and Bobby…" He shakes his shaggy head. "Forget it."

"What?"

"I said 'forget it.'"

I trust Adriano with my life, but it's difficult to know where he stands on anything that isn't breaking someone in half. He's not entirely Italian. A criminal with no ties to organized crime. He has few needs and he's never liked women. Never, to my knowledge, had a girlfriend. But his loathing of January is unprecedented. And irritating.

"You'll be at dinner," I tell him. "You'll dress appropriately, and you'll behave like a human being and not some vicious *cafone*. Understood?"

He says nothing as he leaves the room, but I know he'll be there. Whatever else, Adriano's loyalty is absolute.

Doc and Bobby wander in. Doc's wearing a shirt. A black one I've never seen before. I gesture at him. "What's all this?"

Doc tugs at his collar. "You said to dress up."

I want to ask, *'Since when do you give a shit about what I say?'* but it would be poor leadership to question someone obeying orders. I collect the carrier bags beside me. "Sit down and have a drink. I'm going to give January her gifts."

"What did you get her?" Bobby asks.

"You'll see."

Doc can't meet my eyes. I'm not sure if it's the shirt

or because I know what he did to January last night. He hoped Bobby wouldn't tell me, but Bobby's my oldest friend. He tells me everything.

What Doc might not realize is that I'm not mad he touched January. I'm pissed at him for stealing my keys and undermining me, but their little pseudo threesome gives me hope.

She let them touch her, which shows with a little persuading she's willing to be touched. And if Adriano was trying to warn me that Doc and Bobby are infatuated with her, that's hardly news. So am I. However this evening plays out, I'm still going to tell Gio she's a virgin.

I unlock January's bedroom door, but she's nowhere to be found. "Miss Whitehall?"

A small squeak from the ensuite. "Mr. Morelli?"

"Come out. I've brought you some things."

She emerges in a towel, water droplets still clinging to her skin. She looks as beautiful as a sunset over the Mediterranean. I want to recline with a tumbler of the world's best scotch and just watch her.

"Mr. Morelli…?" she repeats, cheeks now scarlet. "What did you want to give me?"

I keep my face stern. She has no idea how attractive she is, but it's better that way. Better she doesn't form bad habits. I extend the largest carrier bag toward her. "For you to wear to dinner."

"Oh." She folds an arm across the towel and takes the rope handles. "You didn't need to… although I guess you did because I didn't have anything else to wear. But thank you."

She sits on the bed and opens the bag. The dress emerges in a rush of cream silk. January looks at me. "It's white…"

"And you're still a virgin, *bella*. Go into the bathroom and get changed."

She hesitates. "It's a gorgeous dress, but I still need to cook the pastina for the brodo."

"Gretzky can do it."

The pinch between her brows makes me smile. "The man can boil pastina, *bella*. It's more important you look beautiful for us. Now go put on my dress."

When she emerges a few minutes later I have to clench my jaw to keep from smiling. She's exquisite. The dress is backless with a deep slit in the side, and it makes her pale skin shine like moonlight. You can see the lines of her abdomen, the swells of her breast, and the shadow between her legs.

She turns self-consciously. "You don't like it?"

"This is how a woman with your figure should dress. Now the shoes."

January returns to the bed, and I pass her the second largest bag. She pulls out the black and white striped box and her eyes widen. "Aquazzura?"

"Surely, you've had them before?"

"No. I wasn't allowed to wear high heels because..." She goes bright red, and I understand. She's tall for a woman. In heels, she'd tower over Parker.

"You don't have to worry about that anymore, *bella*."

"I know. I mean, thank you."

She opens the box, unveiling the sparkling rose-gold heels. "They're *beautiful*."

I watch as she slides the shoes onto her toes. I don't usually care for feet but hers are gorgeous, small and white with tiny pink nails.

I hold out the small bag from Bergdorf's. "Makeup. I'll leave you to apply it, but I'd like you to wear red lipstick."

"You picked out makeup for me?"

"I described your coloring to an assistant. I want you to be subtle. Do not overpower your face."

"Yes, Mr. Morelli."

I like the way she talks, husky and sweet, just the way a woman should be. "There's one thing left," I tell her.

Her green eyes shine up at me. "Yes, Mr. Morelli?"

I pull the ruby necklace from my pocket, the stones glittering in the bedroom light.

She pulls away from me.

"You don't need to panic. No promises will be made because you wear this necklace. I just want to see it against your skin."

She shifts back even further onto the bed. "I don't think... I just..."

My good mood vanishes. For all her beauty and gratitude, she's acting like a child. I shove the necklace into my pocket. "Fine. Put on your makeup and come downstairs."

Her face falls. "Mr. Morelli...?"

"Do not keep me waiting."

I find my men sitting around the freshly cleaned dining table, all of them well-groomed and drinking wine. This is how Velvet House should be.

I sit at the head of the table and raise the glass of Montalcino that's been poured for me. "Salut."

"I was just saying Parker's acting strangely," Bobby tells me. "Sealing himself in his office with his counter chief."

"You were expecting him to do something else?" I ask.

"I was expecting threats. Him biding his time worries me."

Doc throws a chunk of bread into his mouth. "Let him sit around and sulk. Gives us more time to look into this Orchard bullshit. I've tracked down an ex-girlfriend of his in Monaco. I'm trying to reach out and ask if she was ever overwhelmingly horny in Parker's presence."

"Good idea," I say. "If we get confirmation we can—"

Everyone turns to the doorway. Bobby goes red.

Doc's jaw hangs. Even Adriano stares. It's January Whitehall, in record time and she looks fucking delicious. I stand and the other three follow.

She raises her hands then lets them flutter back down to her sides. "Hi everyone…"

"You look like a movie star," Bobby blurts out, then looks mortified. I expect Doc to make fun of him but he seems incapable of speech.

I move toward her and hold out a hand. When she takes it, sparks run up my arm. I lead her to the seat at my left.

"What a pretty dress, Tesorina," Doc says slyly. "Did Morelli buy it for you?"

"Yes."

Doc raises his glass to me. "Good choice."

I bite back a smile as I fill January's wine glass from the decanter.

She touches a hand to her blood-red lips. "I probably shouldn't drink."

"You shouldn't be rude either, *bella*," I say, passing her the wine. "I'm your host."

She raises the glass with two hands and sips, a tiny shiver passing through her.

"Do you like it?"

"Yes," she says with an unconvincing smile.

"My sisters were given a splash of wine in their lemonade as children," I tell her. "Would you prefer that?"

She takes a much larger sip. "You don't have any lemonade. Only orange soda."

Bobby laughs and she looks gratified.

Gretzky and Schnee serve the food. They're not happy to be treated like waitstaff, but they know better than to complain. I dip my spoon into the broth and taste home. Oil and salt, cheese and pasta. I eat a few mouthfuls and look up to see January staring at me. She hasn't touched her food. She looks even more uncomfortable than when Adriano fucked her mouth with a gun. I smile at her. "It's good, *bella.*"

Bobby nods and even Doc grins. "You'll never be allowed to leave now, Tits."

January flushes and picks up her spoon.

We could keep her. It would be risky, letting her stay where Parker could so easily find her, but what is risk to men like us? And it might take time to make her trust us, but time isn't an object. While we wait for her more prudish tendencies to be broken, we could eat together like this. The table laid out with good food and wine. We could laugh and relax, reclaim something that's been lost to us for far too long.

Doc asks Bobby about the Czech ceramics he's just sourced for a private collector in Hudson.

January perks up when he mentions blown glass. "I think I saw something like that at The Met last year." She says it in a nervous rush, as though expecting us to punish her.

Doc smirks. "The only time I've been to the Met is to sell weed."

January's eyes widen. "Really?"

"Yeah, he was some doctor's kid who wanted to meet in the European sculpture and decorative arts section…"

January listens with rapt attention as Doc tells the story. Bobby intervenes, correcting Doc's errors and deflating his egotistic proclamations. I watch all three of them with a smile. My brothers are happy. Even Rossi doesn't look so fucking miserable. It reminds me of being back in my Nonno's house, surrounded by his friends and cousins and their wives, all of them drinking wine, and telling stories.

Gretzky returns with the meat course and it's as good as anything my nonna ever served. I have to fight not to praise January. As with her beauty, my appreciation of her cooking has to be tempered or it will ruin her.

I notice her wine glass is almost empty. For someone who didn't want any, she's getting through it fast. There's a glow in her eyes and her movements are more languid. I refill her glass.

We finish our second course and the mood becomes even lighter. As January, Doc, and Bobby laugh and flirt, I consider where we should take her after this. We could go back into the living room, but my bedroom has full-length mirrors and a minibar—and I want to see everything.

Bobby gestures at his empty bowl. "This was perfect, JJ."

"Thank you," she says. "The pastina was a little overdone."

I can't help laughing. "Are you sure you aren't Italian, *bella*?"

January turns pink but I know she likes the question. "I suppose I'm used to my Zia Teresa giving me feedback."

"A maid correcting your behavior? Did you get angry at her?"

She looks shocked. "Of course not. You can't improve without correction."

I study her over my wineglass. It's a rare thing, a woman who can receive criticism without taking it personally. I think of my vow to send her to Gio. To let some other swine possess this jewel of a girl.

"Where's Gretzky?" Doc demands. "I want dessert."

January draws a breath. "Oh, I'm sorry. I didn't make anything."

"I know you didn't," I tell her. "I had Harvey pick up some cannoli."

She gives a shy smile. "That sounds wonderful. I love cannoli."

"Good," Doc says. "I'm going to handfeed you in my lap."

January barely has time to react. There's a loud rap on the door and Schnee comes into the room. "Sorry to interrupt. We have an issue."

"What?" I say. The warm, date-like atmosphere immediately vanishes.

"A crew has shown up to the north river warehouse. It looks like they're trying to burn the place down."

"Shit," Doc hisses. "How many?"

"Two dozen. Fully armed as far as we can tell."

Doc stands, pressing a napkin to his mouth. "So much for the lack of threats. Basher?"

Bobby's already on his feet. "We'll take the chopper," he tells Schnee. "Tell Piscopo we'll be there in twenty minutes."

Adriano drains his wineglass. "Fucking assholes."

"Go," I say. "Contact me as soon as you have news."

"Wait, where are you all going?" January asks.

Doc walks to her side of the table and kisses her on the cheek. "You're lucky, Tits. You get to keep your virginity another night."

He points at me, and I nod behind January's back. I'm a lot of things, but I'm not cruel. I won't fuck her without Doc watching.

"Thanks for dinner, JJ," Bobby says.

January hides her smile behind her hand. "Anytime."

Both their cheeks are red.

"Awww," Doc says. "Isn't this cute?"

"Very," I agree.

"Fucking hurry up," Adriano growls.

I don't go with them. I want to, but it's a bad look for a boss to assist with what will probably end up being a minor incident. But as I watch them leave, my chest tightens. It's never easy, sending people you love into danger.

January stares after my brothers like a little lost lamb. "Please, Mr. Morelli? Where are they going?"

"To sort out a problem with your ex-fiancé."

Her hand lifts to her throat "Mr. Parker is burning down your warehouse?"

"No. Men who work for him are *attempting* to burn down our warehouse. They won't succeed."

"But why would he do that?"

"This is our life, *bella*. It's not all of what we do, but it's a part of it. And considering what we did to Parker, we expected this sooner and worse."

She looks down at her half-eaten dinner. "I can't believe this is all real."

I briefly close my eyes. In the past week January Whitehall has surprised me with both her intelligence and naiveté. I need to know if she has a stomach for criminal activity or if she'll continue to bury her head in the sand. "What do you know about how Parker made his money?"

"Um, I know he works in technology?"

"Very good. And do you know where he got the money for his company?"

January's gives me a look of beautiful confusion. "He's… a self-made man, isn't he?"

I snort. I will never understand the American obsession with the underdog. In Europe, you're admired for your connections, and your family name. Here, everyone wants to be known for working their way up from nothing.

"Parker is self-made as much as this…" I rap my knuckles on the dining table. "… is twenty-four-carat gold. He inherited his money. Although that's still being too diplomatic. 'Laundered' is the correct word."

"Mr. Parker's money was dirty?"

"Yes, *bella*. It was filthy. His father ran drugs for the Mariucci family. Hash and heroin and coke. And before you say Parker had no control over who his father was, he worked for him. He discovered how to launder drug money through cryptocurrency and online poker. In that sense, he was a tech entrepreneur."

January sucks on her lower lip. "Does he still sell drugs?"

"No. He changed his mind."

"What do you mean?"

"Parker's father died when he was twenty. Zachery took over, but he had no appetite for the business. He took what money and manpower he could and went legitimate. That's why a few years later he was running a tech company and courting your father, hoping to marry into your family."

January's eyes move from side to side as she processes this. I appreciate her response. A woman who goes still when confronted with bad news is a pleasant surprise.

She blinks twice, and her gaze returns to mine. "How do you know all of this?"

I pour myself another glass. "I just do."

"Does it have something to do with why you stole me or—"

"Enough." I push back my chair. "Why are we wasting our evening talking about that ugly man? Come here, *bella*."

Her cheeks go pink, but she doesn't move.

I open my arms. "Come, little doll. And bring your wine."

She lifts her glass and carries it carefully toward me. The pearl polish on her fingernails is chipped, probably from cleaning the kitchen. When Parker is dead and I've hired staff to clean and serve dinner she can get her nails done. Blood red. Or palest pink. She sits delicately on my lap, and I pull her closer, settling her against my chest. "Drink your wine."

She sips obediently and I watch her throat work, tucking a curl behind her ear. I can't get rid of her. I will put my rubies around her neck, and she will belong to

Velvet House.

She turns her head and inhales deeply.

"Is something wrong?"

"Your cologne…" she purrs, a little slur at the edges of her voice. "What kind is it?"

"Do you not like it?"

"Oh, no I do, it's just… I don't think I've smelled lavender on a man before."

"Is it embarrassing, *bella*? Unmanly? Do you want me to be like Adriano and smell like leather and blood?"

She shivers against my chest. "He hates me."

"Don't take it personally. Adriano hates anything that makes him feel and that includes desire."

She shudders and I wrap my arms around her, burying my face in her neck. She smells clean and sweet and I want to lick every inch of her. Bobby said she mewled like a kitten while she came on his face. I want to hear that soft, slightly pathetic, sound. I skim my hands down the sides of her body and she twists in my lap, soft thighs working against mine. "Mr. Morelli, have you given me that drug?"

I pull away smiling. "Is that what you think?"

Her head tilts to the side.

"*Bella*, we both know you wanted me from the moment you laid eyes on me."

"But then why did you give me Orchard last night? I already wanted… I mean… you didn't have to…" She buries her face in my shirtfront. "I shouldn't be saying this."

I shift against her so she can feel my hard cock. She draws in a sharp breath, but she doesn't move away.

I run a hand up her thigh, toying with the split in her skirt. "We gave you your Orchard because we thought it would be fun to send you into a frenzy. But you're full of surprises, aren't you?"

"So are you." She taps my chest. "You're nicer than you pretend to be."

I tug the split a little wider, exposing more porcelain thigh. "Is that right?"

"I think so." She swallows. "Will the others be okay? Doc and Bobby and… and Adriano?"

"Are you worried about them? Have you changed your mind about us?"

"No. I mean, *you're* the ones who want to get rid of me."

I laugh. She's sassy tonight. Maybe it's her natural state, emerging with wine and a sense of safety. I slide my palm between her thighs. "I could have changed my mind, now I know you can cook?"

She inhales. "I was so nervous. I've never cooked for men before."

I like that she was nervous. "What else can you cook?"

"A bit of everything. Pasta mostly."

"You mean boiling water and throwing it in?"

"No. I can make potato gnocchi and tortellini and ravioli. Lots of things. Although I'd need a rolling machine."

I kiss her neck, so she won't see me smile. "What a delightful little girl you're turning out to be."

"T-thank you."

Whether she's aware of it or not, she's spreading her legs, practically daring me to dip a hand between her folds.

"Is that what you want in a wife?" she asks. "A woman who cooks pasta?"

"My wife will not cook."

"Because she'll be too fancy to get her hands dirty?"

Here it is again. The teasing sass. "Exactly, *bella*. My mistress, on the other hand…"

"So, you want a woman who cooks, but not as a wife or mother to your children?"

I sigh. "I couldn't explain to an Americano like you."

"Didn't you grow up in America?"

"I did, but that doesn't make me American. Italians bring their homeland wherever they travel, as the Romans did."

She smiles. "Did the Romans have mistresses?"

I nip the side of her neck. "Yes."

She giggles. "Ah, I see."

"Having a mistress is not a shameful thing. Marriage

is an arrangement between two families. Your wife is your business partner. A mistress is a person you chose for pleasure."

January considers this. "Is that what your father did?"

"My parents married for love."

"Really?"

"You're confusing that statement for a happy one, *bella*. My parents were miserable."

"What happened?"

I raise my palms and close them over her breasts, squeezing her lightly.

She squirms. "Mr. Morelli…"

As soon as I hear that wild, desperate note in her voice, I drop my hands. I'm no horny teenager. If January is to be mine, she needs to learn these games will go on as I see fit. That she cannot control me with her body any more than she could control me with tears.

"My parents met on a holiday in Borneo. My mother was engaged to an Earl and my father, Vincent Morelli, was a financial investor. It was love at first sight. Three days after they met, my mother gave back her ring and my father handed her his."

January's eyes shine like stars. "Wow. So, they got married?"

"They did. My mother's family were furious. My Nonno threw her out of the house."

She gapes at me. "But the Morellis are one of the

richest families in New York!"

"True, but to my Nonno, all American money was new money." Her incredulous look makes me smile. "My mother came to live with my father in Manhattan. They were married and a year later I was born."

"Did they have a big, beautiful wedding?"

"They did. Then they had a short, unhappy marriage."

"Why?"

"My mama was used to travel, to diamonds, to writing cheques without thinking. My father was wealthy, but he wasn't an Earl. After I was born mama patched things up with Nonno and took me back to Naples and lived in his household for weeks on end. Sometimes she wouldn't even tell my father she was leaving. He would just come home from work and find us gone."

"She *kidnapped* you?"

I snort. "Don't be melodramatic, *bella*. She always returned to New York. Not that it did any good. After my sisters were born, things got worse."

January gapes at me. "How?"

"It just did. My father loved my mama, but he couldn't make her happy. They separated not long after my brother was born."

"Oh." January lifts her glass and takes a deep swallow of wine.

I raise my knee, jostling her. "Did I disappoint you?

Do you want to think love conquers all?"

She doesn't smile. "Do think your parents' marriage would have been better if your father had a mistress?"

"I think people should be rational about what makes marriage work."

"And have you ever been married?"

I frown. Sass is one thing, impudence is another. "No, and neither have you, Miss Whitehall."

January holds her tongue. I shift my hand to her abdomen, feeling her flat belly tense beneath her dress. "Are you so sure you don't want to live here and play mistress, *bella*?"

"Do you mean to you? Or to… all four of you?"

I rub my cheek against hers, stroking her silky skin with my stubble. "Does it matter?"

"I guess. I thought you wanted me all to yourself?"

"I did, but seeing how happy you made my brothers tonight, I'm considering other options."

January finishes her wine.

Amused, I take the glass and put it on the table. "Is that a 'yes?'"

"I don't think I can…"

I bite back a smile. From what she's already done with Doc and Bobby, there's nothing she'd like better than being our little whore. But she's not ready to know that about herself yet. I'll have to show her. I kiss the side of her neck. "Well, what do you want to do with yourself, Miss Whitehall?"

"I'm not sure. It changes every day."

"I very much doubt that. You're domestic. You want to sing and prepare food and prance around a pretty kitchen being a beautiful little girl."

Her mouth falls open. "That's so... I don't want that."

"Ah, *bella,* don't protest. It's lovely."

"But you're saying I'm an idiot!"

"No, I'm saying your heart belongs in your home. And it always will." I press my hand between her legs. "Would you like me to buy you a pasta machine? Fill the cupboards and let you cook us dinner every night?"

My fingertips brush the wet petals between her legs, and she squirms against me.

"I don't want to be your mistress."

"Being a mistress is a purer love than being a wife. It's all affection. All pleasure. It's precious."

"And what about the others?"

I laugh. "Ah, the real question. *'Would I have to give up Doc and Bobby?'*"

"No! That's not what I mean!"

I smirk. "You don't need to lie. I heard about last night."

"You did?"

"Of course. My brothers and I have no secrets." I rest my thumb against the soft button between her legs.

"Would you like to be shared?"

"Shared? What does that even mean?"

"You're not a stupid girl, I'm sure you understand."

"But how would it work? Monday nights I'm with Doc, Tuesdays I'm with Bobby?"

"Maybe," I say evenly. "We can make up our own rules. That's the fun of it."

"And you would… approve of that?"

I rub my thumb against her, lighter than a whisper. "As long as you're not my wife, I don't mind if you take pleasure from my brothers. In fact, I'd be happy to see it."

"You can't mean that!" she gasps. Whether from shock or my touch, I'm not sure.

I move faster, stroking her clit in gentle circles. "*Bella*, you're young and you've never had a boyfriend. You don't know much about men."

"No, but I don't think most men are like you."

I scrape my teeth along the side of her pale neck. "When you've settled in, I'll have Doc take you to Dreams. Men watch their friends get lap dances; they talk about women's bodies with one another. When they're close—and my brothers and I are very close—men can find pleasure in sharing a beautiful woman together."

There is a heavy silence and I know what she's thinking. I grin. "What a dirty little mind you have, *bella*. But no, none of us are attracted to men."

"Then why…?"

"There's a saying," I murmur in her ear. "*'It's nice to drive a Ferrari, but then you can't watch it go by.'* You are that Ferrari, January. Sometimes I want to drive and sometimes I want to watch you be driven. To loan you to someone I trust because that is my pleasure."

"I… I'm not a car, I'm a girl."

"A pretty, obedient little girl," I say, bringing my second hand between her splayed thighs. Her cunt is soaking, and there's no resistance as I slide a fingertip inside her. When I pump, she whines like a lost kitty—just like Bobby said she would.

"My brothers and I are busy men, *bella*. We travel and work long hours. We don't have time to date. Sex is easy to come by, but home comforts are another matter."

I pulse my fingertip inside her, careful not to penetrate too deeply.

"The longer you're here, the more I think it might be practical to keep you. A little woman for us to play with."

Her head tips back onto my shoulder, her green eyes glazed. "I don't know…"

"So don't know. Let me know for you. I'm telling you that there is nothing you would like more than to live in my house and cook and sing and get fucked by four men."

Her cunt ripples around my hand. "No…"

"Don't deny it. Just the thought of being ours has you coming all over my fingers."

She tosses her head from side to side. "But Adriano hates me."

"And sometimes it's a pleasure to fuck what you hate."

I rub her in firm circles and she grips my wrist and tries to push my hand away. I shake her off, pulsing and stroking at once.

"No…" She whispers. "Please."

Her inner muscles clench tight around me, practically drawing me in. I'm going to make her come. Show her where she belongs.

She twists against me, gasping. "I don't want to be a mistress. I want to be special to someone."

"Have you not listened to a word I said? You'd be special to all four of us."

"No. You're lying. You're just scared to love someone the way your father loved your mother."

The words are a knife in my chest. I stand, letting her tumble onto the floor. She cowers below me, shock written across her face. "Apologize, Miss Whitehall. Now."

January's eyes are already bright with tears. "I'm… I'm sorry, Mr. Morelli."

"Not good enough." I grip her hair and yank her to

her knees. "I am not nicer than I pretend to be. I'm a thousand times more cruel. You forget yourself. You forget where you are. It is for my amusement you were given a choice between myself and my brothers. There's no way out of this situation in which you won't be tied to a powerful man, bent over, used and made to have his children."

"I'm sorry." The dam bursts and tears stream down her cheeks.

"I know you are. Now you'll prove it. Unzip me and take me out."

"But—"

I tighten my hold in her hair. "Now, Miss Whitehall."

She reaches for my belt, unbuckling it with fumbling fingers. I let her wallow in her own clumsiness. If she wanted me to be gentle, she should have kept her idiotic mouth shut. She pulls my belt open and undoes my pants. She hesitates when she gets to my underwear.

"Have you seen one before?" I demand.

She swallows and I remember the previous evening. "Doc, stroking himself in front of you?"

She nods.

"That man is always ruining things. Never mind, Miss Whitehall. My cock will be the first you taste. Take me out and suck."

She pulls me from my briefs and my stomach clench-

EVE DANGERFIELD

es at the tentative touch of her lips. They close over me and she sucks, quite literally, drawing on me without moving. It's good, but it won't get the job done. I pull her hair, guiding her back and forth. "Like this."

She seizes on the rhythm, and I groan. "That's a good girl. Deeper. Concentrate."

All the muscles in my body tighten as I strain into her mouth, and I become aware of the weight in my pocket. The ruby necklace. The final crown for the princess on her knees.

"Do not stop sucking." I release her hair and take out the necklace. I fasten it around her throat. Mine. All mine. She looks up, her mouth full of cock, my rubies shining against her pale skin. "Beautiful."

I scrape a tear from her cheek and put it to my tongue. She gives a tiny moan of helplessness that vibrates down my shaft. I smile. "There is more you need to learn than just how to make a man come. You're here now. And you're ours. You've showed some strength, but if you want to be worthy of the world you've found yourself in, to be a woman I would be proud to call my own, you'll need to be more than just a pretty mess."

A bang on the door. January starts but I grip the back of her head and hold her in place. "Come in."

Gretzky enters, his expression blank. "Doc needs to talk to you."

I look down at January, still working back and forward, tears puddling on the ground below her. "Is it urgent?"

"Very."

Gretzky doesn't exaggerate. I pull myself from January's mouth and swipe a thumb over her swollen lips. Her face is paper pale.

"Take Miss Whitehall to my bedroom and lock the door."

"Yes, sir."

I stroke January's tear-stained cheek. "Be ready. When I return, you will do your duty by me. And if the others come back alive, you will do your duty by them, too."

CHAPTER SIXTEEN

January Whitehall

I'M RUNNING THROUGH a burning house, grabbing paintings and vases for mom. I'm the only one who can do it. Mom said the fire can't touch me. But maybe she was lying because flames are crowding in, licking my heels, and turning my hair to straw. I run faster, stacking things on top of each other, trying not to drop anything…

"Tesorina?"

A cold hand shakes my shoulder and I gasp. I smell whiskey and cigarettes. "Domenico?"

A low chuckle. "Yeah, baby. Basher's here, too. And Morelli."

I rise and see dark shapes moving at the foot of Eli's bed. It's twice the size of mine, big as an ocean. Doc's icy hand closes on my shoulder. "Did you miss us?"

I want to say no but as his weight sinks into the

mattress, I smile. There's a sense of rightness in him being here at odds with everything else. "You're all okay? None of you are hurt?"

"We're fine, Tesorina. Kiss me."

Before I can protest, Doc's mouth descends on mine. I fight for a second then give in. He's such a good kisser. There's no urgency, just a slow exploration like we've got all the time in the world. A bedside lamp flicks on and color rushes at me. I see the bright gold of Doc's hair, the dark tattoos on his forearms.

Another weight settles at my back. "JJ…"

A warmer hand cups my jaw, breaking my kiss with Doc. Bobby. He kisses me, fast and rough. I feel Doc slide beneath the covers, putting his cold knee between my legs. I'm still wearing my white dress and Eli's rubies are heavy around my throat. I tried to take them off but the clasp is impossible to undo alone.

Bobby moans into my mouth, his hands winding through my hair. There's a sound of something being dragged across the floor and I pull away. Eli is settling into a chair at the foot of the bed, his dark eyes gleaming. "Hello, *bella*."

I recall the feel of him in my mouth, his promise before he left that they would all take me. A sizzle of fear runs down my body.

"Bobby's been a brave boy," Eli says. "He was stabbed."

I gasp. "What?"

Bobby glares at Eli. "You had to tell her?"

Doc laughs into my neck. "Show her your war wound, tough guy."

With a scowl, Bobby leans back and I see a bandage where his t-shirt meets his collarbone.

"Oh my God!"

"It's nothing, JJ. Just a graze."

Eli laughs. "You're going to have to make Bobby feel better, *bella*. Give him another kiss."

He says it lightly but it's an order. I press my lips to Bobby's and heat surges between my legs.

Doc licks a line across my cleavage. "What about me, Tesorina? I've been brave too."

Bobby releases me. "Go on, Jay. Kiss him."

The next moment Doc's tongue is back in my mouth, licking softly. Just like falling asleep after what Eli did, it's easier than I want it to be.

Bobby's hands brush over my ass. "God, you're sexy. The girl of my fucking dreams."

My insides go molten, and I kiss Doc even deeper. He smirks against my lips, reaping the benefits of Bobby's compliment. My cheeks burn. I should be stopping this. Or at least not moaning and pressing up against the two of them while sparks light up my body.

Doc breaks the kiss and lowers himself, panting, to my nipple. "Make out with Bobby. I wanna do this."

He pulls my dress open and draws me into his mouth. My gaze finds Eli. He's lounging in his armchair like royalty, watching his men put their hands all over me. He said he wanted to be my first, but Bobby is pulling up my dress and Doc is sucking my nipple and he's just watching, his stare as heavy as his necklace.

He smiles. "Don't worry, *bella*. Just enjoy yourself."

Bobby's hand is between my legs, his fingers rubbing lightly. As my eyes roll back, Doc kisses me again.

"You look so pretty between them, Miss Whitehall. I'm going to watch you get fucked and then I'm going to take my turn."

I make a panicky noise and Doc swallows it with his tongue.

"I did want your virginity," Eli says. "But my brothers were so brave tonight, they deserve that honor. Bobby will be the first man to finish in your mouth. Domenico has earned the right to take your cunt."

Bobby's fingers run along my slit, spreading the wetness like cream. I moan and Doc grunts in response, his jeaned cock pressing into my thigh. We all fit together so easily, like pieces of a puzzle.

"There's still your tight little asshole, *bella*. That will be mine. But I'll let the boys take their pleasure first."

Shock ripples through me. If that's true, when they're done I won't be any kind of virgin. And what will happen then? Eli won't want me as his mistress. Bobby won't make me his wife. Doc can't auction off my body. Adriano will kill me. I push a hand into Doc's chest. "Please don't take my virginity?"

He growls. "This bullshit again."

"Miss Whitehall, we discussed what was and was not possible at dinner," Eli says coldly.

"I know. But my virginity is the only valuable thing I have."

Bobby makes a disturbed little noise. He might disagree but he still can't save me.

"It's ours," Eli says. "You have no choice."

"If you let me stay a virgin, I'll do things for you. For all of you. With my mouth and my hands."

"You'll do that anyway."

"Yes, but I'll be… enthusiastic. I'll dress up. I'll be happy. You won't have to threaten."

Doc pushes me onto my back and climbs on top of me. His butterfly knife is in his hand. "Lie still."

My eyes fill with tears. "Domenico, *don't.*"

He lowers the knife to my throat. "You don't get it, do you? Threatening you makes my dick hard."

"But please—"

His mouth twists in that Elvis sneer. "Forcing myself on you will make me come so hard I'll go blind. I've earned you and I'm gonna fucking have you."

I look at Bobby. His face is shadowed, his eyes unreadable. The flat of Doc's knife digs into my skin. "You think Basher'll come to your rescue? He loves you, Tits, but he loves me more."

Bobby holds my gaze, saying nothing.

A tremor runs through me. "This can't be happening…"

"It is." Doc sits back, his hips pinning me to the bed. He shoves his knife between his teeth and unbuckles his belt. His hands dip into his jeans and he pulls out his cock. It's hard and thick and shining at the head.

"Please stop?"

He ignores me, shifting forward to sit on my chest. He fists my hair, jerking my head up. "Open wide," he says around the knife.

I part my lips and he drives into me. He's thicker than Eli with a raw taste that makes me think of bloody steak. It's harder to give a blowjob on my back but I slurp and suck and rock back and forward the way Eli showed me. If I do a good enough job maybe I can protect my virginity.

Doc opens his mouth and the knife falls into his hand. He holds it to my throat. "Morelli? Can I fuck up this dress?"

"Go ahead."

I moan around Doc. The silk is so lovely and expensive.

Eli laughs. "Sorry, *bella*. We like ruining beautiful things."

Doc swings a leg off me and brings his knife between my breasts. "Hold still."

I freeze as he cuts. The silk barely makes a sound as it splits. It falls away from my body like autumn leaves and my nipples pucker. Doc grins, grabbing my breast. "Fuck, these are huge. What size are you?"

I whimper as he pinches me.

Doc taps his knife on Eli necklace. "Come on, bitch. Say it."

"30G," I whimper.

"30G?" Doc gives a low whistle. "You couldn't tell under all those nun clothes."

"What about her wedding dress?" Eli asks. "I've never seen a bustier bride."

"Yeah, Parker's a tasteless fuck. But I thought it was a push-up bra or whatever."

Despite their casual conversation—or maybe because of it—there's a wildness in the air. A sense that anything can happen. I try to sit up, but Doc presses the knife to my neck. The next second he's back on top of me, gripping my hair and forcing himself into my mouth.

The mattress shifts and I hear the rustle of zips and buttons. My body stiffens.

"Deeper," Doc snarls. "Suck my fucking cock."

Hands close around my calves, lifting my legs onto either side of a warm, hairy chest. My pussy splits open, wetness pouring down my thighs.

"Bobby, no," I try to say.

"Fuck," Doc groans. "When she talks, I can feel it up my dick."

Something smooth and hot slides between my legs and I shriek. I know what it is, Bobby dragging his hard cock through my pussy.

"Watch it, Basher," Doc snaps. "That cherry's mine."

"Just playing," Bobby groans, as he rubs himself through my wetness. I don't want to like it, but he's gliding over the place he licked last night making everything tingle.

"You look beautiful, *bella*," Eli calls. "Naked and trapped. Take Domenico into your throat. Swallow him."

I obey, widening my mouth and letting Doc go deeper. As long as I'm sucking him, he'll stop Bobby from taking my virginity.

"Pretty girl," Eli says. "Does Bobby's cock feel nice against your cunt? Do you wish he'd slide himself inside you and fill you up?"

Doc pauses. "Morelli, I killed three men and kept Basher alive. She's *mine*."

"I know," Bobby pants. "But until you free up her mouth, I'm gonna keep doing this."

As they work at opposite ends of my body, orgasm surges inside me, like lava rolling over the earth. Bobby's cock vanishes from my folds. There's a moment's relief before his stubbled cheeks are against my thighs and he's licking me again. I moan, unable to keep myself from grinding against his face. My pussy feels lush and empty. I need something inside me even more than I did when I was on Orchard. But I can't lose my virginity.

Doc pulls out of my mouth. "I'm gonna nut if we keep going. I've been on edge for too long. Basher, go take a knee."

Bobby gives me a last lick then moves to the end of the bed. Doc tosses his knife on to the bed and peels off his shirt. Sliding off me, he strips away his jeans. His thighs and shins are covered in tattoos. Roaring lions and twisting thorns and skulls with knives in the eye sockets.

My heart jolts so painfully I'm almost sick. It's going to happen. I'm really going to lose my virginity to a violent psychopath.

Doc kneels between my legs, his cock in his hand. "Now, how should I do this? From behind? Make you ride me and give the boys a show?"

I lie frozen, naked except for Eli's necklace, knowing the moment I've been dreading is here.

"I could do it nice and traditional," Doc says. "Missionary."

"Please?" I manage to whisper.

"Please do it missionary? Fine." He braces above me, one hand on the bed, and rubs his cock through me. It's thick and round as a baseball bat. "You ready to become a woman?"

"Domenico…"

He flashes a smile at the others. "You watching, Bash? Ten bucks says she comes as soon as I'm all the way inside her."

He moves the head of his cock through my folds like Bobby did and his eyes find mine. There's a question there. *You want this too?*

Yes, I think. Yes, I want to know what sex feels like. Yes, I want to know what it feels like with this man. But there's more to it than 'yes.' There's Mr. Parker paying millions to never touch me. Eli warning me that wherever I go I'll belong to a powerful man. Adriano telling me I'll die as soon as the others are done with me.

I shake my head and for a heart-breaking second, Doc looks crushed. The next his knife is at my neck.

"Fuck you. I know you want to. Say it."

I can't. I push back against Doc's blade and a sting edges at my throat.

Panic blurs his handsome features and he lifts the knife. "The fuck, January?"

"Domenico." There's a warning in Eli's voice. "If she's going to hurt herself, you need to put the knife away."

Doc presses a thumb to the stinging place at my neck. "Is that right, Tits? You'd rather behead yourself than fuck me?"

I hear the hurt behind his anger, but I also hear Adriano telling me he'll end my life. If there's any way I can get out of sleeping with Doc—with any of them—I need to take it. I say nothing.

Doc lifts his thumb and there's blood, as red as Eli's rubies smeared across it. He raises it to his lips and sucks it away. "You don't know how fucked you are."

My skin crawls, but before I can scream, his hand is over my mouth. He drops the knife and climbs onto my chest, his lean, wolflike body pinning me to the mattress. He spits on me, smearing my breasts with his saliva and cups me roughly. He slides his cock into my cleavage. It doesn't hurt, but it feels strange. He pushes forward, his fingers biting into my breasts. "I'm gonna paint you a little mental picture, before I paint your rack with my cum, Tesorina."

I feel the gulf between that sweet nickname and how Doc actually feels about me, and it stings. But I've won. My virginity has been spared. I bend my head forward and draw the head of his cock into my mouth as much as I can.

Doc lets out a guttural moan. "You're gonna stay here at Velvet House with us. No chance of getting out now. You've got Morelli's rubies around your neck and my cock between your tits, and you can't lie for shit. We're not sending you to Italy so Eli's cousin can find out we gave him damaged goods. *Look at me.*"

He smiles, the same cold smirk he offered as I made my way up the aisle a million years ago.

"No one wants a wife who's been servicing four criminals. So you'll stay here, cooking and cleaning for us. And we'll let you be a virgin, because who gives a fuck? There's plenty of pussy around."

The words slice through me, more painful than his blade. The thought of him sleeping with another girl, any of them sleeping with another girl, is awful.

"You'll suck me off whenever I want it though. While all your idiot friends are getting married and having kids, you'll be here at Velvet House with your collar on, blowing me." He runs a finger across Eli's necklace, pulling it tight as he pumps between my breasts. "And you'll stay here until I'm fucking done with you."

As I suck him, I know this is the price of denying him my virginity. He has to humiliate me. To be the winner. It didn't have to be like this. Doc came into the room smiling and kissing me. But I made my choice. I wanted to stay a virgin. And as Doc grunts and pulls it out of my mouth, I think of my first night at Velvet House. Eli saying I've never made any real choices. I made a choice tonight and it led me here.

Doc comes, the spray thick across my breasts. He rubs his palm through it, wiping cum all over me. His smile is hard as nails. "What if Zia Teresa could see you now, huh?"

It's so cruel, the air rushes from my lungs. I press a hand to my lips and wait for someone to make him apologize.

"Clean her up and get out of the way," Eli demands.

Doc doesn't move. "Not yet."

He clucks his tongue. "What do you—"

Doc falls to his knees beside the bed. He clasps my hips and pulls me to the edge before settling between my legs. "Don't move or you'll get cum all over Morelli's sheets like the dirty whore you are."

Then he licks me. The same tongue that said such ugly, unkind words laps so sweetly, my body convulses. I want to hate it, to scream in protest, but my body is tight with longing, orgasm only a breath away. I curl my toes and brace for the end when something hard presses into me. I sit up, my stomach muscles clenching. "What's that?"

Doc ignores me and keeps licking my clit, pumping whatever's between my legs in and out. Pleasure surges through me and I collapse onto the mattress.

"*Domenico*," Eli warns.

Scowling, Doc raises his head. "It's only an inch. Your precious flower's still a virgin."

He lowers his mouth and continues lapping as he thrusts the hard object inside me.

I screm. "Seriously, what…?"

But as I say it, I already know. The handle of the butterfly knife that cut my throat. "Oh my *God*."

I try and sit up again but Doc pushes me back down. "That's right. If you won't take my cock, you'll fuck my knife."

He lowers his mouth to me, sucking and licking like an animal until I come. My orgasm detonates like a bomb, and I scream until my lungs give out.

Doc watches me, his eyes black with hatred. "There," he says, pulling his knife from me. "You're not better than me, are you, you rich cunt?"

Shock whips through me, turning my rubbery muscles to stone. He hates me. He really, really hates me.

"Clean her up," Eli says coldly.

"Do it yourself." Doc shoves himself to his feet. He uses his toes to scoop up his clothes and leaves without another word.

It isn't Eli that cleans me. It's Bobby. His fingers are steady as he wipes me with a damp cloth and then a dry one until no trace of Doc remains. I hold back tears as he does so. It's like I've been broken apart in the dirt. Bits of me scattered wide across a huge stretch of land. I want Bobby to comfort me, to pick me up and hold me, but his touch is dutiful, and he won't meet my eye.

When he steps away, Eli looks me over and clicks his tongue again. "Little Miss Whitehall... What am I going to do with you?"

I don't say anything.

"I'm going to offer you another chance to make things right. Will you let Bobby take your virginity?"

Bobby stands naked and impassive at Eli's side, but I can see red staining his cheeks. He still wants me. He still wants this, but what was true for Doc is as true for him. I shake my head.

The brightness in Bobby's eyes departs, and they turn to empty shells.

"Fine," Eli says. "You'll pay a different way. Bobby, show Miss Whitehall what you like."

Bobby looks at him, brow raised.

"I mean it," Eli says. "Move before I change my mind."

My blood runs cold. What could he do to me that Doc hasn't already?

Bobby scrambles onto the bed and hauls me to all fours. He seems bigger naked, dark hair dusting his muscular chest. He pushes hard into the small of my back until my ass is in the air. "Stay still, JJ."

I open my mouth to ask what he's going to do and he spanks me.

"Ow!" I look behind to make sure it's Bobby—my sweet math tutor—doing this.

His expression is stony. "Turn back around."

I feel a surge of anger. "Or what?"

Bobby's mouth thins. "I'll spank you until you can't

sit down. Don't test me. I'll do it."

Looking into his brown eyes I know it's true and the indignity of it makes me cry out, "You're supposed to be nice!"

Elliot laughs but Bobby's hard expression doesn't change. "Fuck being nice. Where's that got me?"

"I *like you*."

"But you respect Doc. You respect Eli. You don't respect me."

"That's not true!"

"Spank her again," Eli says lazily.

His hand comes down hard, and I arch my back at the sting. Red heat spreads through me, followed by a shameful truth. This *doesn't* feel bad. Not the way it should. Bobby grips the back of my neck. "Turn, January. Watch."

I do and the sight of him makes my pussy clench. I imagine him taking me while I'm on all fours like this, his heavy muscles flexing as he slams into me. As I watch, he spits into his hand and slicks it over his cock. "I'm gonna make you come now."

"Bobby…"

His gaze softens. "I'm not gonna hurt you."

My throbbing butt says that's not true, but I know what he means. He won't take my virginity. And he doesn't. He notches his cock between my legs, pushing my thighs tight around himself, the way Doc did to my breasts.

He pulses forward, brushing my aching clit and the sensation's so sharp, I gasp. "Bobby!"

He gives a guttural moan. "You don't know how good this looks, January. Your ass bouncing up against me. Your little pussy soaking my dick."

My muscles tremble as I struggle to hold myself up. I can't believe this is Bobby being so disgusting, but his cock slides against me, and bright spots rush across my eyes.

"She's going to come again," Eli says, sounding amused. "Move slower. Steady."

Bobby swears but he does as he's told and as his swollen flesh drags across me, my body shakes. I can't need to finish again. Not after Doc just made me. I'm *not* a whore. I don't like this.

But the pressure between my legs builds and Eli's necklace slaps into my skin and I'm doing what Bobby said I was, soaking his cock with my needy, disobedient pussy. I can feel Eli watching, I can picture Doc going down on me, thrusting into me with the handle of his knife. My ass is burning and in the back of my mind, I see Adriano Rossi, his gun trained on my forehead—

"That's it," Bobby pants. "Just like that, sweetheart. Come on me."

My vision blurs and my whole body stiffens. Somewhere I can hear myself screaming, but inside everything is still. Bobby tunnels through my soaking flesh, forcing stimulation into me until I feel like I'm going to pass out.

"You're dripping all over me," he snarls. "Fuck. Fuck. *Fuuuuuck*!"

His hips slap into mine and wetness sprays across my stomach. I collapse forward, pressing my face into the sheets as Bobby pumps between my thighs. More wetness comes, sliding in thick ropes down my abdomen to the underside of my breasts.

Bobby blows out a breath. "Sorry about your sheets."

I mumble that it's okay, then realize he isn't talking to me.

"It's fine," Eli says. "Are you staying or…?"

"Nah, I'll go."

And like Doc before him, Bobby scrambles off the bed and collects his clothes, leaving without a second glance. I press my face into the covers as my heart zigzags. I've been used again, left again, but I'm still a virgin.

"My turn, *bella*." Eli's voice is as soft as the velvet that makes up his name. "Are you going to be a smart girl and spread your legs?"

He already knows the answer, I can hear it in his voice. He's daring me to deny him to his face.

I keep my head buried in his sheets. "I'm sorry, Mr. Morelli. I can't."

"Of course, you can't." There's a snapping sound and a strong, sweetish scent fills the air. I raise my head and see Eli has lit a cigar. He exhales a cloud of silvery smoke above our heads. "I thought you were smarter than this, Miss Whitehall."

"Maybe this *is* me being smart."

His jaw hardens. "Perhaps Adriano is right about you. Perhaps you are more trouble than you're worth."

Cold slithers through me. "I don't want to disappoint you, Mr. Morelli. I just want to stay a virgin."

Elliot draws on his cigar, and the end burns orange-white. "In some ways I admire you, Miss Whitehall. There isn't a woman in a million who could have withstood Orchard the way you have, and your childish insolence has its charm. But I laid out certain expectations tonight and you have failed to meet them."

His even tone is worse than Doc's threats. More unnerving than Bobby's anger. "I'm sorry, Mr. Morelli."

He points the cigar at the floor in front of him. "On your knees."

My heartbeat pounds in my ears as I crawl across the bed toward him. I eye his cigar and remember the fire from my dream. Was it a warning? Is he going to burn me?

Elliot blows out a cloud of smoke. "I will not ask again."

I collapse at his feet.

"*Bella*." The cigar hovers above me. "You're running out of time and options. Do you know that?"

I nod, trying not to keep my face away from the burning end. I already feel the heat of it on my cheek, the threat of it in my heart.

"You're going to finish what you started in the dining room. You're going to suck me like your life begins and ends with my cock. And while you do it, I'm going to sit here and smoke this…" he tilts the cigar at me. "… and think about why I should let you live."

My mind goes blank. Fear obliterating thought.

Elliot moves his hands to his armrest. "What a mess we've made of you."

I touch my hair. It's a rat's nest from being grabbed and pulled and I'm still covered in Bobby's cum. Eli's judgmental smile makes me want to curl into a ball and hide. But I'm frozen, hypnotized by the burning cigar tip.

"You're filthy," he says with satisfaction. "Now take me out and suck."

My hands shake as I undo his fly and pull him into my palm. On my wedding day, I nearly fainted at the thought of doing something like this to Mr. Parker. Tonight, it's a compromise I need to make to stay alive.

I fist the base of Eli's cock and take him into my mouth. As I bob in his lap, I watch the cigar. Fear has me moving twice as fast, sucking as though he's something delicious.

"Did you enjoy what my men did to you tonight?"

It's a trick question. He's only saying it to taunt me. I re-double my focus, running my tongue along his shaft.

"Fine," he says curtly. "Don't respond. The reason I ask is because like Bobby, I have something I enjoy in bed. Do you want to know what it is?"

The hairs on the back of my neck stand up. I've already been spanked, already had a knife against my throat and between my legs. What more can these men do to me that's not sex?

Elliot shifts forward, the movement forcing his cock deeper inside me. I retch, readjusting my jaw and try to swallow. The fingers of his free hand close around my throat. "I like choking. Knowing I'm holding a woman's life in my hands as I make the blood rush to her head."

I gag.

"Good girl," he croons. "I look at your pretty white neck, dressed in my rubies, and think how easy it would be to end you, Miss Whitehall. How convenient."

His grip tightens. The sensation is unnatural but no more uncomfortable than having his cock thrusting between my lips. I lap at him, trying to be better than I was in the dining room. Trying to make him come. Trying to finish the night a virgin.

Elliot's fingernails dig into my throat and I taste a burst of salt. My head spins at the lack of air, but I keep going, pushing, knowing he must be close.

"*Bella*," he breathes and semen floods my mouth. I swallow and he moans, shuddering helplessly above me. He's so ruthless, so utterly controlled, but I made him weak.

I sit back on my heels and wait.

After a long moment, Eli tilts my chin to look at him, his chest heaving. "Have you had enough, or should I send for Adriano?"

My heart stops. He wouldn't let me negotiate my virginity. He would sleep with me just to humiliate me—and then end my life. "No please," I say, thick-tongued.

"Fine. Maybe next time." He holds out a hand to me. "Come, *bella*. You need sleep."

I hesitate, wondering if this is just more games.

"No tricks. Let me help you."

I place my hand in his and he lifts me to my feet. "How do you feel?"

The answer to that question is too large for me to say. I just nod.

He gives me a sad smile and nudges me toward the bathroom. "My ensuite is through there. Shower. I'll wait for you."

I wash in a jumble of disjointed movements, water running through my hair. I won. I kept my virginity. I negotiated my way out of a dead-end deal, all on my own.

I creep out of the bathroom, expecting Eli to be sitting where he was, but he's standing by the bed as Bobby lays down fresh sheets.

"Here." Bobby says when he's finished, throwing open the covers and beckoning me.

I look to Eli. He moves toward me and tucks a strand of hair behind my ear. "I need to go, but you are to sleep here tonight."

I open my mouth but no sound comes out.

Elliot leans down and kisses me softly on the forehead. "Lie down. Bobby will stay with you and keep you safe."

I climb into bed and Bobby slips in the other side. We lie there together, almost touching. Is he feeling the same as me? That he'd like to hold me but he's not sure if it's appropriate? I shift, brushing my shoulder against his. Bobby presses back, his skin warm as sunshine. "JJ?"

"Yes?"

"Can you sing for me?"

My heart squeezes. "Um, sure. What would you like to hear?"

"That French one."

I know what song he means. 'La vie en Rose.' "Are you sure Eli or someone won't be mad if I make noise?"

His fingers weave through mine. "I'm positive. Please sing for me."

I close my eyes and sing as quietly as I can, my voice cracking over the lower notes. And as I whisper the words to 'La vie en Rose' Bobby lets out a soft breath, as though something inside him has released. And when I'm finished, we lie together, holding hands.

"WE'RE GONNA NEED to head out there today. Make sure…"

"… But not if…"

"… Yeah, that's a better idea…"

Light presses against my eyelids. I ignore it. I'm so tired and my whole body aches.

"What else?" a man asks.

It's Bobby. I can feel his legs beside me, hairy and warm, like a big friendly teddy bear.

"Not much, we're just stuck dealing with the fall-out."

That's Mr. Morelli. He must be standing by the bed.

"There were always going to be casualties," says a third voice. The sore patch on my neck throbs. It's Doc. Is he here because he's forgiven me? Is everything okay?

"What if it's a coincidence?" Bobby asks.

Doc snorts. "Parker moves in on the warehouse and the next morning the old woman's in the hospital?"

The sound of flesh hitting flesh.

"*Chiudi quella cazzo di bocca*," Eli hisses. *Shut your fucking mouth.*

I feel all three pairs of eyes on me. I let tiny trickles of breath run in and out of my nose, the rest of me is still as stone.

"Thank fucking Christ," Eli mutters. "This conversation is over. Get dressed and come downstairs."

The covers shift and Bobby's warmth leaves my body.

The old woman's in the hospital. Why would one person being hurt matter if the warehouse was attacked and lots of people were hurt? My body feels it before my mind understands. A sharp cramp in my stomach. My eyes fly open. Doc and Eli are at the bedroom door, Bobby has frozen, his t-shirt halfway on.

"Zia Teresa is in the hospital," I say. "Mr. Parker attacked her."

They have no time to lie. The answer is written on each of their faces.

Elliot starts to say something, but a hole is opening inside me, a hole where Zia Teresa stands, smoking and telling me what to do. I scream and the sound comes from deep inside and goes on and on and on.

Bobby presses his hands to his ears. Doc bolts from the room. In a stride Eli is beside me. He grips my cheek and slaps me across the face. But I keep screaming. I scream until my head swells and my eyes blur. I will scream until I die.

Out of the haze comes Doc. With a needle. He jabs it in my arm and darkness falls.

Chapter Seventeen

January Whitehall

I SPEND SEVEN days alone, locked in the east wing. Every morning Harvey or Mr. Gretzky brought me food I didn't eat. I pleaded with them to tell me something—anything—about my Zia, about what the others were doing. They never did. One time Mr. Gretzky asked if he could have Eli's ruby necklace back. "If he wants it, he can get it himself,' I told him.

Eli never came.

On the third day I tried to pick the lock on my door with a pair of nail scissors. I had no clue what I was doing and the scissors slipped and cut my hand. Doc burst into the room with another needle. When I woke up, anything I could use to break stuff or hurt myself was gone. He left the necklace though.

On the morning of the eighth day, I come up with a plan. It's terrible and probably going to get me killed, but I don't care what happens to me now. If Zia Teresa got hurt because of Mr. Parker, then nothing else matters. She has four daughters and eleven grandkids and she's already giving her whole life to me. I need to get out of here and make sure she's okay. Besides, everyone from my old life must already think I'm dead by now. I have nothing left to lose.

I put on my lightest dress, strip off my socks and braid my hair, tucking Zia's St. Christopher into the tightest folds. The wind is howling outside, bending the great big trees almost in half.

When I hear someone coming, I press my ear to the hardwood floor. A slow, even tread says it's Mr. Gretzky bringing me breakfast. He's who I was hoping for. He always comes further into the room than Harvey and he seems more inclined to deal with a problem himself than contact the guys.

I open the bedroom window as wide as it will go, then creep behind the door. Part of me knows this can't work. It's a childish trick Margot and I played on each other when we were kids. Hiding behind the door then jumping out and yelling 'boo!' But it's the best I have.

Mr. Gretzky knocks on the door. "Miss Whitehall? Your breakfast."

He unlocks the door, and it swings out, concealing my body. My heart pounds against my chest so hard I'm afraid he'll hear it. He takes a step forward and puts the breakfast tray on my dresser. "Miss Whitehall?"

I try not to breathe.

"Oh shit," Mr. Gretzky says, and I hear a flurry of footsteps.

I peek out from my hiding place. He's at the open window looking down. It's my moment. I slip around the door and then I'm there. On the other side. With a rush I see he's left the key in the lock.

"Hey!" Mr. Gretzky yells.

Time slows down. I pull the door closed as he lunges toward me. My fingers fumble at the key and I'm sure he's going to reach me before I can lock it, but then the metal turns with the sweetest little click.

Mr. Gretzky's body slams into the wood so hard it pushes the door forward like a wave. "Unlock it! Let me out!"

"Sorry, Mr. Gretzky." I take the key and run, the dusty carpet soft beneath my bare feet.

I dash down a banister, breathing fast. I never expected to get this far. My plan ended with Mr. Gretzky tackling me. From the loud bangs echoing behind me, he won't be locked in my room for long. I sprint faster. I just need to get to Eli or Doc or Bobby—

A door to my right swings open and a huge, scarred man steps into my path. The only person I didn't want to see. There's no time to change direction. I slam into Adriano Rossi at a hundred miles an hour. His body feels like cinderblocks. I struggle backward but his hand closes on my shoulder, biting down. "*You.*"

There's a crash behind us and Mr. Gretzky appears, panting. "I'm sorry, sir. She was hiding. I thought she jumped out the window."

Adriano glares at Gretzky. "You let her escape."

"I'm sorry, sir."

"She can go back in the cage."

"No!" I scream, desperately trying to organize my thoughts. "I need to talk to you!"

"Shut up." Adriano snarls. "Gretzky. Cage."

"I know something! Adriano, I know where Mr. Parker keeps the Orchard."

His fingers tighten on my shoulder. "What?"

"He has a secret safe. I heard him talk about it on the phone. I bet the Orchard is in there. And even if it isn't, I bet a heap of important stuff is!"

Adriano's green eyes burn into mine. "You're lying."

"I'm not smart enough to lie!"

His face shifts, eyebrows drawing together.

My heart jolts. He believes me.

"You heard Parker talking about a safe?"

"Yes."

"Where is it?"

"I'll… I'll tell you if you take me to my Zia Teresa."

Adriano shoves me to the floor. "I'm done with you." He raises a boot as though to step on me.

I throw up my arms to cover my face but I force myself to keep talking. "If you kill me, you won't find the safe."

A moment of silence and I'm hauled to my feet.

"Mr. Rossi?" Gretzky says.

Adriano turns to him. "You got something to say?"

"No, sir."

"Good."

Adriano drags me up the hall and through the door he came through. Black spots pop in front of my eyes and I see different futures stretched out like invisible roads. Life. Death. Naples. Zia Teresa. Mr. Parker. I wish I'd been brave enough to run away at my wedding. To stop all of this before it happened. Adriano steers me up wooden staircases and down sweeping halls. His hand is as cold as the gun he put in my mouth. I wish I could shake it off, but I know better. He might be leading me to my death, but it's a chance I have to take to get closer to Zia Teresa.

He opens a set of double doors with his thumbprint and practically throws me inside. The room is a gothic hell chamber. Knives on the walls and paintings that would give children nightmares. Monsters shrieking in front of red skies, crows, bones, scaly long-fingered dragons. There's an art to it, but it's ugly. Mean. In the middle of everything is a huge bed with black sheets. It's hard to believe Adriano Rossi does anything as vulnerable as sleep. He should prowl the grounds of Velvet House at night, tossing back his horns and bellowing at the sky.

"You have one minute. Tell me what you know."

"I… can you take me to see my Zia Teresa?"

He pulls his gun from his shoulder holster. And a snort of hysterical laughter escapes me. "Are you going to put it in my mouth again? Is that why we're in your bedroom?"

Adriano does something to the gun so it sounds more ready to deliver death. My blood turns to ice. "You can't kill me. If you kill me, you won't find out what I know."

His nostrils flare, but I can see him turning the dilemma over in his mind. My gaze falls to a bottle of vodka on his bedside table. "I'm sorry, can I… can I have a drink?"

His eyes skim my face, reading me like a novel he hates.

I fight back another crazy giggle. "I'm pretty sure I'm about to die. And if I am, I don't want to do it sober."

He stares a little longer then shrugs and stomps to the bottle, tossing it to me. It's not vodka, it's grappa, and when I twist off the lid, the oily scent almost makes me gag. I swig from the neck and choke and sputter. Adriano watches me. I can tell he's enjoying himself. I drink again.

"Parker's safe. Where is it?"

"What happened to my Zia Teresa?"

He crosses the space between us in a stride and presses his gun to my head. A cold little circle. He smells like earth and stone. An ancient forest hiding behind mountains. "You want me to do it?"

The liquor burns down my stomach in a scorching trail. "If you kill me, I bet the others will be angry."

"The others. If they weren't so cuntstruck, I'd have killed you weeks ago."

"Sorry," I say icily.

He gives me a look I can't read. Maybe scorn. Maybe just plain disgust. "How the fuck have you convinced them to let you stay a virgin?"

A lump rises in my throat. "Maybe they didn't want to hurt me?"

"That makes three of them." He presses the gun harder to my forehead, but I don't feel any fear. The alcohol is whipping through me like trails of light, lending me fire. "Mr. Rossi, I just want to know what happened to my Zia. Haven't you ever loved someone so much you'd go crazy if they were hurt?"

"No."

I keep my gaze locked on Adriano. I have green eyes too. Maybe like his mother or his sister. "Please?" I whisper. "Please, Adriano?"

His mouth twitches, opens almost against his will. "She got jumped leaving your stepmother's house. Broken arms, fractured face."

Air leaves my lungs in a swoosh. "She was mugged?"

"It was a put-up job. Parker reminding us what he can do."

Tears well in my eyes and roll down my cheeks. I leave them where they are. I don't deserve to wipe them away. "Why? Zia's not even my real family."

"Use your head. Parker's not going to go to war with the Whitehalls. He picked someone who'd send a message but didn't have the resources to protect themselves." Adriano's voice is bitter.

"Is that what he did to you?"

I didn't know his hold on the gun had slackened until he presses it harder against my skull. "The safe. Now."

"Mr. Parker and I were walking through Central Park when he took a call from a guy installing a safe in a tree in his backyard."

"A tree?" Adriano rams the gun into my head. "A fucking tree?"

"A-A hollow that was being expanded. They were going to install a biosafe then plant something over it. It was high up. Like fifteen feet in the trunk."

"And Parker said this in front of you?"

I think back to that frosty winter afternoon, my red mittens and my excitement at choosing my own Starbucks order—a Venti caramel with whipped cream. That girl feels so stupidly young, like a little sister who's gone away to boarding school.

"Mr. Parker thought I was an idiot," I say. "He drugged me in front of my whole family. Do you really think he was afraid to take business calls in front of me?"

Adriano lifts the gun. "You were still going to marry him though."

"Yeah, I already told you I'm not smart." I raise the grappa and drink. This time I barely choke.

Adriano watches me swallow. "What do you think of Parker now?"

"He's a creepy asshole."

Adriano smiles.

I would've said whatever I thought he wanted to hear but the insult comes out sweet as caramel. I want to do it again. "He's a perverted, disgusting criminal."

His smile vanishes. "You've told me what you know and I told you about your Zia. You'll go back in the cage until we repair your bedroom door."

"Wait!" I reach out to him, and almost stagger sideways. "Sorry, this grappa is crazy-strong."

Adriano's face softens. "So, stop drinking, Pryntsesa."

The nickname—whatever it means—gives me strength. "Adriano, please take me to see my Zia?"

His gaze falls from my mouth to the front of my dress. It's ivory lace. Whoever is dressing me still favours white. I push my shoulders back. "Please?"

He huffs. "You trying to seduce me?"

"I…"

"Let's get something clear. You're a dog, January Whitehall. A yappy little dog. And if it were up to me, I'd put you down like one."

I stagger backward as though he shoved me, dropping the grappa so liquor glugs all over the floor.

Adriano grins and the scars on his face twist like lighting. "You're going back in your cage."

The cage. The small dark space where I sang and practiced ballet alone. "Okay."

Adriano heads for the door. My limbs are loose as I stumble after him, my chest a raw tangle of nerves. He presses a thumb to the panel sensor, and I remember how he used to wait for me at the ballet studio. Whenever I walked past him, I held my breath, wishing I could disappear. His gaze seemed to follow me through locked doors and around walls, as if he was everywhere I went.

My head is rushing like it's travelling down a freeway. He was there at my studio watching me dance. He was there when they gave me Orchard, competing to be my first.

Adriano Rossi is *lying*.

I tug the straps of my dress down and it falls to the floor. I'm naked except for my cotton panties. I thought I had nothing to lose, but I do. My virginity.

Adriano turns. His face morphs into a grotesque patchwork of pain and battle and murder. My legs go weak, and I'm barely able to hold myself up but I trace a hand across my shoulders, down to my breasts. "You loved watching me dance. Would you like me to dance for you now?"

The silence is so loud it stings. I cup my breasts, running my palms over my nipples. Heat zaps through me and I let out a surprised little *'oh.'*

Adriano's jaw tightens. "What do you want?"

"Promise to take me to my Zia and you can be my first."

His lip curls. "You'd let me ruin you?"

I trail my fingers over my abdomen hoping he can't see the shake in my hands. "There are more important things than purity."

"What's to stop me fucking you then slitting your throat?"

I take a small, controlled breath. "I don't think you *can* kill me."

He steps toward me. "What?"

Every muscle in my body thrums. If I jumped, I might break right through the ceiling. "I don't think you can kill me because of how I dance."

Adriano turns his face away and I know I'm right.

"You want to get rid of me," I say quiet as a prayer. "But you can't end my life and the others don't want to let me go. So, take me to see my Zia and then I'll run and never come back."

He closes his eyes, and I realize Adriano Rossi is almost handsome, with his thick hair and full mouth. Even his silvery scars are kind of pretty. Then his eyes flick open and all I can see is that cold, empty gaze.

"You think my brothers will let me lose you?"

"They'll forgive you. What you four have is bigger than me."

"It was. You fucked everything up."

"I'm sorry, I just—"

"Heartbroken," he spits the word like it sickens him. "All three. Not talking. Not eating. Because of you."

His eyes fall to my breasts, and I feel him turning like a handle on a door. He shoves his gun back into its holster. "I'll fuck you then I'll take you to your Zia. Then you can get on a plane to South America. Chile or Colombia. You'll have to figure out everything on your own. Learn the language. Probably clean houses or suck cock for money."

I ignore the sudden pressure in my stomach. "I don't care."

He moves closer. "You'll never see the others again. If you even dream about contacting them, I'll kill you."

I think of Eli waiting for me as I showered. Doc sidling up to me in the kitchen. Bobby asking me to sing. "Fine."

"Then it's done."

I freeze, waiting for his next move. He reaches down,

cupping my pussy in his palm. His other hand closes around my neck and he steers me toward the bed. The pressure between my legs hurts, but I keep my mouth shut. Whatever happens I will not cry out in pain.

He pushes me onto the mattress and pulls off his shoulder holster and his shirt. His chest is covered in mottled scars and bruises and tattoos. He tears open the button on his jeans, yanking down the zip. He's not wearing underwear and his cock juts through the V. It doesn't look the way it did at the cathedral. It's thick and hard and red at the tip, the tattoos stretched tight around his skin. He bends forward and skims a palm across the flat of my stomach. My body contracts. I feel like I'm going to pee but yet there's another sensation behind it, a hot, warm, alive feeling.

"You'll fuck me for your freedom?"

"Yes," I whisper.

He settles over me and I'm sure he's going to sink his teeth into me. Then his lips find mine and his big tongue strokes into my mouth. I'm so surprised my eyes roll back. Not only is he kissing me, but *I like it*. It's as easy as kissing Bobby or Doc. His hands pin mine above my head and he kisses me so deeply I feel like I'm drowning. Up close his scent is musky like the forgotten corner of a library. I've been alone for days and my hunger for touch roars up like a beast. I wrap my legs around him.

Adriano grunts into my mouth, his hips rolling onto

mine. If it's like this, it won't be too bad. But then his hand locks around my throat, holding my skull like I'm a bobblehead doll. He tears his mouth away from mine. "Little whore."

I cry out and he squeezes tighter. "Say you want me."

"I want you," I gasp, unsure if it's true or not. Heat pulses between my legs and I try not to think about his long, tattooed cock.

His teeth lock around my earlobe. "You fingered yourself?"

"Not... not on the inside."

"But you've been licked by Doc and Basher. And Doc shoved his knife in you."

"Just a bit of the handle. Please don't do the same?"

He slaps me, and the side of my face goes white hot. I cry out and he squeezes my throat harder. "Lie still or I'll kill you."

I lie like a board as Adriano reaches to one side and pulls out a length of black cord. He binds me to his headboard, like I'm a dead deer he's strapping to his car.

"Keep your fucking mouth shut." He moves down my body and parts my folds with a thick finger. I wait for more, but he just stares into my pussy. Do I look disgusting? Disfigured? But there's a stillness in Adriano's scarred face, a pleasure I didn't expect to see. He catches me looking at him and slaps my clit. "You're soaked. Doc told me you liked dick, but who fuckin' knew?"

I whimper, unsure of what to say. My wrists already hurt from how tightly he's bound me. He rubs a rough, tattooed thumb through my lips and my pussy flutters. I wait for him to force himself inside me, but instead his shaggy head lowers and his tongue laves my clit. It's softer than any part of him should be. He sucks and the whole world tilts again, this time in a way that has nothing to do with alcohol. "Oh my God!"

He looks up at me from between my thighs. "Quiet."

He returns his mouth to me, and as his tongue rolls through my aching pussy, I bite the inside of my cheeks to keep from screaming. Adriano is the third man to do this to me. They've all been so different. Bobby was precise. Doc was lazy and practiced, but Adriano laps at me like a bear at a river. Like it's a primal act. I was going to pretend I liked whatever he did to me, but I don't have to pretend to like this.

He growls as he licks, slow and steady. He likes it too. His beard tickles my thighs and I arch against him, my toes curling. "Adriano..."

He pulls away, swiping his hand over his mouth and I scream like a little brat.

I brace for a slap, but he lets out a rumbling laugh and fists his tattooed cock. I can't imagine how much it would hurt to get tattoos on that part of your body. The only purpose must be scaring the women he sleeps with. So, they know how much pain he can withstand. He kneels above me pumping. My pussy tightens, hot with displeasure. It wants Adriano's mouth again.

"Please?" I mumble. "Adriano?"

His furious green eyes find mine. "When I'm done fucking you, you'll leave the country?"

"Yes. Anything you want, Mr. Rossi."

His mouth becomes a tight line. "You fucking liar, telling me whatever I want to hear. Maybe you won't go to Colombia on your own. Maybe I'll follow you."

I shudder.

"Don't like that, do you?"

I shake my head.

He drops onto his elbows, the hair on his chest brushing my nipples. "Too fucking bad. I know how to follow people without them seeing. I've done it to you for years."

He strokes his cock through my folds and I whimper. His mouth has me so on edge that I can hardly think, and as scary as the rope is, I'm glad it's there. It means I'm being forced to this. To feel this way.

"Maybe wherever you end up I'll get an apartment nearby," he mutters. "Maybe you'll feel me watching you while you go to work. While you sleep at night."

I imagine Adriano out there, looking through dark windows and standing just out of sight on the packed streets where I make my new home. A feeling I didn't expect comes over me. Warmth.

"Maybe I'd feel safe," I whisper. "Maybe I'd feel like you were protecting me."

He shudders, big shoulders shaking, then he reaches up and releases the rope holding my hands. I let them fall to the bedhead, throbbing with blood.

"I can be your pet monster," Adriano mutters. "Come out at night and fuck you while you're unconscious. You'll have no idea until all your kids come out looking like me."

I should be terrified, but there's a note in his voice that if it was sung would make me cry. I brush a hand over his back feeling the smooth furrows of scar tissue. "Adriano, I'm not afraid anymore. I'm giving myself to you."

He throws his head back, avoiding my eyes. His fist is still pumping his tattooed cock and I can see a pearly droplet swelling at the head. "I don't want what you have to give," he says.

"But…"

"You're already mine, January."

Everything inside me goes still.

"I watched you dance and you were mine. Parker wants your last name. Your stepmother wants money. The others want your body, but I *saw you*. I watched you dance. And every night since I've dreamed about you."

I can't breathe. I can't think.

"Your hair. Your mouth…"

Adriano's free hand traces my lips. Then he screws his eyes shut, pain and embarrassment warring on his face.

The frenzied death I thought was gone, hovers close again. If I upset this man right now, if I offend him, he will kill me just to save his heart. I touch his scarred cheek. "Adriano, I need to go. I need to see my Zia."

His green eyes bore into mine. "I saw you."

My heart aches, because he did. He watched me dance when no one else would. Too tall and too busty to be a ballerina, he didn't care.

His breathing is ragged now, his fist still working his cock and as scared as I am of him taking me, I'm more scared of what will happen if he doesn't.

"You hunted me," I whisper. "You caught me. Please take me."

He closes his eyes, green lamplights dimming. It's just the two of us alone in his bed. The last people in the world. The hand on his cock slows and he angles himself between my legs. My body aches, my clit is flushed, and I know I'll come while he fucks me. I'll come screaming and shaking and pleading for more, and my husband, whoever he ends up being, will not be the first man to make me feel these things. Adriano Rossi will be. I close my eyes, waiting for the moment my pussy stretches to let this brutal murderer inside me. "Please be my first," I whisper, as a small tear drops from my eye.

The head of Adriano's cock rubs against me but doesn't penetrate.

I buck my hips, urging him inside me. "Take me. End this."

"Pryntsesa…" Adriano rears back like a stallion, looking me right in the face. I don't know what he's trying to see but he doesn't find it. He bares his teeth and then he's above me, his fist juddering across his cock, one hand grasping my breast.

His cum is thick and warm as it rushes across my hips and stomach. He throws his head back in a snarl, a grizzly bear straining against a trap. It's over. Adriano finished without penetrating my body. I am still, somehow, a virgin.

He turns away and I hear a zipper snarl. "Let's go."

"Adriano?"

He looks at me, his expression as hateful as the night I arrived in Velvet House. "We're leaving."

CHAPTER EIGHTEEN

Adriano Rossi

JANUARY SITS BOLT upright in the car seat beside me. I told her to put on makeup, enough that anyone who knows her wouldn't recognize her right away. She's done a good job. Heavy gold eye shadow, pink cheeks, shiny red lips. The clothes help. A thin little nothing of a dress and the ruby necklace and sky-high heels Eli bought her. She looks like a snotty little socialite.

She stares straight ahead, her green eyes vacant. I want to break her head open and read her thoughts. Is she thinking about what we did? Or is that calm, empty expression for her future?

After I was done with her, she picked up one of my T-shirts and wiped my cum off her stomach like she'd been doing it her whole life. "Can I go see my Zia now?"

It was like my head had been turned inside out. I'd finally touched the girl who danced in my dreams and the only reason she'd allowed it was to get her own way. I wanted to throw her back in her cage and hide the key. Instead, I pushed myself to my feet. "If I take you to see your housekeeper, it'll be the last thing you do on US soil."

She looked at me, her back straight and her mouth steady. "I know."

She packed her bags, and I shaved and dressed. By the time we collected an unmarked BMW from the underground garage, neither of us looked like ourselves.

January's already got a new identity. Eli had it made when he was still deluding himself that he'd send the girl to Naples. Isabella Bianco. I've got her passport, driver's license, and an AMX card with ten grand on it. When we get to international departures, I'll shove her on a plane with all three and watch her fly to freedom. Morelli's going to be livid, and Doc and Bobby will throw hands, but eventually, they'll appreciate why I did it.

This girl is trouble. Abducting her was a needless risk that all of us undertook for different reasons. Or maybe it was the same reason in the end. We all wanted her closer and that was a mistake. As long as she's with us, things cannot be right. Sending her away is the only thing that can bring the scale back to balance.

Teresa Calderoli is a patient at St. John's Private Medical Center. It looks more like a mansion than a hospital and the parking lot is full of Porches. Considering Calderoli's a housekeeper, someone stumped up serious cash to keep her here. Parker or the Whitehall bitch.

I park the car and scan for anything suspicious. Bobby's intel says Parker's men abandoned the hospital after three days without us or January showing up. Still, no reason to make things obvious. I reach into my glove box and pull out a pair of clear black framed glasses. The scar on my face is always identifiable, but clean-shaven in a tailored suit and glasses, I don't look much like Adriano Rossi. I turn to the girl. "Ready to go?"

"Do you usually disguise yourself as a stockbroker?"

She seemed so serious in the ballet studio, so solemn and small. But here she is making fun of my clothes. And back in my room, she acted like me gun-fucking her mouth was a kink of mine. It must be Doc's fault. He's always been a bad influence.

"Can we go?" she asks, one hand already on the door. "*Please?*"

I hold up a finger. "Why are we here?"

"To visit my Aunt June. She broke her leg falling off a bike."

"And who are you?"

"Elizabeth Mills. A first year at the Fashion Institute."

I point at myself. "Me?"

I expect her to blush, but she just smiles coolly.

"You're my father, Anthony Mills."

"Good. Let's go."

I fold her arm underneath mine as we walk to the hospital. I don't want to touch her but she's shaking like a junkie. She leans into me, and I try not to breathe in her scent. Like sweet nectarines and moonlight.

The outside might be fancy, but the inside of St. John's smells the way all hospitals do, like disinfectant and microwaved beef. Heads turn as we make our way to reception, men and women staring at January. Unavoidable. I could have made her wear jeans and scrub her face, but the girl's too good-looking. Nothing short of a potato sack would have helped and that would have been even more noticeable.

"Five minutes," I mutter in her ear. "Then we're out of here."

"Yes, dad."

"Morning," I say to the bored-looking woman behind the front desk. "Anthony Mills. My daughter and I are here to visit June Mills."

I pulled the name off Bobby's scouting notes. Some old girl we can pretend to be visiting if Parker's still checking the guest register.

"Ms. Mills is on the third floor," the receptionist says. "Sign in then take the elevator to the left."

I scribble a fake signature on the guestbook then steer January to the lift. She sticks her heels into the ground.

"Can't we buy Auntie flowers?" She gestures at the stand beside reception.

I grit my teeth. "Fine." I get a bunch of stupidly expensive yellow roses and January does a decent job of looking bored as she picks her nails at my side. She should really be on her phone, but I'm not giving her one. She can buy something when she gets to where she's going. It'll be safer that way.

"Here," I say handing her the roses. "All yours."

The corner of her mouth twitches. "Thanks, *dad*."

As we make our way to the elevator, I think of her father, Nicholas Whitehall. He gave in to cancer without stopping his viper of a second wife from doing whatever she felt like after his death. He knew what she was, warned her not to meet with Parker, but he never took steps to protect his daughter.

If I was January's father, I'd have sold off my foreign properties and tied up the money in trust funds the stepmother couldn't touch. I'd have sent January to a Swiss boarding school to grow up in the snow and soft skies. Made sure she came into millions as soon as she turned eighteen. But that's rich idiots. Always thinking nothing can hurt them, even once they're dead.

When we're in the elevator I hit the button for the sixth floor. Zia Teresa is in room 612. As the elevator moves, I hear January's shallow breathing and think about her sprawled in bed, my tongue between her legs.

She was under me, moaning and seconds away from coming. All I had to do was plant my cock inside her and end it. But I couldn't take her virginity. I don't know why. Only that I'd have cut my dick off before I slid into her.

Maybe she'll fuck a man as soon as she lands wherever she goes. Get rid of the thing that everyone wants. Maybe she'll even fall in love with the guy. Some nice, normal guy who vows to protect her and give her the safe little world she craves.

I'll still find her. I've tasted her cunt and watched her dance. I was the first man she offered herself to. We're joined now. As long as she's alive, she's mine.

We exit at the sixth floor. January walks too fast up the hall. I yank her shoulder, make her slow down. She's crying already. Tears splashing onto her slutty pink dress. I turn my face away. I can't stand women's tears. We pause outside room 612.

"Five minutes," I repeat.

Her eyes are fixed on the door. "Of course."

I grab her chin. "Your Zia looks bad. She might not be conscious. You scream or make any noise, I'm coming in there and shoving my hand in your mouth."

She looks me right in the eyes. "I promise I'll be quiet."

I release her. "Then go."

She keeps staring at me. "Adriano. Thank you."

I clench my jaw and say nothing.

She opens door 612 and slips inside. I give her a couple of minutes before I stick my head in. The room is dim, with thick curtains drawn over the windows. There are cards and flowers everywhere. January sits beside the bed, her face buried in Teresa Calderoli's sheets. The old girl looks bad. Her face is a mess of purple and both her arms are in casts. Whoever worked her over went beyond the call of duty. She's unconscious or the stuff in her IV is helping her sleep. They're probably more generous with meds in a place like this.

"You okay?" I ask.

She lifts her head, makeup smeared around her eyes. "Is it time?"

I want to lock her in the basement. Hide her away from everything that makes her look like this. "Not long," I say, closing the door on her.

We passed a coffee machine on the way from the elevator. I find it, prepared to shove any amount of money into a slot to get some. It turns out to be free. I press a button and watch the freshly brewed beans pour into a paper cup.

My phone buzzes. Eli ringing me. I've already got messages and missed calls from Bobby and Doc. So, it begins.

I shove my phone away and take my coffee. It's too hot but I empty the cup into my mouth anyway. I was hoping January's Zia would be awake. I wanted to see if the relationship was mutual or if the girl had projected a mother onto another disinterested party. Looking into my empty cup, I find myself hoping it's real. That someone loved January the way Magdalena Rossi loved me. Stupidly. Against all her better judgment.

Mama feels close in this hospital, so different from the one where I watched her die. Eight hospital beds crammed in a room, dead-eyed doctors giving distracted updates, their minds already on the patients who might live. Eli wanted to pay for a private hospital, but I knew it was too late. I was just waiting for her to go. I close my eyes and see her in our tiny green kitchen, folding varenyky and singing along to the radio. I'm older than she was now and everything about that is wrong. I was supposed to die young.

A noise behind me. A squeak like a scuffed shoe.

Time folds backward, peeling away like the point of a blade. I pull my Glock from my shoulder holster but it's too late. I know it like I know my name. The bullet slices my side. I turn, clipping a short guy through the forehead, but I've barely had time to aim at the massive blond behind him before someone grabs me. I heave against them, breaking their hold but they jam their fingers into my bullet wound, tearing downward. My head splits open in agony.

"Take him down!"

The massive blond sprints toward me, I raise my gun as his fist slams into my nose. The pain whips the air from my lungs. I collapse onto my knees, gagging on blood.

A woman screams. January? I push my foot into the floor and try to stand but the blond kicks me in the chest. I sprawl onto my back and my fake glasses go flying. I hear them splinter on the floor. An ambush. A stupid run-of-the-mill ambush.

The metal tang of blood goes down my throat and I hack it up. The blond takes my gun, and spits in my face. "Fucking scumbag."

Another feminine scream. "Adriano! Help me!"

I see January in her tiny pink dress, sitting next to her Zia Teresa. I remember the feel of her under me. I should have fucked her. Why didn't I fuck her?

"Hello, Rossi."

It's funny how little Parker's changed in twenty years. His face is unlined, his round blue eyes still flicking around for more money, more pussy, more power, more pills. An empty void swirling around nothing. I cough, spraying more blood up and back over my own face.

Parker laughs. "I'm going to kill you, Rossi."

He's going for Morelli's light confidence, but his voice is shaking.

"So, fucking do it."

Parker licks his pink lips. "You and January checked in as father and daughter. Was that a joke or have you violated my fiancée?"

I laugh. "You don't know the half of it."

Parker's gaze goes black. "Shut up."

"I had her on my face an hour ago, naked and begging me to—"

Parker's not strong, but a boot in the ribs is still a boot in the ribs. I feel another dull crack and my breathing twists off like a rusty tap.

"You've grown a tongue, bootlicker. What happened to letting your friends do the talking?"

I laugh even though it makes my insides scream. "You're fucked, asshole. You kill me, there's three more coming."

Parker pulls a Beretta from somewhere and hovers it over my face. "Time to die, huh?"

I don't speak. Better men than Parker have held a gun to my head. I wouldn't insult them by begging for my life. Death was always a possibility, and this is my fuck up. I deserve it. All I can hope is that the others find January. That Morelli marries her and lets Doc and Bobby fuck her whenever they want. And they have dinners like the one we had.

I look into the barrel of the gun. "Hurt January and the others will make you pay."

Parker bares his teeth, and the world goes black.

✧　✧　✧

RED LIGHT THROUGH paper cracks.

Slow, seeping heat.

A man screaming. That horrible insect whine.

Sirens.

"Mr. Mills?"

A woman in white is pressing something to my head, saying something I can't hear. I blink. White walls with a leaf border. Mica flecked floor. I'm still in St. John's hospital. I try to push myself up and collapse, blood streaming into my mouth like poison. I press my hand to the bullet wound and go again, staggering to my feet. The pain is there but a street or two away. Someone else's problem. They must have given me drugs.

A girl behind me screams and the doctor says something else. I ignore them and stagger forward. Zia Teresa's door is open, the cards and flowers and candy exactly where it was. The old woman is still in bed and for a second, I think it's okay. Then I see her blank brown eyes.

She's dead and January is gone.

EPILOGUE

January Whitehall

"Y**OU DISGUSTING, DEGENERATE slut.**"

I sit across from Mr. Parker in a limousine. The windows are blacked out. If he hits me no one will see.

Zia Teresa is dead. A masked man put his hands around her throat and killed her. I saw him do it. I heard the awful sounds. Adriano is shot. I don't know if he's dead but when I was dragged past him, he wasn't moving.

These are the facts. They can't be argued with or cried at. They can't be changed.

Mr. Parker leans forward, steepling his fingers. "Ten years. Ten years I've been paying your bitch of a mother for you to get snatched away at our wedding. Millions of dollars pissed down the drain."

Mr. Parker's bodyguards have glazed looks on their

faces. It seems like my ex-fiancé has been ranting about this a lot since my abduction.

I fix an understanding smile on my face. "I'm so sorry, Mr. Parker."

"Don't smirk at me, you little cunt. You know, your mother thinks I stole you. Why the fuck would I do that?" He looks at me expectantly.

"I'm not sure, Mr. Parker."

"Of course, you're not, you stupid bitch." His expression is gleeful. I'm sure he's been dying to talk to me like this. It was probably hard for him to buy me flowers and take me for walks when this is the relationship he really wanted to have.

He leans in close, tapping a finger to the ruby necklace. "Have you been fucking Eli Morelli?"

His breath is sweet and sour like rancid soda. My throat constricts. "No."

Mr. Parker gives a high wobbling laugh. "So, you fucked Adiano?"

"I… who?"

He looks at me like I'm a worthless patch of dirt. "Adiano Rossi."

I smile. "It's pronounced 'A-dree-ah-know.'"

Pain explodes across my face.

"You worthless whore," Parker hisses. "You fucked them. You fucked all four of them, didn't you?"

My lip is split. I touch the tiny part in my skin, feel the blood drip through like oily water. I was struck by the others, but this feels completely different. When they did it, my pulse picked up and resentment and heat fought for space inside me. Looking into Mr. Parker's eyes, all I feel is dull, quiet disappointment.

"I'm still a virgin," I tell him.

"You're a lying little bitch."

I lick my upper lip. I hate the taste of blood, but I don't have any Kleenex and I don't think anyone is going to give me any. "I swear on my Zia Teresa, I'm still a virgin. None of them slept with me. Nobody has."

Mr. Parker narrows his eyes. "And if I have a doctor examine you? You'd still be intact?"

I'm pretty sure the hymen doesn't work like that. That if it did cover the hole you wouldn't be able to have your period. But I'm not going to tell Mr. Parker that.

"Of course, I'm intact," I say, trying to sound sad but lightly offended. "You can have a doctor examine me. I want you to. I'm still a virgin."

He sits back in his seat. He still doesn't believe me.

"They would have filmed it. If they took my virginity, they would have filmed it and showed you."

Mr. Parker traces his teeth with his tongue. "We never got any recordings of them fucking with you after the first one. I thought you were dead."

He sounds mildly annoyed, as though he'd lost a wallet. He grips my wrist, crushing it in his fleshy, too-hot hand. "Why didn't they keep filming you? Why didn't they force themselves on you?"

I think back to that dinner at Velvet House. The five of us sitting around the polished dining table eating and drinking and laughing. I should have said yes to staying there. If I had, I'd be safe and Zia Teresa would still be alive.

I touch a finger to my shoulder, where my St. Christopher is hiding beneath my dress strap. Zia Teresa is with me now. I carry her in my heart. And she once told me not to blame myself for what other people do, but to focus on my own survival.

Mr. Parker is still watching me, waiting for an answer.

"I think they had feelings for me," I say quietly. "They didn't want to force me. They wanted me to choose them."

He gives a giggling snort. "That's fucking hilarious."

His bodyguards grin obligingly.

I bite back my own secret smile. Mr. Parker believes me. He knows I'm still a virgin. He'll keep me alive just to mock the men who stole me from him. As his limousine whirrs through the city, I repeat their names like a mantra. *Elliot Morelli. Domenico Valente. Roberto Bassilotta. Adriano Rossi.*

They're murderers. Dangerous, violent men. And they will come seeking bloody revenge. I just have to survive until they find me.

✧   ✧   ✧

Thank you for reading VELVET CRUELTY by Eve Dangerfield! We hope you loved this breathtaking and scorching hot romance with January and her four beautifully dangerous men. Find out what happens after January is taken by Mr. Parker in SILK MALICE...

My heart tells me I don't want to belong to one man. I belong to four.

But the criminals I love are proud. Too proud.

Their brotherhood is in tatters.

They fight for me. And they possess me, even as the enemies close in. Even as the foundation of our twisted family crumbles. Even as the dark legacy threatens to consume us all.

Remember Elliot's sister Sasha? She also appears as the best friend in the dangerously spicy book in KING OF SPADES, a modern dark retelling of Alice in Wonderland.

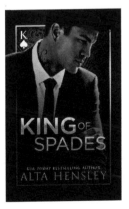

He demands my virtue as payment.

I'm falling into a world of luxury and sin.

With every twist and turn, I need more.

Except this is not a man to love.

This is a man to fear.

The warring Morelli and Constantine families have enough bad blood to fill an ocean, and their stories are told by your favorite dangerous romance authors. See what books are available now and sign up to get notified about new releases here...

www.dangerouspress.com

ABOUT MIDNIGHT DYNASTY

The warring Morelli and Constantine families have enough bad blood to fill an ocean, and their brand-new stories will be told by your favorite dangerous romance authors. These series are now available for you to read! There are even more books and authors coming in the Midnight Dynasty world, so get started now...

Leo Morelli is known as the Beast of Bishop's Landing.

He'll get revenge on the Constantine family and make millions of dollars in the process. Even it means using an old man who dreams up wild inventions. And his daughter. The college student must spend thirty days with the ruthless billionaire.

"Secret Beast is the dark and delicious Beauty and The Beast re-telling I've been craving. Leo Morelli is an EPIC hero and I could stay in his world forever!"

– M. O'Keefe, USA Today bestselling author

Eva Morelli is the oldest daughter. The responsible one.

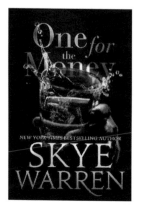

She doesn't have time for her own interests. Especially not her interest in the charismatic, mysterious Finn Hughes. A fake relationship is the answer to both their problems.

Until it starts to feel real…

"Skye Warren like you haven't seen her before! This book is emotional, angsty, and had me holding my breath."

– New York Times bestselling author
Corinne Michaels

Meet Winston Constantine, the head of the Constantine family. He's used to people bowing to his will. Money can buy anything. And anyone. Including Ash Elliot, his new maid.

But love can have deadly consequences when it comes from a Constantine. At the stroke of midnight, that choice may be lost for both of them.

"Brilliant storytelling packed with a powerful emotional punch, it's been years since I've been so invested in a book. Erotic romance at its finest!"

– #1 New York Times bestselling author
Rachel Van Dyken

"Stroke of Midnight is by far the hottest book I've read in a very long time! Winston Constantine is a dirty talking alpha who makes no apologies for going after what he wants."

– USA Today bestselling author Jenika Snow

SIGN UP FOR THE NEWSLETTER
www.dangerouspress.com

JOIN THE FACEBOOK GROUP HERE
www.dangerouspress.com/facebook

FOLLOW US ON INSTAGRAM
www.instagram.com/dangerouspress

ABOUT EVE DANGERFIELD

Eve Dangerfield has loved romance novels ever since she first swiped her grandmother's paperbacks. Now she writes her own stories about complicated women and gorgeous-but-slightly-tortured men. Her work has been described as 'genre-defying,' 'insanely hot' and 'the defibrillator contemporary romance needs right now'...and not just by herself or those who might need bone marrow...OTHER PEOPLE! She lives in Melbourne with her boy and a bunch of semi-dead plants. She can generally be found making a mess.

COPYRIGHT

This is a work of fiction. Any resemblance to actual persons, living or dead, business establishments, events or locales is entirely coincidental. All rights reserved. Except for use in a review, the reproduction or use of this work in any part is forbidden without the express written permission of the author.